ABOUT THE AUTHOR

M. L. Tompsett is an emerging author of action paranormal fantasy romance. This is her second book published.

A bit about the Author

M. L. Tompsett has been creating worlds to escape to since she was a little girl. Years later, she is still enjoying her writing in her imaginative make-believe worlds with interesting characters. Finally, moving forward to the big, wide, scary world of digital and print publishing.

M. L. Tompsett is married to her childhood sweetheart. They live in Victoria, Australia, and have two fully grown, extremely talented sons.

Her books are now out in print, softcover books, ebooks, and now venturing into Audible. She is excited to see something she has been working on for far too long finally become a reality.

When M. L. Tompsett is not busy tapping away on her keyboard, creating her next page-turning book with a cup of tea and a bag of licorice, you will find her either creating digital book files for one of her talented clients or taking random photos around Australia.

facebook.com/M.L.TompsettAuthor

instagram.com/mltompsett.author

bookbub.com/profile/m-l-tompsett

ALSO BY M. L. TOMPSETT

In the Series

Sex, Lies And Family Secrets

The Guy Next Door - *Book one*

Dark Surprises - *Book two*

You Never Know - *Book three*

It's You - *Book four*

What You Know - *Book five*

OTHER VAMPIRE BOOKS

Her Vampire Fated Mate

Paranormal Fantasy, *including Vampires and Witches*

Plus many more…

OTHER BOOKS

By M. L. Tompsett

DIFFERENT GENRES

Contemporary Romance

SECOND CHANCE AT LOVE- SERIES

Insta Bride

The bodyguard's convenient marriage

Ghost of a chance in love

Secret Heiress

Urban Fantasy

Shifter Romance

Kept in the Dark of Love and Lust

Kept in the Dark of Lies and Deceit - Book Two

Paranormal Urban Fantasy *including Dragons, Shifters, and Elves*

Plus many more…to come

NON-FICTION

My Travel Log

All books are available at all good online book outlets and Audible stores.

SEX, LIES AND FAMILY SECRETS, SERIES

Book Two

DARK SURPRISES

M. L. Tompsett

Tompsett Publishing ™

Book Two: **Dark Surprises**
Sex, Lies And Family Secrets
Copyright © 2017 by M. L. Tompsett
ISBN: 978-0-6482507-4-6
Large Print ISBN: 978-0-9953858-5-6
ebook ISBN: 978-0-9953858-4-9

Cover Art designed by **Tompsett Publishing**™. Cover images licensed via Adobe Stock and DepositPhotos. This book in the series edition published by **Tompsett Publishing**™ & **M. L. Tompsett Author**™ Victoria, Australia

Tompsett Publishing™

For all your digital book formatting requirements

eBook and Print Books

www.mltompsett.com

Disclaimer: This book is a work of fiction. All characters in this book have no existence outside the imagination of the author and have no relation to anyone bearing the same name or names. Any resemblance to actual individual persons, living or dead, or actual events is purely coincidental. Characters, businesses, places, events and incidents are either the products of the author's imagination or used in a fictitious manner. The town of Darshia doesn't exist but is a fictional location. Except for the original material written by M. L. Tompsett Author™, all songs, song titles and lyrics contained in this book are the property of the respective songwriters and copyright owners. This ebook is intended for readers 18 years and older.

NATIONAL
LIBRARY
OF AUSTRALIA

A catalogued digital record of this book is available from the National Library of Australia.

This book is written and edited in Australian/UK English. Which means spelling will be different. This book contains coarse language, adult sexual themes, blood, vampires, young love, soulmates, violence, nudity, and handsome-muscled men. If you are offended by any of themes, this book is not for you.

M. L. Tompsett Author™ Revised Print book edition 2026

In these trouble times.
Take the time to look after yourself.
If you do not look after you — who is going to do it?
Be kind to yourself.
Be the best you can.
Remember — tomorrow is another day.
As for today, we are living it.
Keep safe.
Keep your distance.
Wash your hands.
Wear a face covering.
Speak with your family and friends, to make sure they are okay —
the internet and phone are a fabulous inventions.
Big hugs everyone.
We will make it through it.
Just one day at a time.

DEDICATION

For my Family

*To all you fabulous readers of paranormal fantasy romance fiction,
there is always a time and place to escape too. To enjoy the life of
your favourite character and submerge yourself into their lives for
even a short while.*

*If you ever wondered if those piles of scraps of paper in the broken
box, hidden away in the cupboard can be transformed into
something for others to enjoy reading, don't just sit there
wondering, break open your imagination and give it a go.*

Your imagination is only as good as you allow it.

*And to all those little helpers, I have managed to wrangle into
assisting me along my journey - thank you. Anth, Emma, Kylie,
Michele, Gwen, Robyn, Alli - just to name a few.*

Enjoy

Blurb

Alexia is back, and finds herself drawn into the paranormal world she thought she had left behind.

We finally get to meet Lucy and see how her life dangerously entwines with Alexia and Drake in the next instalment of Sex, Lies and Family Secrets: Dark Surprises.

What happens when your sexy husband is mistaken for someone else and kidnapped by violent, evil, men? You take charge and organise a rescue of course. Finding out Witches are real, and her best friend Lucy comes from a family of Witches. With Lucy by her side, they soon find themselves fighting for their lives against the Dark Witches, who are out for blood.

Alexia finds herself learning and using Lucy's spells and gifted magical charmed necklace to rescue Drake from a Dark One traitor. Can Alexia save Drake in time or will this spell the end for our loving couple. And, then there is the mysterious woman in the shadows, who is she and why does she seem so familiar?

DARK SURPRISES

In a world, you prefer to live in,
A world, you would prefer to stay, and thrive in,
A place which can be all your own and enjoy every minute,
A world you can love, with no restraints and rules.
A world you can be - you.
~ ~ M. L. Tompsett

CHAPTER ONE

Basking under the unexpected summer-like heat on this beautiful sunny Spring day, I relax on my naked front, enjoying the sun's rays while stretched out in my secluded oasis pool surrounded by lush greenery.

My playful husband stealthily approaches me. From across the pool deck, I sense his presence long before he reaches me. It's still hard to believe I'm married to the handsome, sexy man heading my way. *HUSBAND!* That is one new word I'm still adjusting to in my new life.

If someone had told me two months ago that I would be married, I would have dismissed it as a dream. If they'd told me a month ago, I would have asked what planet they were from. They'd have to be out of their minds to even think it. And yet here I am, married to a man whose physical presence is irresistible, like a delicious feast for the senses.

So much for my thirty-minute escape for myself, time I desperately need to relax and unwind.

Unless... hmm. A smile forms on my face.

Maybe my new handsome husband is exactly what I need to unwind, my body already humming with erotic anticipation for his loving, sensual touch.

The cheek of the man — he probably thinks I'm fast asleep and that he can sneak up on me as I lie here in the shallows of the solar-heated, crystal-clear pool water. The warm water laps against my side, rocking my body gently and lulling me into a blissful state. I listen to the soothing sound of water cascading over the pool's waterfall — a beautiful formation of rock and sculptured boulders, the water spreading out over the stone and falling into the pool below, forming bright rainbows in the mist.

It's nearly time for me to roll over to continue my overall tan. My husband of two weeks continues his not-so-sneaky progress toward me, most likely wondering how I'm out here all by myself — and most of all, where my guards are. Now that is a feat in itself: being alone and outside in the pool.

My thoughts drift back over the last few weeks and what a surreal time we've had. All because of teenage hormones, sex, and the scrumptious guy next door. Yes, my next-door nearly eighteen-year-old neighbour. The person I've lived beside for the past fourteen years. The guy who has been my best friend, who became my boyfriend, then my lover, and now my husband. I'm still coming to terms with the idea that we're parents. Oh yes — parents of newborn twins. Can you believe that! I'm still coming to terms with it all. Seriously, though, our gorgeous twins, Alley and Damien, are my life, and I will do anything to protect them.

The other gigantic piece of life-altering news I received was about another race of people known as Dark Ones. Most people know them as vampires, and guess what… I'm now one of them. Oh, and did I happen to mention I'm also their princess?

Shocker, right? Who would have guessed?

Me — a royal princess and a Dark One.

These past few weeks have been hectic chaos — finding out my then-boyfriend had to leave me because his live-in guardians witnessed him consuming my blood. As a result, they sent him away to hide his big family secret. They believed I was human, and as a human, I wasn't allowed to know anything about their world.

After confessing to my mother the true nature of my relationship with my best friend and boyfriend, my loving mother dropped a massive bombshell on me in return. That revelation led to Mum and me leaving home for a three-day drive to meet and confront our relatives — our long-lost secret family. A family I never knew existed. A family of Dark Ones.

On top of all that, what I first thought was a simple bug turned out to be something a little more serious. I soon discovered I was pregnant — me, nearly eighteen, pregnant, and with no boyfriend to be found.

From the first day I arrive in the secret place named Darshia, my life is constantly under threat as I narrowly escape death on multiple occasions. Assassins lurk around every corner, each attempt more determined than the last. I find my next-door neighbour again, and together we celebrate the arrival of our newborn twins before secretly marrying.

A few days later, I save my husband's life, which ends with me shooting my father-in-law — who, as it turns out, wants me dead. He nearly succeeds in his final attempt. Geez, who needs enemies when you have a family like mine?

With my life hanging by a thread, against all odds, I find the strength to survive and make my way back to my beloved family, defying death and the relentless pursuit of my would-be killers. When I wake up in the hospital, I find myself cradled against my husband's firm chest, wrapped in the warmth of his arms.

Drake explains how I saved his life by giving him my blood before medical help arrived, and how I confronted my father-in-law. As he was determined to kill my gorgeous twin babies, my mother, and me. We fight one another until I manage to defeat him and protect the ones I love — but not before being critically injured.

From my hospital bed, I arrange for the head of security to assist me in taking charge of and running my ancestral secret family home — which is a small country in itself — Darshia, to keep everyone safe and bring back balance and peace after the attack. Grandma Ma, otherwise known as Alexettia and the Queen, had been severely injured and nearly died in the attack against everyone in the Darshia castle. Now she's healed, Grandma Ma takes charge of her royal throne once more. Don't get me wrong, I appreciate having Grandma Ma back, but... hmm. Something seems different with her — I just cannot place my finger on it.

With Grandma Ma finally back to rule and on her royal throne, I can travel back to my hometown and live next door to my parents with my husband and our twins.

As of this morning, I return to my old human teenage life. After far too many hours, I finally complete all my set school assignments. Thus, I'm enjoying the rare sunshine and heat out by the pool before we go back and start the last school term of the year, which just happens to start in less than eighteen hours — officially.

Now, back to my husband... I roll onto my back, feeling the cool water against my heated skin as he positions himself between my feet before manoeuvring his sexy, hard-muscled body over mine.

I slowly open my eyes and look straight into the gorgeous brown eyes of my sexy husband, Drake. Drake Smithlyn, with his six-foot-three hard-muscled, ripped body, powerful jaw and straight nose, scruffy short golden-brown hair, and the most panty-dropping smile, with his very kissable and lickable lips. Never forgetting his washboard abs and that V of muscle pointing down from his hips. Hmm-mmm, I love that V of muscle. All that yummy toned man flesh. Oh yes, a scrumptious body — and all mine.

Drake slowly glides the tip of his nose along mine before ghosting his kissable lips gently against my own in the barest of touches, sending erotic tingles down my spine and through my body.

"Hello, husband," I say through smiling lips, knowing how much Drake enjoys me addressing him that way, even though we're both still adjusting to such monikers.

"Hello, wife," Drake replies with a big, cheeky smile that reaches his eyes and makes his whole face glow. "Here, I brought this flower for my beautiful wife."

Oh my. Wife. Ha. Hearing that word from Drake's sexy lips leaves goosebumps across my body. I have to keep reminding myself this gorgeous and very sexy male is all mine. Hmmm, yummy. I wonder if I will ever get used to hearing that word wife.

Drake and I have only just started our very long life with one another — a very long life, leading into many centuries of wedded bliss. Oh, and him showering me every day with beautiful flowers. I'm a lucky girl.

With my own smile just for him, I reply, "Thank you, Drake."

Drake slowly brushes the soft petals of the flower against my warm naked skin, between and around my full, upturned breasts, causing my nipples to harden. But then, Drake has that effect on my body anyway.

"Alexia, I'm not complaining, but why are you naked in our pool?"

Ah, I was wondering if Drake would mention that little detail. Glad to see my husband is observant, especially as his body is slowly responding to mine. Hmmm, yep. I'm glad to see I'm not the only one naked.

I lift my eyebrow at his panty-dropping, smiling face.

Especially since I can feel one of my new toys against my leg. It seems to be growing on me. Literally. As it gently taps to its own beat against the warm skin of my wet, naked thigh. Hmmm, yummy.

Let us play.

CHAPTER TWO

Smiling into my husband's eyes, I reply, "I do not want to start having tan lines." I give my shoulders a slight shrug. "Plus, I make sure my security detail is not able to see me. They've been warned to give me some privacy. Nobody should be able to see me from this position."

I watch Drake glance up and around our surrounding area.

Instantly, my mind connects with Drake's; I can see and hear his thoughts — a benefit of being a Dark One princess and soulmate. While he searches for my security detail, I see everything through his eyes, and right now he's just discovered my guards, making sure they're not close enough to see our naked bodies entwined in the shallow water of the pool.

Now that I'm next in line for the royal throne, a full-fledged Princess of Darshia, I have to have personal 24-hour security. The all-male team is slowly learning not to mess with me. Only a select few of my primary security team know I can access any of their minds whenever I want and look into their deepest secrets. That's why the guys are allowing me my privacy here in my own backyard pool — they know I'm powerful in mind-reading and excellent with a gun.

Relief glides over Drake when he realises the guards are giving me space; now we can enjoy some alone time. He slowly lifts himself, raising his body just enough from mine, and with his eyes he casually surveys my naked body. I notice his tongue making an appearance, sweeping between his kissable lips.

With his eyes lifting back up to mine, Drake slowly lowers his head and brushes his nose around and against my pebbling nipple. Sexual tingle sensations start to move through my body whenever he's near, but when he touches me — well, there are times I might, and have, mind you, been able to orgasm from his sensual touch alone. Even his bite can send me into an orgasmic state.

Yes, the bite and the blood consumption are part of my new life. A big part of our world, a part of a world I never knew existed. A world containing a mystical entity known as a Dark One. Some people call them bloodsuckers, leeches — otherwise known as vampires. The difference between a vampire and a Dark One: vampires are turned, and Dark Ones are born. Both drink blood straight from the vein.

In my case, as a mated soulmate, I can only consume Drake's blood, and he can only consume mine.

We are soulmates who have just completed the embarrassing Joining Ceremony, and we are now life-bonded mates.

To top off my life, my doctor recently confirms that Drake and I are once again pregnant. Oh yes, the joy of facing another pregnancy. The red tape that comes with two royal Dark Ones going down the path and joining in a Dark One Joining Ceremony — which boosts our Dark One abilities — is just an extra perk. Can you pick up on my sarcasm?

Just wait until my parents find out about that little piece of trivia: their only daughter pregnant again before I even turn eighteen. I think I might inform them over the phone, because they will not be happy whatsoever. And just think — if my mother had gone down the same path I have, she too would be mated and consuming blood every day as a Dark One. But no, my mother chooses to remain fully human.

Even though my mother, Amelia, does seem to exhibit some Dark One abilities, her limited talent will never extend to full Dark One abilities, as she is still human — and a successful lawyer.

Please don't get me started on our grandmother, Grandma Ma — otherwise known as Alexettia. The time I spend with her is great, but at times, a little confusing. Alexettia manages to teach me some of her royal techniques and even reveals a few of her hidden chambers around the castle.

But my internal senses keep warning me: something is definitely wrong with Grandma Ma from the moment I first meet her. I think I'm going to need to speak with Mum and my security team about Grandma Ma, because sometimes Alexettia's behaviour is Jekyll and Hyde.

Hmmm. Yes. More.

My back arches, offering my breast toward Drake's warm, talented mouth, inviting him closer, urging him without a single word for his talented tongue. He never makes me wait. His breath skims my skin, sending a rush of heat spiralling through me. The light brush of his lips against my diamond-tipped nipple sends a shiver racing down my spine, and then he lowers his head, his mouth closing over my breast with a hunger that makes my whole body respond.

Oh yes. That feels so good. Pleasure floods my system so intensely my eyes start to roll back in my head.

Drake's voice cuts through my haze of bliss.

'Babe, I think I might continue my exploration of tasting every inch of your delectable, delicious body.'

Ooooh, yes. I can absolutely go for that right now.

'I think Nanny Sharonia can handle the twins when they wake for their next feed. There's bottled milk in the kitchen fridge. Speaking of milk...' My mind barely registers his words until...

Twins. Milk. What?
Nanny Sharonia?
Oh, crap on a stick.

I pull my mind away from Drake and his maddeningly talented body long enough to focus. I send Nanny Sharonia a quick mental message. Thank the goddess, I can communicate via my mind with whoever I want.

'Drake and I are not to be disturbed. If the twins wake before I'm back in the nursery, please feed them the expressed bottled milk in the fridge.'

Her reply comes instantly.

'Relax. I can handle the twins.'

Knowing my babies are in safe, capable hands, I shut out every distraction and focus solely on Drake. His mouth, his warmth, the way he knows exactly how to unravel me. His lips close around me again, drawing a sharp breath from my chest as my back arches in response. His hand glides along my skin, confident and sure, coaxing every part of me to respond to him, to him alone.

It isn't long before I feel a tingling in my breast, signalling that my hind milk is about to be released. Hearing Drake suckle more intensely tells me he's getting a steady flow of breast milk.

Once the rush of milk from my sensitised breast diminishes, Drake runs his warm tongue around both nipples, cleaning off any remaining milk before kissing each hard, erect bud. Keeping his head low, Drake continues to journey down my body, focusing on his favourite spots. I can't disagree, as my body responds by arching again, craving more of his sensual touch.

Further down, his solid body travels, kissing, licking and nipping my heated, tantalised flesh.

'Drake, please. Please, babe. Fill me up, with your delicious cock.'

Feeling Drake smile against my wet flesh, followed by hearing his cheeky laugh echoing in my head.

'Sorry, baby. No can do. I am a little busy at the moment. You must learn to have patience.'

Patience. Did he just tell me to have patience?

Drake is sensing my physical reply. He quickly uses his hands and lifts and spreads my legs wide apart, with my knees up to my chest. Exposing my heated, wet and swollen folds, before his hungry mouth.

Still trying to fill my lungs with much-needed air, Drake swoops down and captures my little bundle of nerves between his lips. Quickly rubbing and gliding his tongue over it, over and over again, while applying suction, causing my stomach muscles to tighten. My thighs squeeze Drake's head as his teeth nip at my clit, sending erotic sensations throughout my body.

Before my mind can gather any coherent thoughts, my body just about flies off into the air when Drake suckles hard on my bundle of nerves, causing my sensitive bundle to scream for a reprieve from the overload of sexual delights as he continues teasing my clit and making it hard and erect.

I feel myself growing wet, the sensation of it running down

between the cheeks of my arse. Oh, this is not fair. I need Drake's mouth lower. I need something in me. Something big would be fantastic right about now.

With my mind once more, I send my plea for Drake to end this torture, this mind-blowing sexual madness. Drake's response is to laugh at my sexual plight. Hearing him laugh across my mind.

'Damn, the man.' I scream out in my head, *'Drake, just fuck me already. Stop this sexual torture. Payback will be a bitch, husband.'*

My tone loud and frantic with need, my lungs fighting for much-needed air.

Feeling Drake reply, caress my mind, with a wicked laugh. *'Do you really think so, my beautiful wife?'*

Before my brain can comprehend Drake's words, he is over my body and with a hard thrust of his narrow, toned hips, spearing me straight into my tight, muscled, weeping channel. His silky, long, thick length stretches and fills me.

What little air I have soon whooshes out of my lungs, and my eyes snap open wide. With a quick swivel of Drake's talented hips, he nearly pulls all the way out to his tip, before thrusting back in, gliding through my warm, silky, wet crevice, tightening around him, not wanting to let go.

With a firm grip of his strong fingers wrapped around my ankles, keeping them raised and spread wide apart, allowing him better access, deeper penetration, touching all my favourite inner places.

My eyes start to roll back into my head from the overwhelming rush of sensation, a wave so intense it steals my breath. Every part of me tightens at once, as my internal muscles tighten and spasm, my body reacting in a way I can't control, a deep, spiralling pull that leaves me trembling under the force of it.

'Yes. Yes. Oh my Goddess, yes. I'm cumming, Drake,' my mind screams, to my busy, hip-thrusting, talented, sexy husband.

CHAPTER THREE

CLIMBING INTO THE BACK OF THE PALACE LIMO, I SECURE BOTH twins in their baby seats, fingers checking each buckle twice. The soft click settles something tight in my chest. Baby lotion, warm milk, and that sweet newborn scent cling to the air. Blankets, bottles, and tiny socks spill everywhere — travelling with the twins feels like moving an entire nursery every time we leave the house.

Drake slides in beside me. His hand finds my leg instantly, warm and steady, but the tension in his touch gives him away. His thumb strokes once… twice… like he's grounding himself. His gaze keeps flicking to the twins, watching their tiny chests rise and fall. That quiet, sharp parental fear hums between us — the kind that never fully switches off.

At the far end of the car, Lucile sits with her spine straight and her eyes alert, scanning every movement like she's mapping out threats before they exist. She's only filling in as Drake's guardian again, but the role settles over her like a second skin. She and Michael raised him from the time he was three, living next door to me, shaping his entire human life.

There's a flicker in her expression — a shadow of the night she and Michael walked in on Drake drinking my blood. The moment everything cracked. The moment she realised she had to send him back to Darshia only weeks ago, tearing him away from the life she built for him, from the boy she raised, from the street where our childhoods tangled together.

She smooths her face quickly, but I catch the guilt. The fear. The fierce devotion. She watches him now like she's afraid that if she looks away for even a heartbeat, she'll lose him again.

Nanny Sharonia hovers close to the twins, arms full of wipes, bottles, and rattles. Every tiny sound from the babies snaps her attention back, even when she tries to sneak glances out the window. Her shoulders stay lifted, ready to spring into action.

Mum sits opposite me. Her fingers tap her briefcase in a restless rhythm, long and elegant but tense. She probably doesn't even realise she's doing it. Her mind is already in the meeting, racing ahead of us, calculating outcomes, preparing for the worst.

The limo hums beneath us, the engine a low vibration through the floor. Outside, the early morning light is pale and cold, washing the world in that too-quiet stillness before school chaos begins.

Mum organised this meeting with the principal and staff. First day back for them. Student leaders only. I remember being one — the pressure, the expectations, the way everyone watched you like you were supposed to have answers. My grades slipping. My job hours dropping. My portfolio barely staying afloat. Dad's lessons saved me, but even then... I let myself get distracted. Parties. Lucy. Bad choices.

Drake never slipped. He built his portfolio into something massive. Multi-millionaire massive. The kind of money that changes futures. The kind of money his father definitely didn't want him to have. After the "conversation" I had with Davelt — the threats, the gunshots, the fight — I doubt he left Drake anything in his will, except for the physical and mental trauma.

Mum's briefcase holds confidentiality agreements — crisp paper, sharp edges, legal weight. Break them, and the consequences are real. Arrest. Court. Jail. Darshia doesn't do warnings.

A knot tightens in my stomach. I want this morning to go smoothly — questions, signatures, done. But the air feels too still, like the moment before a storm breaks.

The limo turns up the school's paved driveway. Empty car park. Silent buildings. The tyres crunch softly over gravel as we stop outside the administration entrance. The twins sleep through it all, tiny chests rising and falling in perfect rhythm.

We climb out — Mum, Lucile, Drake, me — leaving Nanny Sharonia with the twins and two guards. When the moment's right, she'll bring them in. If the staff are going to know I've had babies, they need to see it. See us. See me feeding them if it comes to that.

Two security cars idle behind us, engines low and watchful. Our entrances look dramatic now. Tomorrow, when school starts, we'll have to tone it down. Four guards pretending to be new students. Drake and I already have a bet on which one gets hit on first. Poor guys. If they step out of line, Grandma Ma will handle them personally.

I scan the grounds — windows, shadows, rooftops. My pulse stays high until I'm sure everything is clear. No students. No threats. Just the quiet hum of morning.

I give my sleeping babies one last look through the tinted glass. Their tiny faces soften something fierce inside me.

Then I turn toward the entry and start walking.

CHAPTER FOUR

With Drake keeping step beside me, our minds brush together in that slow, warm slide that always feels like a breath against my skin. We don't even need to decide to mind-talk — our thoughts just reach for each other, drawn together like magnets. One of the perks of being what we are — Dark One soulmates. Our conversations intertwine, intimate and private, kept hidden from the world.

Drake lingers at the edge of my mind shield, his presence a soft pressure, like fingertips tracing a line along my thoughts.

'Alexia... how are you feeling? This feels surreal. Walking back into this school after everything that happened over the break.'

His voice in my mind is deeper, smoother than when he speaks aloud. It curls through me, warm and familiar. I glance at him, and the look he gives me — concerned, protective, a little overwhelmed — hits me right in the chest. I nod once, the movement small but enough for him to feel the agreement through our link.

'We left here as kids. We're walking back in as something entirely different — married, parents, bound by a soul-tie that hums between us with every step.'

'Yeah,' I whisper back, letting my thoughts brush against his, *'it's surreal.'*

His eyes soften. The warmth that pours through the link wraps around me like a slow embrace. I look ahead toward the principal's office, but I can still feel him watching me.

'The staff are going to freak when they see the twins,' I murmur. *'And when Mum announces the royalty thing... and the bodyguards... Goddess, this morning is going to be a circus.'*

His response slides into my mind like velvet.

'Alexia... be confident. We rise above this. Always. And I love you. My wife. My soulmate. My beautiful, impossible girl.'

The affection in his thoughts spills over into mine — a gentle heat, a pulse of longing he tries to hide but can't. Images flicker at the edges of his mind: our warm bed, my skin against his, the quiet safety of home. The things he'd rather be doing than walking into a room full of teachers who still think we're just students.

A soft breath escapes me. A longer break would've helped — more time to learn the rhythm of the twins, more time to breathe, more time to just be with him. We're lucky to have my parents and a live-in nanny. Without them... I don't even want to imagine it.

The principal's secretary stands as we approach, her smile polished and professional. Her heels click softly against the floor as she steps out from behind her desk.

Instinctively, I reach out with my mind. Her aura brushes mine — layered, masked, not fully human. Interesting.

Her thoughts rise like steam.

'Oh my, it's the gorgeous hunk of maleness. Drake Smithlyn... those arms... those hands... wait. Is that a wedding ring? And Alexia too? Well, that's new. Shame for the rest of the female population... I wonder if I can pick up their thoughts...'

Oh, shite.

'Babe,' I snap through the link, *'mind shields up. Now. She's trying to read us.'*

Drake's reaction is instant — a tightening of his mental presence, a protective flare that warms through me like a heartbeat. My face stays neutral, but he feels the confusion I can't hide. She's not human — but what she is, I can't place. A shifter? A witch? Something else entirely?

I flick a warning to Mum and Lucile. Mum's response is immediate — she's suspected this woman for years. Ms Lexington hides her nature well, but not well enough today it seems.

The secretary's expression twitches when she realises she can't get into any of our minds. She masks it quickly, pasting on another smile.

"Good morning. You're here for your appointment with Mr Smite and the school staff. They're expecting you. Please follow me."

We keep a few feet behind her, our shields locked tight. Her thoughts keep slipping — frustration, curiosity, a spike of fear when she realises we're not what she assumed. Her shoulders stiffen. Her own shields snap higher.

Poor thing has no idea who she's dealing with.

She glances back. Our eyes meet.

I give her a polite smile. She tries to return it, but it wavers at the edges, her emotions bleeding through.

I send a soft whisper into her mind. *'Ms Lexington... breathe. Relax.'* My smile widens just a touch. *'We're not the bad guys here.'*

CHAPTER FIVE

I HEAR THE SECRETARY'S BREATH CATCH — A TINY, SHARP SOUND she tries to swallow. Her eyes widen, and her pulse spikes so fast it thuds against my senses. My Dark One instincts flare, picking up every shift in her body: the tightening of her jaw, the way her shields snap higher like she's slamming mental doors shut.

She scans the four of us again, her gaze lingering on me a fraction too long. Poor woman. If she keeps forcing her shields like that, she'll give herself a migraine. They won't stop me — but I let her believe they might. For now.

Her four-inch heels click-clack across the polished concrete, each step sharp and precise. The sound echoes down the hallway, too loud in the early morning quiet. We reach Principal Smite's office door. She taps twice — crisp, controlled — then pushes the heavy wooden door open.

"Mr Smite — Mrs Steele, Ms Alexia Steele, Mr Drake Smithlyn, and Mrs Clayton are here for the 8:00 AM meeting."

She turns back to us with a bright, brittle smile that never touches her eyes. Then she slips away toward her desk, her thoughts still buzzing like static at the edge of my awareness.

Inside the office, every teaching staff member is already seated. Every single one. The sight hits me harder than I expect — a wall of faces, all watching, all waiting. The five empty chairs at the front feel like a spotlight.

I don't wait for the principal to acknowledge us. He doesn't even stand. Just sits there in his plush leather chair like a king on a throne he doesn't deserve.

Fine. Two can play rude.

I walk straight to the empty seats. The others follow. As soon as we're behind our chairs, we sit. Mum on my left. Drake on my right. Lucile beside him.

Mum sets her briefcase on the desk. The click of the latch sounds like a warning shot. She pulls out the confidentiality agreements, her movements smooth but edged with steel.

"Good morning, everyone. For those who don't know me, I am Mrs Steele — Alexia's mother."

Her gaze sweeps the room, cool and assessing, until it lands on Principal Smite. The look she gives him could peel paint. He still doesn't stand. Doesn't greet us. Doesn't even pretend to be professional.

Unbelievable.

"Before we begin," Mum continues, "each of you will be required to sign a confidentiality agreement. The subject matter discussed today is highly confidential. No one outside this office is permitted access to it. Anyone who breaches these clauses will face legal consequences — including court and potential jail time."

The reaction is immediate. A chorus of sharp breaths. Eyes widening. Shoulders tensing. Even the principal's face twitches — and his is the most entertaining of all.

Until I slip into his thoughts.

And then my breath catches.

His mind is a sewer.

Images slam into me, disgusting images — twisted fantasies of bending me over his desk while his friends watch, of using me like I'm nothing but a toy. Another man forcing himself into my mouth. Laughter. Power. Control.

My stomach lurches. My skin crawls. A cold, oily disgust spreads through my chest.

I push deeper, needing to know how far this rot goes.

It goes far.

He's imagined the same things about my mother. His secretary. Several female staff. And worse — he's acted on some of them. Students. Vulnerable girls. Manipulated. Threatened. Used. All hidden behind fake charm and carefully buried records.

A low, dangerous heat coils in my gut.

This man will never be near another girl again. Even if we can't prove anything here, Darshia has ways of dealing with filth like him. Permanent ways.

Movement flickers at the edge of my vision. The secretary has slipped back into the room, quiet as a shadow, and taken a seat beside Lucile. She's taking notes.

Oh no, Ms Lexington. I don't think so!

Not today.

CHAPTER SIX

I REALLY NEED TO LEARN HOW TO STAY PHYSICALLY ALERT WHILE diving into someone's mind. My focus drifts for half a second — enough to make my shoulders loosen — and I snap myself upright again. Practice. I need more practice.

I brush against Mum's mind shield, a gentle tap.

'Excuse me, Mum...'

Her thoughts pause mid-stride, sharp and controlled.

'Yes, Alexia?'

'The secretary's taking notes. And the principal... he's filth. Sick, dangerous filth.'

I push a brief flash of his memories into her mind — the worst of them, the ones that still make my stomach twist.

Mum's mental tone hardens instantly.

'Thank you, Alexia. I'll handle it.'

Relief washes through me. For once, I get to sit back and not carry the weight of the room. For once, I get to be a teenager. The feeling lasts all of three seconds — because something in my gut already warns me it won't last long.

Mum moves through the room, handing out confidentiality agreements. When she reaches Ms Lexington, she stops, clears her throat, and her voice slices through the air.

"Ms Lexington, note-taking will not be permitted today. Please read the agreement and sign it."

The secretary flicks a glance toward Principal Smite, silently asking for direction. Mum answers before he can even open his mouth.

"Ms Lexington. Due to the nature of this meeting, you are legally bound to follow my instructions. No notes. No electronic data. No video or audio recordings. Read the agreement. Sign it."

Ms Lexington's shoulders tighten. She places her tablet on the table with careful fingers, turning it off before she even sits. Smart woman.

I let my awareness expand, slipping through the minds around me. Their thoughts ripple like disturbed water — confusion, shock, curiosity. One teacher thinks this is a prank. Another wonders if there's a hidden camera crew. If only they knew the truth about their boss.

Only one staff member notices the rings on Drake's and my fingers. Their first thought: *She must be pregnant.*

Cute. If only that were the strangest part of today.

But speaking of cameras…

I refocus on Principal Smite. His mind is a swamp, thick and foul. I push deeper, searching for the flicker I saw earlier.

There.

A camera.

No — several.

Hidden. Wired. Recording.

The lowlife is recording everything happening in his office, right this minute.

My pulse spikes. I scan the room with a slow, casual sweep of my eyes. Tiny red glimmers blink from the corners — barely visible unless you know where to look. Five cameras. But his mind says seven.

I dig deeper.

One under his desk.

One in the air vent above us.

Disgust curls through me like smoke and gritty smog.

I reach out to my security detail. Riley answers instantly, his mental presence crisp and alert.

'Yes, Princess Alexia. How may we be of service?'

'Riley, do you have anything to block video feeds or shut down surveillance cameras?'

A beat. Then his tone sharpens.

'Is someone filming you without permission? ...Actually — no one should be filming you at all.'

'Yes, Riley. The principal has hidden cameras. I want them off. Now.'

'Give me a moment, Princess. I'm on it.'

'And Riley — send a team to his house. Search everything. Collect evidence. Once we leave this office, search here too. Photograph everything. Especially the three-wall safes. His video

collection is... extensive. Bag it all. Strip the office. Strip the house.'

'Right away, Princess Alexia.'

Using my mindlink, I send him the safe locations and codes. His acknowledgement snaps through the link like a salute.

While I wait, I update Mum, Drake, and Lucile with a single mental burst. Their reactions hit instantly — shock, fury, revulsion. All three whip their heads toward Principal Smite.

Oh no.

Their anger rolls off them in waves, thick and hot. If I don't intervene, someone is going to launch across the desk and strangle him.

'Hey — cool it,' I warn, pushing calm into the link. *'We need proof before we act. Riley's handling it. Sit. Wait. And do not mention the royalty thing until Riley gives the all-clear. I am not joining Smite's little collection of blackmail victims.'*

Drake's voice cuts through, tight with worry.

'Alexia, what do you mean? Why would he blackmail anyone?'

'Drake, I'll explain later. Right now, we wait for Riley.'

DRAKE NOTICES THE WAY MY FOCUS SHARPENS. HIS GAZE FOLLOWS mine, sweeping the room with that quiet, lethal calm he gets when something feels wrong. I watch the moment he spots the blinking red lights. His jaw tightens. His shoulders shift.

Oh no. He's going to speak.

"Mr Smite," Drake says, voice steady but edged with steel, "why do you have cameras in your office? And why are you recording this meeting? Everyone heard Mrs Steele say there is to be no recording of any kind."

The room erupts.

Teachers twist in their seats, scanning the walls, the corners, the ceiling.

Murmurs rise.

Then voices.

Sharp. Accusing. Angry.

"What is this, Marc?"

"Why are we being filmed?"

"Turn the cameras off!"

"Why do you have so many?"

Even Mum and Lucile join in, their voices low and dangerous.

Mr Smite narrows his eyes at Drake, then at me. A slow, oily glare.

Great. Now he's going to be difficult.

Mrs Hoyt — vice principal, backbone of the school — stands abruptly. She strides to the door, throws it open, and turns back to the room with a look that could silence a riot.

"Everyone," she says, voice clipped, "I think you'll be more comfortable in my office. Without recording devices. Ms Lexington, please arrange extra chairs."

Ms Lexington flicks a nervous glance at Smite. His expression doesn't shift, but the tension in the room spikes. She swallows, picks up her tablet, and nods.

"Certainly, Mrs Hoyt."

She hurries out.

Within minutes, we're all in Mrs Hoyt's office. Chairs line the walls. The air feels tighter, safer — until Smite rolls in his own office chair like a throne on wheels.

The moment I see it, my stomach drops.

A camera. A listening device. Hidden in the chair's frame.

Of course he brought it.

I slip the information to Mum through our link. Her expression shifts — a tightening around the eyes, a subtle flare of anger — before she turns her full lawyer presence on him.

"Mr Smite," she says, voice smooth as a blade, "I've already informed everyone about the rules of this meeting. Remove your chair. Now. If you don't, you'll be in breach of contract. And before you claim you haven't signed anything — my daughter's bodyguard is outside this room. If her safety is compromised, he will act. You do not want to test him."

Smite gulps. His face reddens. His anger simmers just beneath the surface.

"Mrs Steele," he snaps, "you are in my school. Do not threaten me. I will have all four of you removed."

Mum pauses — calculating, dangerous.

I feel her strategy forming before she speaks.

"Mr Smite," she says, "I'm sure the police would be very interested in your office full of surveillance equipment. Especially considering you often meet with female students alone. Perhaps Ms Lexington should call them now."

Gasps ripple through the room.

Teachers stare at him.

Some look sick.

Mum continues, voice calm, almost gentle — which somehow makes it worse.

"We did not consent to being filmed. And there is no school policy allowing you to record staff meetings."

Oh, crap on a stick.

She's going for the jugular.

Smite pushes up from his seat.

No.

No, no, no.

I shoot a message to Drake. *'Stop him. He cannot leave this office.'*

Drake's hand finds mine, warm and grounding. *'What's going on, Alexia? Why can't he leave?'*

'Because Riley's team is in his office right now collecting evidence. And after this, they're going to his home. We need him contained.'

A beat passes then Drake's mental voice hardens. *'Understood.'*

He stands, moving with deliberate calm, placing himself between Smite and the door.

"Mr Smithlyn," Smite snaps, "move."

"Of course," Drake says smoothly. "Allow me."

Before Smite can react, Drake grips the chair, wheels it out the door, and leaves it in the hallway — far from any ears or lenses.

He returns to my side, squeezes my hand once, then sits.

Mrs Hoyt's voice slices through the tension.

"Marc — I mean, Mr Smite. Sit down. Stop being rude. We have an important meeting."

She turns to Mum. "Mrs Steele, you mentioned confidentiality agreements. What exactly are they for, and do we require them?"

CHAPTER SEVEN

We keep the staff contained in Mrs Hoyt's office — a controlled space, a safer space — and I make sure Principal Smite stays exactly where he is. The teachers settle into their chairs, flipping through the confidentiality agreements with stiff fingers and darting glances. Their confusion thickens the air, but it keeps them busy. Keeps them distracted.

Meanwhile, through the thin thread of my mind-link with Riley, I feel the quiet hum of movement. My security team sweeps through Smite's office like shadows — cameras pulled, listening devices disabled, files copied, cloud accounts cracked open and emptied. Every disgusting video he's ever taken is now in our hands.

Riley's voice brushes my mind, crisp and efficient.

'Princess, all devices removed. All footage secured. We've placed our own surveillance in his office and home. We'll know everything he does from this moment on.'

A pulse of satisfaction warms my chest.

My men are terrifyingly good at what they do.

Electronic warfare, surveillance, infiltration — they move like a hybrid of FBI tech ops and Navy SEALs. And they're mine.

'Thank you, Riley, and let the men know I appreciate all their hard work for me.'

'Roger that.'

Fifteen minutes pass. Every staff member except Smite signs their agreement. The teachers grow impatient, their irritation turning into open hostility.

"Marc, just sign it."

"We want to get on with this."

"Stop stalling."

Their voices push him into a corner he can't escape.

I shift my attention back to the room, watching the staff's reactions ripple as Mum explains the truth — that Drake and I are royalty, that I'm a princess, that the security isn't for show. Disbelief rolls through them like a wave. Some still expect a film crew to burst in yelling *Gotcha!* Others stare at me like they're trying to reconcile the girl who won trophies for the school with the princess standing in front of them.

Their eyes flick between Drake and me, searching for cracks in the story.

They won't find any.

Outside, I feel my security team settle back into position — a quiet perimeter around the building. Another team from Darshia is already combing through the evidence, piece by piece.

Then Mum gives me the signal.

Time for the twins.

I reach out to Nanny Sharonia.

She's already on her way.

Drake's head lifts, his eyes softening.

'Babe, I feel them. They're awake. Nanny Sharonia's bringing them in.'

His smile is pure warmth — the kind that melts every sharp edge inside me. The love he has for our children radiates through the link, bright and fierce.

'They're outside the door,' he adds. *'I'll let them in.'*

He stands — smooth, controlled — and every staff member watches him like he's performing a magic trick. He opens the door, steps aside, and Nanny Sharonia wheels in the pram.

The room shifts.

Curiosity.

Confusion.

Shock.

The staff look from the pram to Mum, to Lucile, to Drake, and finally to me.

Their expressions say everything:

Twins? How? When?

Drake catches my eye, then bends over the pram. His hands move with practised ease, unbuckling the twins. The moment he touches them, both Alley and Damien light up — wriggling, reaching, tiny hands grasping for their father.

Alley's head swivels like a tiny queen surveying her kingdom. She spots Mum first and beams a gummy smile. Then she finds me.

And I feel it — the soft pressure against my mental shields.

She pushes.

Hard.

And slips straight through.

'Ma ma mama. Pick me up. Hug, Alley.'

Her voice is bright and warm inside my mind, full of mischief and excitement. She's confused by the room, by the strangers, by the tension she can feel but not understand.

'Hello, my beautiful girl, I whisper back. Do you want Mum to hold you? Remember — you and your brother must behave. These people don't know we can talk like this. They're not like us. Be good, little one.'

Alley's expression shifts — thoughtful, processing. She understands more than she should. Born Dark Ones learn fast. Too fast.

I rise and lift her from the pram, her tiny body curling into me instantly. She tucks her head under my chin, warm and trusting. Drake mirrors me, lifting Damien and settling him against his chest, rubbing slow circles on his back.

When I turn back to the staff, their faces are priceless.

Mouths open.

Eyes wide.

Shock rolling off them in waves.

And it only deepens as they watch Drake and me with the twins — the quiet murmurs, the instinctive touches, the natural rhythm of two young parents who shouldn't exist in their world.

Two students they thought they knew.

Two royals they never expected.

Two Dark Ones, they can't begin to understand and never will.

CHAPTER EIGHT

NEARLY READY TO LEAVE.

My nerves prickle beneath my skin, a restless flutter that won't settle. I grip the edge of the vanity, breathing through the tightness in my chest. What am I doing? I have two babies who need feeding. A husband who — okay, yes, can take care of himself, but he's still mine to look after. A household to run. And as I place my hand over my belly — A new life to protect.

The thoughts tumble too fast, tripping over each other.

I'm babbling.

I know I'm babbling.

I can't stop.

There's school.

There's Darshia.

There's training.

There's the crown waiting for me like a storm on the horizon.

And then there are the rules.

So many rules.

My jaw clenches.

Grrrr.

I lift my gaze to the mirror.

The girl staring back at me looks familiar and foreign all at once.

Where did she go—the girl who only worried about exams, athletics, and whether her hair looked decent in the morning?

Now I'm a wife.

A mother.

A princess.

A future queen.

My other hand drifts to my lower stomach before I even think about it. Warmth blooms beneath my palm. The tiny life growing inside me stirs something fierce and protective in my chest.

Another daughter.

Another princess.

"Alexandra," I whisper to my reflection. "Alex."

The name feels right.

Strong.

Bright.

Hopeful.

I pray she grows in a world kinder than the one I've had to survive.

One thing is certain: my children will never be helpless. They will learn to fight. To defend themselves. To stand their ground. No child of mine will rely solely on guards. Not when danger can slip through any crack. Not when I've already come too close to dying.

Dad's training saved my life. Without it, I wouldn't be here.

I finish adjusting my school uniform, smoothing the fabric over my hips. My maternity bra sits comfortably, nursing pads clean and dry. My hair is pulled into a high ponytail — practical, neat. A light sweep of makeup brightens my tired face: soft pink lipstick, a touch of mascara, a whisper of eyeliner. Enough to look human. Enough to hide the sleepless nights.

I smile at my reflection.

A real one.

Small, but real.

If I'm going to be a wife and mother, I can at least try not to look like a zombie. The twins haven't slept properly since we arrived. They fuss in their new beds, restless and unhappy. They sleep better at my parents' house. I don't know what Mum and Dad did, but the twins adore it there.

Drake and I try to handle the nights ourselves. We want our children to know us — not just the nanny. Nanny Sharonia deserves rest too, unless something urgent happens.

A soft tug in my chest pulls my attention.

The twins are awake.

Hungry.

I glance at my watch.

Enough time for one last feed before school.

My heart squeezes.

I'm going to miss them today.

I grab my school bag on the way out of — Drake's bedroom.

No.

Our bedroom.

The thought warms me.

I head toward the nursery, mentally checking my supplies.

Spare nursing pads in the nursery.

More in my bag.

A second locker at school with a change of clothes.

Two breast pumps.

Clean bottles.

Even nappies in case the twins come to school.

Prepared.

Organised.

Trying my best.

I push open the nursery door, and the soft sounds of my babies reach me — tiny breaths, tiny movements, tiny lives that anchor me more than any crown ever could.

Time for cuddles.

Time for their last feed.

Time to hold them close before the world pulls me away again.

CHAPTER NINE

THE MOMENT I SHUT MY LOCKER, HEAT PRICKLES ACROSS THE BACK of my neck.

A glare.

No—several.

Sharp, hostile, aimed straight at me.

I turn casually, like I'm just stretching my shoulders, and catch them in my peripheral vision. A cluster of cheerleaders. Arms folded. Lips curled. Eyes full of petty, simmering hatred.

Fantastic.

Nothing like starting the morning with a pack of hormonal piranhas.

Their thoughts brush against my senses — sharp, jealous, ugly.

They're waiting for a show.

Waiting for me to slip.

Waiting for Drake. So they can entice and paw him.

I send him a warning through our link.

'Drake, your little cheerleader fan club is giving me death glares. Brace yourself. They're coming for answers.'

His annoyance flares instantly, hot and protective.

'Thanks, babe. I'll handle it.'

That's it? That's all he has to say…

'Be careful, I warn. They're planning something.'

His irritation shifts—this time aimed at me.

'Alexia. I said I'll take care of it. They tried to get me into a three-way last semester. I turned them down. They're immature. They don't interest me. You're my soulmate. My wife. The mother of my children. I go home with you. I want you. Only you.'

The words hit me like a storm — then the link slams shut.
He blocks me.
It stings.
Not because he can keep me out — he can't, not really — but because he's choosing to.
So I give him space.
I head to class, only to have one of the cheerleaders slip in ahead of me.
Tabatha.
Of course.
Her name alone makes me want to laugh — *to-bath-her* —but the humour dies when she turns, eyes narrowed, posture sharp. She's all long golden hair, pouty lips, and nipples that could take out an eye. She's been after Drake since forever, and she hates that he's always chosen me.
Just wait until she notices the rings.
I walk toward my usual table — three years, same seat — when a spike of movement hits my senses.

Fast.

Targeted.

Her.

I sidestep without thinking.

Tabatha slams into the desk instead, bouncing off and landing flat on her arse.

How I don't laugh out loud at her foolishness, I never know. I place my books down, then look at her with polite confusion.

"Tabatha, what are you doing on the floor?"

Her mind is a storm of rage and humiliation. She wanted to knock me into the desk. She wanted a scene.

Too bad.

I glance toward the front—no teacher.

Of course, there isn't. That's why she targeted me.

I turn to the boys nearby. "Someone help Tabatha up. She's fallen."

Her head snaps up, eyes blazing. "How dare you push me!"

"I didn't touch you," I say calmly. "I walked in and put my books down. That's it."

She flicks a look at her little group of admirers.

I feel the lie forming before she opens her mouth.

"Oh boys, you saw Alexia push me. She hurt me."

Two of them rush over, hands all over her as they haul her up. She milks it — fake tears, trembling lip, the whole pathetic performance.

I roll my eyes.

Quietly.

But not quietly enough.

"Tabatha," I sigh, "stop making a fool of yourself. You nearly slammed into me. Why did you try to hit me?"

Her eyes widen — caught.

"Don't you dare accuse me!"

I step closer, lean in, and whisper near her ear, "Every

classroom has new security cameras. Your little stunt is recorded. So maybe get your head out of your arse and sit down."

She jerks back, scanning the room.

To her, as far as she cared. No cameras in sight.

Her smile turns smug. "I don't see any. You're lying."

Goddess, she's dense.

"If you'd bothered to come to school yesterday, you'd know about the new security."

I leave her standing there and take my seat.

The whispers start immediately — her fall, her drama, her terrible acting.

I ignore them, flipping open my notebook.

Tabatha's thoughts scrape against my mind — rage, humiliation, and a desperate need to claw back control.

Pathetic.

The teacher finally walks in, oblivious. Students scramble. Tabatha slinks to her seat, still fuming, still plotting. Her intentions brush my senses like barbed wire.

She's not done.

Drake nudges the edge of our link — hesitant, cautious.

'Alexia... I'm sorry. I shouldn't have shut you out.'

I keep my eyes on the board.

'We'll talk later. I need to focus.'

He doesn't like it. Too bad. Maybe he should have treated me better.

He accepts my reply anyway.

Good.

The bell rings. I gather my books quickly, wanting to slip out before Tabatha—

Too late.

She blocks the doorway, arms crossed, chest thrust forward like she's trying to weaponise her nipples.

"Alexia," she says sweetly. "We need to talk."

"No, we really don't," I calmly reply.

I step left.

She steps to my left.

I step right.

She steps to my right. Blocking my path.

"You think you're special," she hisses. "Just because Drake is giving you attention."

I lift my left hand.

The ring catches the light.

"We're married."

Her face freezes.

Her thoughts explode.

"You're lying!"

"Ask him."

I brush past her.

Her shock is delicious.

But beneath it, something darker coils — sharp, determined, venomous.

She isn't giving up.

And whatever she's planning…it's aimed straight at me.

I SLIDE INTO MY USUAL SEAT, THE ONE I'VE CLAIMED FOR THREE years, in my English class, and glance at the clock.

Five minutes late.

No teacher.

The room buzzes with low chatter, restless energy building as students realise Ms Lallown still hasn't arrived. She was at the meeting yesterday. She should be here.

I open my novel, pretending to read, but my senses stay sharp. A flicker of movement at the doorway catches my eye — tall, still, deliberate. Not a student.

I look up.

A stranger steps inside, strides to the teacher's desk, and drops his bag with a thud. The room quiets around him, whispers rising like smoke.

Relief teacher.

But why?

Students start asking questions before he even turns around.

He answers in a loud, arrogant voice that grates across my nerves.

"Morning, students. I am your new English teacher, Mr Stragoft. I am replacing Ms Lallown. She was involved in a car accident early this morning and is recovering in hospital. She will not return until the end of term."

Gasps ripple through the room.

Shock. Confusion. Fear.

My stomach drops.

I look at Tabatha. She's smiling. A slow, smug, poisonous smile.

I slip into her thoughts — and the truth hits me like ice water.

Mr Stragoft is her great uncle.

She knew. She planned this.

My gaze snaps back to him. I push deeper, brushing against his mind.

His thoughts ooze with satisfaction. He's pleased Ms Lallown is hurt. He's already planning to fail half the class — not just fail us, ruin us — and the delight he takes in that curdles in my stomach.

A cold ripple crawls down my spine.

Because of Tabatha. Because of her petty, jealous, vindictive little tantrum, she's dragged her great-uncle into this school to sabotage anyone she doesn't like.

The realisation hits me like a punch.

He can't do that. But he intends to.

The thought snaps through my mind, sharp and hot, tightening something deep in my chest.

This is bad. Very, very bad.

"Okay, students. Quiet down and take your seats."

His voice slices through the room. His eyes sweep across us — beady, dark, predatory — cataloguing faces, weighing weaknesses, deciding who he'll break first. When his gaze lands on me, something inside me twists hard.

I force a polite smile, lower my eyes to my book…and that's when it hits.

His thoughts slam into me like a shove.

Recognition. Interest. And beneath it — something slick and foul, the kind of intention that makes my skin crawl.

He knows who I am. He's already imagining things he has no right to imagine.

His mind is oily, thick with fantasies he thinks he's hiding. He has no idea I can hear every one of them.

I keep my head down, breathing slow, and reach out to Laif.

'Laif. Have you read his thoughts yet?'

'Not yet, Alexia. But the way he keeps staring at you... I'm already uneasy.'

'You should be. He's here to make things difficult for me — and for a few others. He's related to Tabatha. The girl who tried to slam me into a desk earlier.'

Laif's mental tone sharpens instantly.

'Should I contact Riley?'

'Yes. Tell him everything. I want a full background check on this man. And I want the truth about Ms Lallown's accident. Every detail. Injuries. Circumstances. Witnesses. Everything.'

'You think she was targeted?'

'Yes. And I think Tabatha helped arrange it.'

A beat of silence. Then, *'Understood, Princess Alexia. I'll contact Riley now.'*

And he calls me Princess Alexia again, and I sigh internally. *'Laif — at school, call me Alexia. If anyone finds out I'm a princess, my life becomes a nightmare.'*

'You mean Tabatha?'

'Exactly. Now go. I need to focus on him.'

I lift my eyes just enough to watch Mr Stragoft begin roll call, his voice dripping with authority he hasn't earned.

His mind pulses with malice. With intent. With plans he thinks he'll get away with.

He has no idea he just walked into a room with a Dark One princess who can hear every vile thought he tries to bury.

And he has no idea that I'm already planning my next move.

CHAPTER TEN

STUDENTS SWARM THE HALLWAY LIKE STARTLED BIRDS, DARTING from one class to the next. I slip through them easily, weaving between backpacks and elbows until the noise fades behind me. The moment I step into the administration wing, the air shifts — quieter, cooler, more controlled.

I slow my pace, scanning for Ms Lexington.

Drake brushes the edge of my mind, gentle but insistent. I let him in.

'Babe, why aren't you in class? Where are you?'

'Administration building.'

His worry spikes fast. *'Why? What's wrong? Are you okay? Did something happen?'*

'Yes and no.'

'Alexia... what does that even mean?'

I exhale through my nose. *'My English teacher was in an accident. She's out for the term. We have a replacement — a man who's already planning to fail half the class. And thanks to your little friend Tabatha, he's targeting me and a few others she doesn't like.'*

A moment of stunned silence. Then— *'What? What does Tabatha have to do with this?'*

Is he actually serious right now?

Remaining calm, I say, *'Drake, she hates me. She wants you. She's related to the new teacher — Mr. Stragoft.'*

'You've got to be kidding me. I never thought she'd take it this far.'

Goes to show how little he knew her.

'Well, she has. So think fast,' I mutter as I spot Ms Lexington returning to her desk. *'I have to go. I'm going to try to transfer into your English class. Or Lucy's old one. If I can, I'll keep Laif with me.'*

'Okay. Just be careful. I love you.'

'I love you too.'

I close the link and focus on Ms Lexington.

"Good morning, Ms Lexington," I say with a smile. "How are you today?"

She returns a polite one. "Good morning, Alexia. What can I do for you?"

"I need to transfer out of my English class. Unless we can get a different teacher."

Her fingers fly across the keyboard. "Why? Did something happen? Did he do something inappropriate?"

I pick up a brochure, pretending to read while I slip into her mind.

'Ms Lexington... do you know what kind of man Mr Stragoft is? He's planning to fail students — especially the ones his niece doesn't like.'

Her thoughts stutter. Her eyes flick up to me, then back to the screen.

'What do you mean he's related to a student? As far as I know, he has no family here.'

'Trust me. Tabatha is his niece. And if he gets his way, he'll be taking advantage of female students.'

Her mental voice spikes with horror.

'What? No. We just got rid of one lowlife.' She exhales sharply.

'Yes, I know all about Mr Smite. Men like that don't belong near students.'

'You're lucky he never targeted you,' I murmur through the link.

'It wasn't luck,' she replies, bitterness flickering. *'But enough of that. What about Mr Stragoft?'*

'I don't trust him. And I wouldn't be surprised if he had something to do with Ms Lallown's accident.'

'Alexia... that's a serious accusation. The accident—'

'When he's near, read his mind. You'll see. Now — can I change classes?'

Out loud, she sighs. "Alexia… according to the system, it's too late in the year to change. I'm sorry."

She brushes my mind again, asking permission. I let her in.

'Once I check his thoughts myself, I'll speak with Acting Principal Hoyt. If he's changed the course structure, that's a violation. I'll handle it.'

"He already changed our reading list," I say aloud. "He told us we're doing two books instead of the assigned one."

"What? He can't do that. The curriculum is set."

"You tell him that," I mutter. "He's made it clear we'll do what he says. I don't have time for this. I have too much to lose."

She nods, jaw tight. "I'll speak with Acting Principal Hoyt. She needs to know."

"You're sure I can't change classes? It's the first day."

"I'm sorry, Alexia. No. You're stuck with him."

Damn it.

Heat coils in my chest — frustration, anger, the sharp edge of fear. I can't let this man derail my final semester. Not when everything is already hanging by a thread.

Something needs to be done.

And I know exactly who to call.

Riley.

If Mr Stragoft thinks he can fail me — fail us — he's about to learn what happens when a Dark One princess decides she's done playing nice.

Fail me?

My arse he will.

CHAPTER ELEVEN

So far today, has been an eye opener. I've already expressed milk twice. Thankfully, one of the guards whisked the bottles away with military precision, swapping out the pump like we're running a tactical operation instead of dealing with my leaking breasts. Motherhood is wild, and my patience is abandoning me.

By lunchtime, my patience is hanging by a thread. Tabatha's voice has been scraping across my nerves all morning — sharp, petty, poisonous. I swear, if she flicks her hair in my direction one more time, I might actually combust. Laif listens while we walk, his jaw ticking tighter with every detail I give him. I don't sugarcoat anything — Tabatha's snide comments, the way she keeps circling Drake like a starving vulture, the way she keeps trying to needle me into reacting.

By the time I finish, he exhales slowly, the kind of breath that says I'm two seconds from removing a problem permanently.

"She's escalating," he mutters, eyes scanning the hallway like he's already planning countermeasures. "Her behaviour is becoming obsessive. I don't like it."

"No shit," I reply, rubbing the bridge of my nose. "If she keeps pushing, I'm going to lose my temper. And you know how well that goes."

"I do," he says dryly. "Which is why we're adjusting our strategy."

I arch a brow. "Strategy?"

"We sit together from now on," he says, tone firm. "Every class we share. No exceptions."

I blink at him. "You're assigning yourself to me?"

"I'm protecting you," he corrects, not missing a beat. "And Drake will agree. He'll want you covered when he's not in the room."

A warm flicker of affection sparks in my chest — for both of them. "We only share two subjects," I remind him. "Four times a week with Drake. The rest with you."

"Exactly." His gaze sharpens. "And I'd rather you sit with me than deal with Tabatha's venom. She's unpredictable. And stupid. A dangerous combination."

I snort. "You're not wrong."

He gives me a sideways look. "I rarely am."

I roll my eyes, but the corner of his mouth twitches — the Laif equivalent of a full-blown grin.

We reach the end of the hallway, and I shift my bag on my shoulder as we head toward the cafeteria, weaving through the crowd. The noise grows louder the closer we get — chatter, laughter, the clatter of trays. Normal school chaos.

We slip into one of the long tables against the far wall. Big enough for eight, maybe more. Perfect. Neutral. Out of the way. A place where I can breathe without someone's drama landing in my lap.

Laif sits across from me, leaning forward, elbows on the table, voice low. "We need to talk about something else."

My stomach tightens. "That sounds ominous."

"It is." His eyes lock onto mine. "Tabatha isn't acting alone."

A cold ripple slides down my spine. "What do you mean?"

"She's been talking to people. Stirring things. Trying to turn students against you."

My pulse spikes. "Why?"

"Because she's jealous. Because she's petty. Because she wants Drake and can't stand that he chose you." He pauses. "And because she's stupid enough to think she can win."

I clench my jaw. "Let her try."

He shakes his head. "No. You're not engaging. Not unless you have to. That's an order."

I glare at him. "You don't get to order me."

"I do when it concerns your safety."

I open my mouth to argue — but he's right to a point. And we both know it.

I lean back, exhaling. "Fine. But if she pushes me—"

"I'll handle it," he says, tone final. "You focus on staying calm. Drake and I will deal with the rest."

I huff, crossing my arms. "I hate being handled."

"I know," he says, voice softening. "But you're not alone in this. Not anymore."

Something warm and steady settles in my chest. A reminder that I'm surrounded — protected — even when the world feels like it's tilting sideways.

Before I can respond, movement at the cafeteria entrance catches my eye.

Tabatha.

Of course.

She glances over her shoulder toward our table, smirking with that evil little grin she thinks makes her look powerful. Then she struts toward a group of boys like she's auditioning for the role of *Most Annoying Human Alive*.

Laif follows my gaze, his expression darkening. "And so it begins."

Sensing Drake getting closer, I reach for him through the link before he walks through the cafeteria door.

'Drake, Tabatha is up to something. Just giving you the heads-up.'

'Thanks, Babe. We're nearly there. I'll grab lunch and join you soon.'

Good. Because I have a feeling I'm going to need him.

He appears a few moments later, grabs his lunch, and with a tray in hand, heads straight for us — until Tabatha's shrill voice cuts through the cafeteria.

"Drake, sit over here! I saved you a seat!"

Oh, fan-fucking-tastic. She's starting early.

Drake doesn't even break stride. "No, thank you, Tabatha. I'm sitting with Alexia and the others. Enjoy your lunch."

Her smile curdles. "Why do you want to be anywhere near her, when you know you'd rather be with me? Especially after last night."

My blood spikes. Oh, my Goddess. I'm two seconds from launching myself across the room. Laif rises with me, ready.

I clamp down on my temper and send a sharp message to my husband.

'Drake... explain to your little friend—'

But he's already moving. He hands his tray to Laif, closes the distance between us in three long strides, and then his arms are around me — lifting, pulling, claiming. His mouth crashes into mine, and the world just… drops away.

Heat. Breathlessness. My fingers in his hair. My legs around his waist. The cafeteria erupts into cheers, but it's all background noise. He kisses me like he's drowning and I'm the air he needs.

When we finally break apart — seconds, minutes, who knows — he presses a soft kiss to my forehead, then my nose, and rests his forehead against mine.

"I love you, Alexia." Loud. Clear. Deliberate.

A message to everyone watching.

Tabatha's voice cracks like cheap glass. "Drake, why are you doing this to us? You know you love me!"

Drake turns, annoyance rolling off him. "Tabatha, quit it. There is no us. Never has been. Never will be. I was with Alexia last night — like every other night. We're together. We're committed. Do yourself a favour and grow up."

Her face cycles through shock, humiliation, rage. "You'll regret this, Drake Smithlyn! Mark my words!" She storms out, the cafeteria cheering her exit like it's the best entertainment they've had all week.

I exhale slowly. Trouble is coming. I can feel it like static under my skin.

'Drake, you know this is only the beginning. Whatever she's planning… it's going to be bad.'

'I know. And I'm sorry, Alexia. I should've shut this down sooner. I'll talk to some of my friends, see what we can do. I'm not putting up with her stupidity anymore. Also… Baby, you need to express. Your breasts look full, and I can smell your milk. I think you're leaking.'

Oh, crap on a stick.

He lowers me gently, my legs wobbling after that kiss. The scent hits my nose a second later — warm, sweet, unmistakable. Damn it. I was hoping to last until after lunch.

I send a quick message to Samual.

'Samual, I require your assistance. Can you deliver a pump and bottles to one of the designated rooms — the one without surveillance.'

'Roger that, Princess. Be there shortly.'

'Thank you. Much appreciated.'

Thank the Goddess for that small mercy.

MILK STREAMS THROUGH THE CLEAR HOSES IN TWO FAST, STEADY lines, warm against my skin as the pump pulls rhythmically. Four bottles fill quicker than I expect. The machine hums softly, the only sound in the small room. I exhale, shoulders loosening. Both breasts empty at once — thank the Goddess. This pump is a thousand times better than the one I used earlier.

The milk disappears into the cooling tank, the unit humming as it chills everything within seconds.

The door clicks.

Drake slips inside with a tray of food balanced in one hand, closing the door behind him with his foot. That grin — the one that always means trouble — spreads across his face the moment he sees me.

"Alexia," he says, voice low and warm, "how are you going? Nearly finished?"

His eyes drag over me — from my bare chest, to the milk still racing through the hoses, to the soft rise and fall of my breathing — before meeting mine again. That cheeky glint in his gaze sharpens.

Uh-oh.

Heat curls low in my stomach. My body reacts before my brain can form a coherent thought.

Not at school, my mind whispers uselessly.

Drake steps closer, slow and deliberate, like he's stalking prey he already knows belongs to him. He reaches for the pump controls, flicks the switch, and the suction releases with a soft pop. The sudden cool air hits my skin, making me shiver.

He notices.

Of course, he notices.

His grin softens into something warmer, deeper — protective and intimate all at once. His fingers brush my skin as he removes the cups, gentle enough to steal my breath. The air conditioning chills the droplets left behind, and goosebumps rise across my chest.

The carry bag seals shut, hiding the bottles away like nothing ever happened.

Drake's eyes darken.

He doesn't say a word.

He doesn't need to.

The room feels smaller.

Hotter.

Charged.

And I know — he's absolutely up to no good.

"COME HERE," HE MURMURS, NOT TOUCHING ME, BUT CLOSE enough that the heat of him wraps around me anyway.

His tone is playful, but there's a seriousness under it — the kind that reminds me he's not just my husband, but my anchor. My safe place. My everything.

I exhale slowly, letting the moment settle, letting the tension ease without disappearing entirely. With Drake, it never really disappears.

Our lips fuse together, our passion infuses with enough heat to warm up a small town. My surroundings disappear. In the far recesses of my subconscious, the hard surface of the wall presses into my back, as the cool air from the air conditioning attempts to cool my naked, heated flesh.

Drake and I become one; our bodies join in the utopia that only soulmates can create. Our love grows, our movements become passionate and heated. If I don't end up with wall burn on my back, I'll be glad. Drake's hips pump hard and faster, chasing our impending orgasms.

A little more, just a little. I'm so close.

My gums tingle, then my canines drop.

Both Drake and I simultaneously sink our fangs into each other's necks, causing our world to burst into a surge of magical love, mate bond, and blood.

The delicious flavour of his ambrosia fills my mouth before sliding down my throat, satisfying my thirst and hunger. With every pull on his neck, the pleasure of his release intensifies, as he does the same to me. My body keeps spasming, muscles repeatedly tightening and relaxing, as my orgasm continues to roll through me.

My tongue glides over the fresh, raised bite marks on Drake's neck, sealing the wound. A stray drop clings to my lip; I catch it with a slow sweep of my tongue — and freeze.

My senses begin to come back online when I finally sense an intruder.

Someone is at the door.

Oh shite.

The bliss evaporates like someone dumped ice water over my head. My pulse spikes. Drake's body is still pressed against mine, pinning me to the wall, both of us breathless and half-lost in each other.

I turn my head sharply.

Too late.

The door is cracked open, and standing there — eyes huge, mouth hanging open — is Lucy.

My Lucy.

My old best friend — Lucy Blachart.

She looks like she's walked in on a murder. Or a porno. Or both.

I breach Drake's mind in a snap. *'Baby, we have company. Someone's here. And they're very, very shocked.'*

'Ha — what?'

He's still foggy, still riding the aftershocks of our high. His hips are still pressed to mine when he finally registers my words.

'What do you mean someone is—'

He turns his head towards the door.

He sees her.

He freezes.

I clear my throat, trying to salvage whatever dignity I have left.

"Lucy, either come in or close the door and wait outside. I need to get dressed."

Lucy blinks. Once. Twice. Three times.

Her thoughts slam into me like a tidal wave.

'Oh my Goddess, when did Alexia and Drake team up? Did I just see her bite him? Holy shit. Alexia is a Dark One? How did I not know? I leave town for nearly two months and miss EVERYTHING.'

What.

How does Lucy know about Dark Ones?

I dive deeper into her mind — fast, sharp, needing answers.

Images flash.

Lucy with a man.

Laughing.

Kissing.

Bodies tangled.

Running.

Hiding.

Loving.

My breath catches.

She's in love.

And he's on the run.

And the man?

Drake's twin.

Just like she said.

Holy shit.

No — holy freaking way.

What has she gotten herself into?

As I sift through her thoughts, something else brushes against my senses — a second presence, faint but unmistakable. I scan the room, then zero in on Lucy again.

Her body.

Her aura.

Her energy.

Oh my Goddess.

No.

No way.

Lucy is pregnant.

You have GOT to be shitting me.

My Lucy girl is pregnant with my brother-in-law's baby.

I check again — seven weeks, maybe. She doesn't know. Not yet.

And then I feel it — the other presence.

An entity.

Magic.

My eyes narrow at my friend.

Lucy is a witch.

What the actual…

Since when?

How did I not know?

My Dark One senses are getting sharper — first the embryo, now this. Witches are real? Since when are witches real?

Lucy finally finds her voice.

"No freakin way." She shakes her head like she's trying to rattle the image loose. "No. No freakin way this is possible. How are you a Dark One, Alexia? How? When? And since when are you and lover boy—"

Her eyes drop.

Way too low.

Hey. Eyes up, girl.

I fold my arms over my chest.

"Yes, Lucy, since when were you a witch? And while we're at it — how did you hook up with Drake's twin brother?"

Her face drains of colour.

Shock.

Denial.

Confusion.

Her thoughts explode again, loud and panicked.

'How does she know I'm a witch? And what is she talking about, Drake's twin? Drake doesn't have siblings. He definitely doesn't have a twin.'

Oh, Lucy.
You have no idea.

CHAPTER TWELVE

WITH OUR CLOTHES BACK ON AND THE THREE OF US SITTING ON the hard plastic chairs, the room feels too small, too bright, too real. The adrenaline fades, and the weight of everything slams into me.

Drake sits beside me, fingers laced through mine. His emotions bleed into me through our bond — shock, confusion, protectiveness, disbelief. He feels the baby inside Lucy, too. He shouldn't be able to. But he does.

His brother. My best friend. A baby.

And Lucy… is a witch.

My mind spins.

I skim the surface of her thoughts — not deep, not invasive, just enough to understand the shape of her fear — and the truth hits me like a punch.

Her step-uncle.

The assault.

The "ceremony."

The cousin.

The coven.

The hatred of Dark Ones — especially for Devlain.

My stomach twists. My hands curl into fists.

I need to hear it from her.

I need her to say it out loud.

"Lucy," I whisper, "what are you doing here? You disappeared last term. No goodbye. Nothing. What happened? Why did you have to leave?"

She lowers her head, breath trembling in and out. When she looks up, her smile is thin and broken. Her eyes are full of sorrow so deep it makes my chest ache.

Her thoughts loosen — unravelling like a knot pulled too tight for too long.

"Hey, A-Babs," she says with a shaky laugh. "Long time, no see."

It's her coping laugh — the one she uses when she's seconds from falling apart.

She inhales again, deeper this time. "Alexia… I'll start at the beginning."

Her gaze flicks to Drake, hesitation flickering across her face. She knows he'll hear everything through me anyway. She turns back to me.

"At the start of last term, I started seeing this guy named Lain Smith." Her lips twitch. "Okay, now that I think about it, he does look a bit like lover boy here. But no — that's not why I fell for him. There was just… something about him. Something I wanted more of, as if he was part of me. Part of my soul."

Her eyes soften — dreamy, aching — and I know she's thinking of Devlain.

"My parents and step-uncle caught us together. And when my uncle demanded he 'test' me in a virginal ceremony, I knew I was screwed." Her voice cracks. "Before I could run, they grabbed me. Transported me back to the coven. Locked me in a room."

Her hands tremble.

Her breath shakes.

Her memories hit me like shards of glass.

"I'd heard about his ceremonies," she whispers. "My cousin told me. How he assaulted her. Impregnated her. She was sixteen."

Anger burns through her words, sharp and shaking.

"He hurt her, Alexia. In front of the family. To 'prove' she wasn't pure. And they let him. They let him do it to girl after girl. He's sick. Twisted. A predator."

A tear slips down her cheek. She doesn't wipe it away.

My stomach churns. My heart pounds. I want to tear her family apart with my bare hands.

Lucy's voice drops to a tremor. "They strapped me down. Completely exposed. Blindfolded. Gagged. I couldn't move. I couldn't see who was in the room."

My breath catches.

"I could hear them, though," she whispers. "Smell them. They were men from the coven. They touched me. Talked about me like I wasn't human. Like I was something to inspect. They said they had to 'check' me. To see what a Dark One had done to me."

Her voice breaks.

"They took turns, Alexia. Fingers. Hands. Using anything they wanted. Laughing. Grunting. Battering my body. Saying they needed to feel the difference. Saying they were purifying me. Cleansing me. Punishing me for being with Devlain."

A tear rolls down my cheek. Those animals were raping my best friend. My fists shake.

Lucy swallows hard.

"My body is in pain. Laughter and exciting voices reach my ears as my step-uncle brought his dog into the room," her voice cracks into a whisper. "He let it near me. I was screaming into the gag. Begging them to stop."

Bile rises in my throat. I move without thinking — sliding

closer, wrapping my arms around her trembling shoulders. She collapses into me, shaking.

Through her thoughts, I feel everything — the terror, the humiliation, the pain. It hits me so hard I almost choke on it. Those filthy, perverted, disgusting bastards.

"Shhh, Lucy," I whisper into her hair. "Stop. You don't have to relive this. What they did to you... it should never have happened."

She lifts her face, eyes red and fierce.

"I have to finish," she says. "You need to know what happened that day."

I hold her tighter.

"Okay, Luce," I whisper. "I'm here."

Lucy's voice drops to a thin, hurting whisper.

"The sounds around me... the way they move, breathe, laugh, encourage each other... it makes my skin crawl. It was like it was on repeat — Something warm hits my body. Wet. Sticky. What felt like every few seconds or so. Hands rub the wet globs across my skin. I can't see anything. I can't stop anything. I'm tied there. Terrified."

My stomach lurches. Acid burns the back of my throat.

How did she survive this?

How did she survive them?

Lucy shudders, breath hitching, and I know — the worst part is still coming.

"With all the noise they're making," she whispers. What she doesn't say outloud, I can hear it in her mind. As if I'm her, I can feel what the flea bag is doing to her. Before I throw up, I slam my mind to hers. Her voice brings me back. "The dog gets worked up. Too worked up. It growls, barks, and snaps. It bites me — hard — high on the inside of my thigh."

I flinch. My hand flies to my mouth. I am going to be sick.

Goddess.

No.

I shove a handful of tissues into her shaking hands. She wipes her face, blows her nose, tries to steady herself — but her voice cracks again.

"When they see the dog biting me, they panic. I hear them yelling — saying it's gone too far. But instead of stopping anything, they run. They leave. They leave me alone with my step-uncle and his dog."

Her voice breaks. "I'm bleeding. I'm in agony. My throat is raw from screaming."

My poor, beautiful friend. What she has been through.

Lucy trembles in my arms; my mind must have lowered, as her memories start crashing into my head like a storm. My vision blurs. I'm crying now — silent tears sliding down my cheeks as I try to hold myself together for her.

"What makes it worse," she whispers, "is feeling the dog's hot breath on my neck. I think it's going to bite me again. Rip my throat out. I truly believe I'm going to die, Alexia. I'm screaming into the gag until my throat feels shredded."

I pull her closer, wrapping my arms around her, trying to warm her cold skin with my own. She shakes violently, breath stuttering.

"Then I feel my step-uncle's filthy fingernails scraping over my skin," she says, voice trembling. "He's laughing. Enjoying that I'm hurt. Bleeding. Terrified. He lifts my blindfold just enough so I can see him — see what he's doing — while he whispers what he plans next. How no one will ever touch me again."

My stomach twists so hard I nearly gag.

My heart cracks.

My rage simmers hot and lethal.

Lucy's voice fractures.

"Just when he's about to... about to hurt me even worse... someone bursts into the room." She hiccups, her breath shallow.

"Hearing Lain burst in is my miracle," she whispers. "Everything explodes. Barking. Yelling. Crashing. Bones breaking. Chaos everywhere."

Her eyes glaze as she relives it.

"Lain pulls my blindfold up just enough for me to see. When my eyes adjust... I see the carnage. Lain has already taken down the dog. And then he goes straight for my step-uncle."

Lucy's voice drops to a whisper as she shakes her head.

"My step-uncle falls. Hits his head on the table I'm strapped to. The angle is wrong — horribly wrong. I hear the crack. By the time he hits the floor... his neck is broken. Can you believe that horrible man dies because of a table?"

She wipes another tear away with shaking fingers.

"Lain unstraps me, removes the blindfold and gag, and carries me out wrapped in a blanket. My mother sees me — shaking, bleeding, covered in you do not want to know — and she screams at Lain, thinking he hurt me."

My breath catches.

Goddess. What a nightmare.

"But when I grab her hand," Lucy says, "I show her everything through our link. All of it. She's horrified. Appalled. And right then, she decides to help me escape. She tells Lain to run. To hide. She thanks him for saving me."

Lucy takes several trembling breaths.

"I told him I'd contact him when I could. But I haven't seen him since. He's not answering his phone. I'm scared for him, Alexia. My step-uncle's family is after him. They want revenge. They don't care — to them, Lain was the predator. They only care that a Dark One killed a witch."

Her eyes lift to mine — terrified, pleading.

"Lucy... was the police ever involved?" I ask softly, even though I already know the answer.

She scoffs bitterly.

"You're kidding, right? That coven protects their monsters. I guarantee some of those men are still doing what my step-uncle did."

My heart breaks — not just for Lucy, but for every girl trapped in that hell.

"My mother has me seeing a special counsellor," Lucy says. "Someone who works with witches. She's helped me so much. At least now I can be in public again. Just... don't let any dogs near me. I can't handle it. If one gets too close, I... react. Badly."

Okay. No puppy for Lucy. Ever.

"And I miss Lain," she whispers. "I need him, Alexia. There's this pull... this feeling that I need to see him soon."

I feel it too — the truth humming beneath her words.

Lucy will need Devlain's blood soon.

For her and the babies' survival.

I swallow hard. It's like history on repeat. I know how dangerous it is for her to go without Devlain's blood.

"Lucy," I say gently, "don't take this the wrong way, but... how long before the attack did you and Devlain — I mean Lain — last have sex? Did you have unprotected sex before the assault?"

She stiffens.

"Why do you ask, Alexia?"

Her thoughts spill — raw, sarcastic, hurting.

'As if I'd have sex again after what happened. Lain is the only one I've ever let touch me. I miss him. I hope I can go near him again. Time will tell.'

I take a breath. "It's just... I'm not sure how to say this, but you need to know. Lucy... I can detect another life force inside you. You're pregnant."

She jerks back like I slapped her. "That's stupid, Alexia. I'm on the pill. How can I be pregnant?"

How do I explain to her about Dark Ones and their soulmates? "Lucy… if you have unprotected sex with your soulmate, you can fall pregnant very quickly."

"What are you talking about? How would you know that?"

Her eyes drop to my hand.

To my ring.

Then to Drake's.

I feel the moment it clicks.

"No shit," she breathes. "You're married. You and Drake are soulmates. You fell pregnant yourself — that's how you know."

"Uh-huh," I say softly. "You could say that."

I ask Drake for my phone. He pulls up the photo app and hands it to me. I turn the screen toward her.

"Lucy… this was four weeks ago."

She glances — then snatches the phone.

"Holy shit. Is this real? You look like you're about to pop. This has to be photoshopped."

I shake my head and swipe to the next photo — me holding the twins in the hospital.

"Lucy, meet Damien and Alley."

Her jaw drops.

"Holy shit on a brick. You had twins? And you're back at school looking like that?" Her eyes rove over my body. " How?!"

"Dark One soulmate pregnancy," I say. "Short. Intense. Fast healing. C-section. Back to normal in days."

Her eyes drop to my chest. They widen. "Holy shit, Alexia. Your tits are bigger."

Of course she says that.

"Thank you, Lucy," I say with an eyeroll, "And yes — breastfeeding twins will do that."

"So you're serious. You've had twins. You're breastfeeding. Where are they? Is your mum watching them?"

"No. Mum and Dad are at work. Our nanny is with them. I express milk during the day and have it delivered home."

Her eyebrows shoot up.

"You have a nanny?"

CHAPTER THIRTEEN

LUNCH BREAK EVAPORATES FASTER THAN I EXPECT. LUCY TALKS like she's trying to outrun the clock — words tumbling out, hands flying everywhere, her energy vibrating between panic and sarcasm.

"So, guess what my mother decides?" she announces, throwing her arms up. "'Lucy needs stability.'" She even air-quotes it, her face twisting like she's tasted something sour. "Apparently stability means shipping me back here like I'm a misbehaving parcel."

She drops into the seat beside me with a dramatic groan.

"And you'll love this part," she continues, leaning in conspiratorially. "She's got me staying with her human relatives. The everyday, basic, *magic doesn't exist* type of humans." Her eyes widen in mock horror. "They have no idea about our world. None. I'm basically undercover in my own family, Alexia. Do you know how exhausting that is?"

She flops back in her chair, arms crossed, muttering, "Honestly, if time could slow down long enough for me to breathe, that'd be great. But no. Apparently, the universe thinks I need character development."

I snort. She shoots me a glare, then softens.

"And I'm still ticked you didn't invite me to your damn wedding," she says, pointing at me accusingly. "I should be furious. But then you explain that whole Dark One Joining Ceremony thing and — yeah, no. I'm relieved I wasn't there. I would've passed out. Or screamed. Or both."

She shudders dramatically.

"And don't even get me started on walking in on you and Drake going at it like bunnies against the wall forty minutes ago. That was enough trauma for a lifetime. I swear, I never want to see you having sex ever again."

I choke on a laugh. Drake coughs into his fist, trying to hide his grin.

Lucy bites her lip, her bravado slipping. "Alexia... I honestly don't know whether to believe you about this whole pregnancy thing. Me? Pregnant?" She shakes her head, still processing. "Fine. I'll come over this afternoon. And don't give me that look — I know you live with Drake now. His house. Next door to your parents. I'm not stupid."

She rolls her eyes, but her voice softens. "I'll use one of those pregnancy tests from that giant multipack your doctor gave you in Darshia. Maybe then I'll actually believe you."

She gathers her books against her chest, exhaling like she's been holding her breath for hours.

"Alright... I'll see you later. I need to get to my next class before I completely lose my mind."

She turns and walks off, her shoulders tight, her steps uneven — like she's holding herself together with sheer willpower.

Drake and I sit in the quiet she leaves behind, the weight of everything she's carrying settling over us like a storm cloud.

DRAKE KISSES ME AGAIN — SLOW, DEEP, KNEE-WEAKENING — AND my legs wobble so hard I have to brace myself against his chest. His heartbeat thuds steady beneath my palm, grounding me even as my mind spins like it's forgotten how to function.

I draw in a breath, tilt my head up, and meet his eyes.

"Drake," I murmur, studying the way his expression softens when he looks at me, "have you been able to speak with your brother Devlain? We need to find him."

His brows lift. "Why do you ask, Alexia?"

"Me... ask?" I fold my arms, pretending to be offended, even though the corner of my mouth twitches.

He gives me that look — amused, patient, maddeningly gentle — the one that makes me want to smack him and kiss him at the same time.

I lean my head back, meeting his smile with one of my own. "I want to meet the pain in the arse," I say with a shrug. "I miss our chats. Maybe he should stick around longer next time. After all, he did say he was at my service." I lift a brow, daring him to argue.

"He said what?" Drake straightens, surprise flickering across his face. "Okay, Alexia. I'll try harder." He drags a hand through his hair, frustration tightening his jaw. "I need to speak to him anyway. Especially after what our father has done." His voice drops, heavy. "Seems my father left everything to Devlain. My mother gets nothing."

My breath catches. I step closer, frowning. "You're kidding me? Your mother was left with nothing? Most of the money was hers."

"Yes, well..." He exhales, shoulders sagging. "My father controlled the accounts. He froze her out of her own money. Left her penniless."

"Drake..." My voice softens. I touch his arm, feeling the tension thrumming beneath his skin. "How is she surviving?"

"I've helped her," he says quietly. "Her family too. She moved back into her childhood home." His jaw clenches. "She found out the hard way — came home one afternoon to changed locks and new security codes. She was… distraught."

My heart twists. I squeeze his hand. "We'll talk about it later at home. I need to go clean up and grab my books for our next class." I sigh. "Which, lucky us, we share."

"Alexia," he murmurs, brushing his thumb across my cheek, "how about I grab your books and meet you there?"

He leans in and kisses me — soft, warm, lingering — and heat curls through me so fast I almost forget where we are. I want to drag him home, lock the door, and forget school exists.

"I love you, my sexy husband," I whisper, tracing a slow line down his chest.

He steps back and strikes a ridiculous model pose. "Ha, you only want me for my body."

"How did you guess?" I grin, shaking my head.

"I know you far too well, my beautiful wife." He taps my nose. "Now off with you. I'll see you in class. Oh, and Alexia…"

I pause mid-step, smirking. "Yes, my husband?"

"I love you, too," his voice is warm, low, and it hits me right in the chest.

Awww. I melt every time he says that.

THE MOMENT I STEP THROUGH THE FRONT DOOR, RELIEF CRASHES over me so hard my knees nearly buckle. I don't even bother dropping my school bag gently — it hits the floor with a soft thud as my gaze locks onto the two tiny humans who own my entire heart.

My babies.

Both twins bounce wildly in their little carriers, legs kicking, arms flapping like excited baby birds. Their faces light up the room

— two cherub smiles, two sets of sparkling eyes, two mouths blowing wet, sloppy bubbles like they're auditioning for "Most Adorable Menace."

"Ohhh, my gorgeous babies," I breathe, rushing to them. "Have you been good for Nanny Sharonia?"

Their minds brush mine before their bodies even reach my arms — warm, soft, needy little pulses of emotion.

Mama.

Pick us up.

Mama.

Cuddles.

Mama.

Boobie.

I laugh, scooping them both up, one on each hip. "You little rug rats. Playing up again, hmm?"

Hopefully that means they'll sleep tonight. Hopefully.

Their tiny fingers curl into my shirt, their little heads nestle into my shoulders, and for a moment the world feels right again.

Then the bond shifts.

I reach out instinctively. *'Drake? Are you home? I've arrived.'*

Silence.

Nothing.

Not even the faintest echo of him.

A cold thread winds through my stomach.

I turn toward Sharonia, adjusting the twins as they squirm for attention. "Nanny Sharonia... has Drake arrived home yet? I thought he'd be here by now."

She shakes her head gently. "No, Princess Alexia. I thought he would have arrived with you."

That uneasy thread tightens.

"No, he had a few things to sort out," I say, trying to sound casual even though my pulse is picking up. "But I thought he'd be finished by now. The boys were arriving back in Samual's car." I force a small laugh. "He must still be busy. I'll check in with one of the security boys later."

The twins nuzzle into my neck, grounding me. I kiss the tops of their soft little heads, breathing them in — baby shampoo, warm skin, pure innocence.

"But for now," I say softly, "I need a shower and clean clothes. I'll feed them in their room. Have they had their bath yet?"

"Yes," Sharonia replies with a warm smile. "Your father came over and helped. You just missed him — he left a few minutes ago."

A pang hits my chest.

Damn.

I would've liked to see Dad.

But right now, with Drake silent through the bond and my babies clinging to me like I'm their whole world... I can't shake the feeling that something is off.

Something is coming.

And I'm not sure I'm ready for it.

CHAPTER FOURTEEN

AFTER A HOT SHOWER AND CLEAN CLOTHES — FINALLY FREE FROM
the sticky reminder of leaked milk — I sink into the rocking chair
and pull Damien close. His tiny hands curl into my shirt as he
feeds, warm and soft against my skin. Across from me, Nanny
Sharonia burps Alley, who lets out a tiny squeak of triumph.

For a moment, everything feels steady again.

Safe.

Normal.

Once Damien is burped and tucked into his bed, I slip quietly
out of the nursery, closing the door with a soft click. My feet carry
me toward the kitchen automatically, my mind already drifting
toward Drake.

The moment I step into the spacious, modern room, my eyes
sweep the space — a habit now, instinctive, protective.

Still no Drake.

A flicker of unease curls low in my stomach.

I reach out through our bond, focusing, waiting for even the
faintest brush of him.

Nothing.

A cold ripple slides down my spine.

He should be home.

He always lets me know if he's running late.

He hates missing bedtime with the twins.

I try again — harder this time.

Still nothing.

My heart gives a hard, uncomfortable thud.

Fine. I'll reach out to our guards.

I reach out mentally, searching for Benji.

Silence.

Marcus.

Nothing.

Samual.

Nothing.

My pulse spikes.

This isn't normal.

This isn't anything close to normal.

Okay. Next option.

Laif.

His response is immediate, steady.

'Yes, Princess Alexia.'

'Have you seen or heard from Drake, Benji, Marcus, or Samual since school this afternoon?'

'I know the boys were with Prince Drake, he replies, concern threading through his voice. He said he was going to sort out the problem regarding Tabatha. But I have not seen them since our last class. Why is Prince Drake not home yet?'

'No. He's not home,' I answer, pacing the kitchen now. *'He's not answering, and I can't sense him or the boys. Something is wrong.*

Notify Riley and have him come to my house immediately. After that, go back to the school and retrace Drake's last steps. Something has happened.'

'Yes, Princess Alexia. Straightaway.'

    Just when I think he is gone he begins speaking again. *'Princess, I should remain with you.'*

'Laif, I will be fine. There are guards here, and Riley will be here soon.'

'But, Princess...'

'Laif, no. Head back to the school.'

He doesn't reply, and the link fades.

My front doorbell rings. I flinch, my nerves stretched thin.

Seriously? Right now? Who could it be…

I reach out with my senses — and groan.

Lucy.

Oh, shite.

I forgot she was coming.

I race to the front door before she can press the bell again and wake the twins. As I run, I extend my senses further — checking for anyone with her.

She's alone.

Her mind is a swirl of nerves — fear about the pregnancy, dread about the truth, and the ticking countdown of her two-hour curfew.

Poor girl.

I pull open the door with a bright smile I absolutely do not feel.

"Hey, girl, welcome to my home."

I wrap her in a hug as she steps inside.

"Wow," Lucy breathes, looking around. "I can't believe you live here now. So…"

Her voice trails off, awkward silence stretching between us.

Right. The test.

"Oh! I almost forgot." I gesture toward the stairs. "Come up to my room. I'll grab the pregnancy test. Want a drink?"

Instead of heading upstairs, I detour to the kitchen, grab two bottles of water, and hand one to her.

"Thanks," she says, twisting the lid. She takes a sip, eyes scanning the room like she's trying to memorise every detail.

"You know…" she starts, "I don't think I've ever been inside the house. I've been out in the pool plenty of times, but not in the actual house. Is that little pool house out back? I remember Lucile and Michael wanted to rebuild it for Summer. Did it ever happen?"

I think of the mess outside — the debris, the chaos — and the relief that the new building was finished before we returned from Darshia.

"Yes," I say. "After the test, I'll show you. Come on, stop delaying. It's time."

Lucy looks down at her feet, shoulders curling inward. Her emotions hit me like a wave — fear, denial, confusion. She doesn't want to know. She doesn't want to face the possibility of being pregnant. And beneath it all, the deepest wound:

Was the baby conceived by love… or by rape?

My heart aches for her.

I turn toward the spiral staircase near the back of the kitchen and start walking.

"Come on, Lucy," I say gently but firmly. "Stop delaying."

LUCY STARES AT THE TINY LCD SCREEN LIKE IT'S A BOMB ABOUT to detonate.

Her hand trembles.

Her breath stutters.

Her eyes widen as the numbers glare back at her.

Positive.

8.5 weeks.

All the colour drains from her face. She shakes her head once.

Again.

Harder.

Like she can physically shake the truth loose.

My heart twists.

Goddess… I know that feeling too well.

I step forward and wrap my arms around her. She's stiff at first, frozen in shock, then she collapses against me, her breath catching on a broken sound.

"Hey," I whisper into her hair, "everything will be okay. If you want, I'll help. I've been where you are. It's a shock — a massive shock — but you'll get your head around it. You adjust. You focus on what has to happen next and you keep moving forward."

I squeeze her shoulders, grounding her, then ease back enough to meet her eyes.

"Remember our motto? Never. Never give up." My voice softens. "You can still live your dream. It'll just take a little longer."

Her eyes glisten. She nods — tiny, fragile — then picks up the test again like it might bite her. She slips it into her pocket with shaking fingers.

"Come on," I say gently. "Let's go outside. But first, I need to check on the twins."

We leave the bathroom and walk through my bedroom, our footsteps muffled by the carpet. Down the hall, I ease open the next door.

The twins are wide awake — of course they are — lying in

their beds, babbling to each other like they're plotting a coup. Cheeky little gremlins.

I push the door open.

"Hey, you two. You should be asleep."

Their little minds brush mine instantly — warm, soft, needy.

'Daddy. Want Daddy.'

My chest tightens.

"So do I, little one. So do I."

I stroke their soft hair. "Daddy should be home soon. Okay? Go back to sleep, and Daddy will be here when you wake up."

Please let that be true.

Lucy steps beside me, eyes widening as she takes them in properly for the first time. The twins spot her and immediately start blowing happy bubbles, kicking their legs like she's the most exciting thing they've ever seen.

"Uh… Alexia?" Lucy whispers. "Why did you say that to the twins? Where's Drake?"

I swallow.

"Ah… Lucy, we'll talk in the kitchen, okay?"

She looks at my face — really looks — and I see the moment she realises something is wrong.

"Oh my Goddess," she breathes. "You do have twins. And look at them… I can see so much of both you and Drake."

Before I can answer, Nanny Sharonia steps into the room.

"Oh, Princess Alexia, I didn't realise you had company."

"That's alright, Nanny Sharonia," I say, turning toward her. "We're heading downstairs. Can you watch the twins tonight? I'll feed them later, but I have a few things to sort out."

"Yes, that is fine, Princess Alexia."

Lucy's head snaps between us, confusion written all over her face.

"What? Why is she calling you Princess Alexia?"

"Because I am a Princess," I say simply. "I'll explain later."

I introduce them quickly, then reach out to Sharonia's mind. *'Sharonia, please call me Alexia when we have guests. Lucy is one of my oldest friends. She knows a little about Dark Ones. We'll speak later. Thank you for minding the twins.'*

'I am sorry if I placed you in an awkward position. It was not my intention.'

I give her a slight smile. *'Just remember — Alexia in front of guests.'*

I turn back to the twins, leaning down to kiss each warm little forehead.

"Goodnight, my loves."

Then I straighten and step out of the room. Lucy follows silently, her mind a storm of questions, fear, and shock.

And beneath it all…she knows something is very, very wrong.

WITH OUR WATER BOTTLES IN HAND, LUCY AND I STEP OUT INTO the warm air and head toward the pool house. Her thoughts keep brushing against my mind — frantic, looping, messy — like she's trying to rearrange her entire life in the span of a few minutes. Annoying, yes, but at least she's finally letting the truth settle.

The last thing I hear before I close my mind to her is the moment she counts the dates…and realises the baby was conceived in love.

Good. She needed that.

But the second we reach the pool house, something shifts.

A presence.

Someone inside. A stranger.

I stop dead and throw an arm out, blocking Lucy's path.

"Lucy, wait here. I need to check something first."

She snorts. "Alexia, I'm used to looking at a mess."

"Lucy," I say, giving her a look sharp enough to cut glass, "just humour me."

She huffs but stays put.

I ease the door open, senses flaring instantly. Someone is asleep inside — deep, heavy sleep — tucked away in one of the spare rooms. I slip in and close the door behind me, the latch clicking softly.

The hallway is dim. Still.

I move silently toward the room where the presence is strongest.

Hand on the handle.

Slow turn.

Quiet push.

A man sprawls across the bed, fast asleep.

Vaguely familiar.

Too familiar.

My stomach tightens.

I brace myself — then kick the edge of the mattress.

Hard.

He jolts upright with a strangled sound. "What the—?!"

"What are you doing at my house, Devlain?" I snap. "And where is Drake?"

Devlain — my so-called brother-in-law — looks like he's been dragged backwards through a storm. Hair wild, shirt wrinkled, eyes bloodshot. He blinks at me, dazed.

"Oh, hell, Alexia," he groans, rubbing his face. "What are you trying to do? Get yourself killed? I could've hurt you."

"Wake up, you idiot," I fire back. "You have some explaining to do."

Footsteps behind me.

Instinct takes over.

I spin, grab the figure, and pin them in a head hold before they can even gasp.

A familiar scent hits me.

Oh shite.

I release immediately. Lucy stumbles back, clutching her throat.

"What the hell, Alexia?" she wheezes. "What was that for?"

"Rule number one," I say, steadying her. "Do not walk up behind me."

I turn back to Devlain — who is now staring past me, eyes widening.

"Is that… Lucy?" he breathes. "Baby, is that you?"

Lucy freezes.

Her gaze flicks from him, to me, back to him.

Her mouth opens, closes, opens again.

"Lain?" she whispers. "What — how — what are you doing here? Why are you—"

She stops mid-sentence.

Her eyes snap to me.

Narrow. Sharp. Accusing.

Oh shite.

I know that look.

"Lucy," I say quickly, "this is not what you're thinking."

"Oh?" she snaps. "And what exactly am I thinking, Alexia?"

"Lucy, I didn't know Devlain was here," I say, hands raised. "I sensed someone inside. I had to check it out. I'm a Princess — I have assassins coming after me sometimes. I wasn't about to risk your life."

Her expression softens.

Barely.

But enough.

"So… you're telling me you didn't know Lain was here?"

"That is correct," I say firmly. "Drake was going to try to contact him after school."

I turn slowly toward Devlain, heat building in my chest — anger, fear, dread all twisting together.

"Devlain," I say, voice low and sharp, "where is Drake? Has he spoken to you today?"

CHAPTER FIFTEEN

I LOCK ONTO DEVLAIN'S EYES, REFUSING TO BLINK, REFUSING TO move, waiting — no, demanding — an answer.

"Alexia," he says, hands lifting like he's warding off a storm, "I haven't spoken to my brother. I came here to talk to him about a few things."

His gaze slides past me and lands on Lucy. Everything in him softens — the voice, the posture, the damn soul. "Hey, baby," he breathes, voice cracking. "How are you? I've been looking for you everywhere. I've missed you so much. Where have you been? Did your mum take good care of you?"

Lucy goes rigid. Completely still.

But Devlain's attention snaps back to me... then to her... then to me again. His face drains. His mouth falls open.

He's just realised we're both pregnant.

Oh shite.

Before he even draws breath, I slam straight into his mind shields.

'Devlain, don't you dare say a word.' My mental voice slices like a blade. *'No one is to know about me. No one. Even Lucy doesn't know yet.'*

His eyes widen as my eyebrow lifts, my tone turning lethal.

'And if you breathe a word, Drake will kick your arse when he gets home — after I've kicked your butt to the kerb. You shouldn't have been able to tell anyway unless it's your twin link. As for Lucy — let her tell you about the baby. She only found out twenty minutes ago. She's still in shock. Take it easy.'

He blinks rapidly, processing, then finally answers through the link.

'Alexia... as long as my brother knows about you.'

'Devlain, I snap, it was your brother who informed me first. So do not even go there.'

His jaw tightens. *'But how — with Lucy? Is the baby mine, or a result of that...?'*

Oh. He thinks I don't know about the assault.

'Well,' I say, *'one way to know is to place your hand on her belly. Fathers can detect it — or something like that. If Drake were here, he'd explain it better. Oh — hang on. I don't know if that works with witches.'*

His mental voice spikes. *'What? What will work?'*

'If you're able to speak to the baby — hear the baby — then it's yours. I don't know if it happens every time, though.'

'I suppose there's only one way to find out.'

'Hang on,' I add, *'did you have sex with Lucy over eight weeks ago? Because the test said she's eight and a half weeks along.'*

I turn slightly — and catch Lucy's expression.

Eyebrow raised.

Jaw tight.

Eyes narrowed.

Uh-oh.

She's getting pissed.

I turn fully toward her, already deciding to give the lovebirds space. Devlain has a mountain of grovelling ahead — especially after giving her a different name and then vanishing like a coward.

"Luce," I say softly, "as you might have guessed, I know him. No, I didn't know he was here. He is indeed Drake's twin. And I'll leave you to speak with Devlain."

Lucy looks like she's about to erupt. My Lucy girl is not a happy little camper.

I smirk as I walk past Devlain, glance over my shoulder, and mouth, *Sucker.*

His mental voice snaps back instantly. *'Shut up, Alexia. We will be talking very soon, sister-in-law.'*

'Bring it on, Devlain. If you hurt her...'

I let the threat hang — sharp, cold, deadly.

My tone shifts inside his mind, turning to ice. *'She's been through too much already. You'll be answering to me. Don't forget*

*that. I'm very good with a gun. Ask your father. Oh — right. You
can't. He exploded into dust the moment the silver bullet tore
through his evil, dead heart.'*

His face pales.

Good.

Message received.

I turn on my heel and walk out.

Behind me, Lucy's voice rises. "What did Alexia just say to
you? I know she was speaking to you with her mind. I've worked
that out myself. She does the same thing with Drake. It's annoying
— and it's rude!"

She yells the last part deliberately, making sure I hear it.

Guilt claws at me. I stop in the hallway and push my words
gently into her mind.

*'Yes, Lucy, I can hear you... and I'm sorry. I didn't mean to be
rude or mind-talk in front of you. I was warning Devlain. If he
hurts you, he'll answer to me. Ask him what I did to his father.'*

Her mental voice spikes. *'What — how — what? Alexia, what are
you doing in my head? How?'*

*'Lucy, it's part of being a Dark One. And a Princess to Dark
Ones. I can do a little extra — more than the average Dark One.
But it's secret. Always remember that. Our lives depend on it.'*

She exhales shakily. *'Oh... shit. Okay, Alexia. I'll speak with you
later. I need to talk with Lain. He needs to know about the baby.'*

'Good luck, Lucy girl. I'll be in the house if you need me.'

I close my mind to her and head inside.

The moment I step through the back door, silence hits me.

Drake still isn't home. Neither are his guards. The emptiness presses against my chest like a weight.

Worry coils tight in my stomach.

Drake and his crew should be home by now. It's not like him to disappear without telling me. It's not like him to miss the twins' bedtime. And the fact that I can't reach him — can't sense him — sets off every alarm bell in my head.

Something is wrong.

Very wrong.

I inhale slowly, steadying myself.

Time to call a meeting with my security boys.

I just hope Laif can find out what happened... and why Drake and the others haven't come home.

CHAPTER SIXTEEN

By the time Riley and the four other security guards arrive, my stress levels are climbing into the danger zone. I'm glad I sent Laif back to the school when Drake didn't answer me — even though he gave me grief about it. He hates leaving me unattended, even with two guards on the property and two more next door protecting my parents.

Riley's mobile buzzes. He frowns. "It's Laif. I'll put him on loudspeaker." He taps the screen.

"Laif, what did you find?" Riley asks, stepping closer to the kitchen bench, shoulders tight.

"Captain, I've searched the school building and grounds. I spoke with several students, including that annoying female Tabatha and a small group of her followers at the gym."

Riley's eyes flick to mine. My stomach drops.

If Laif is calling and only spoke to students… he hasn't found Drake.

"What have you discovered, Laif?" Riley presses.

"As we already know, that Tabatha is a lying bitch."

Riley's lips twitch. I bite the inside of my cheek to stop myself from rolling my eyes or laughing. *Yes, Laif. We know Tabatha is a bitch. Groundbreaking news — not.*

"Tabatha is still trying to push the issue and tells anyone who'll listen that she and Drake are an item."

What a cow. That's getting old fast.

"And the little so-and-so is spreading nasty rumours about the Princess — that she's been seeing other people behind Drake's back."

What! As if I would ever cheat on the man I love.

"Laif, did you read her mind? Did she have anything to say about Prince Drake's disappearance?" Riley demands.

"Yes, I read her mind. No, she has nothing to do with the prince's disappearance. That female has left me feeling dirty and unsanitary."

Damn. Where is my husband?

"Oh — Tabatha is planning to make trouble for the Princess tomorrow at school."

Seriously? What kind of trouble this time?

Laif continues, "I spoke with Prince Drake's old football friend Martin. The fool noticed the Prince and the others fighting with five strangers."

Hang on — what?

"When I questioned Martin further, all he said was that he thought the guys were playing around."

Playing around?

"Martin didn't think anything was wrong. He turned and left to catch up with his girlfriend Julia before she left for work."

Seriously!

"Did you get a description of these other men?" Riley asks.

"Yes. Big, dark, wearing hoods and black from head to toe."

"Anything else?"

"Martin mentioned a strange van parked not far from where they were fighting."

"Okay, thanks, Laif. Come back here. I'll follow up on the security camera footage."

Riley moves fast, making arrangements for the school's surveillance footage.

As I make a cup of tea, I watch him from the corner of my eye — phone in one hand, laptop in the other, coordinating his team as they access the new cameras. Thank goodness most students don't know they exist yet.

He ends a call, flips the laptop around, and the screen fills with school surveillance footage.

My heart shatters into pieces.

We finally know what happened to Drake and the three Darshia guards.

Shock hits me like a punch. Anger follows, hot and violent. I don't know whether to scream or break something. How the hell did this happen? The footage looks like a nightmare.

Riley slows the video down as Drake and the three guards — Benji, Marcus, and Samual — appear. They're talking as they walk toward Samual's SUV in the student car park.

Seconds later, a dark, modern van with no side windows screeches to a halt beside them.

Five hooded men — black from head to toe — spill out and surround Drake and the guards.

The fight is fast, brutal, and over in minutes.

Drake and the guards collapse. Unconscious.

What in the world just happened?

The hooded men haul Drake and the three guards into the van, slam the door, and speed out of the car park.

How can this happen? What could knock out not just Drake, but three trained Darshia guards?

The only explanation is chilling — these men know Drake and the others aren't human.

I turn to Riley, voice low and steady. "When do we leave?"

Before I can say another word, Riley cuts me off. "Sorry, Princess. With all due respect, you're not going anywhere. You stay here. You're to be protected at all costs."

My eyes narrow. I give him the deadly stare. "Riley, I'm not sitting here waiting. Something needs to be done. Action is required — now."

The outside door opens. All of us turn.

In a heartbeat, every man in the room has a gun raised.

Lucy walks in mid-sentence, oblivious — until Devlain, behind her, freezes at the sight of the weapons. He moves instantly, shifting Lucy behind him.

My mind is already open to the men.

'Stand down. Now.'

I move toward Lucy and face my security.

Out loud, I say, "Everyone, this is my dear friend Lucy, and the guy with her is Drake's brother Devlain. Some of you might know of him."

Through the mind link, my tone sharpens. *'Stand. Down. Men. Now. Put your weapons away before someone gets hurt.'*

Riley presses against my shields. I let him in. *'Princess Alexia, what is Devlain doing here? I thought he was in hiding because of his father. And who exactly is Lucy?'*

I turn to Lucy — she'll be pissed if I keep mind-talking in front of her.

"Everyone, meet my oldest and best friend, Lucy. And before you say it — yes, Lucy is a witch."

I gesture to each man. "Lucy, these are my security personnel and bodyguards. Riley, my head of security. Laif — you've seen him at school. And the others: Jackson, Travis, Blackstone, and Goffery."

I give her a small smile, letting her know it's okay.

My men lower their weapons slowly.

They nod. "Nice to meet you."

Even though they're still bombarding my shields with questions, all I want to do is leave — find Drake — and bring him home.

CHAPTER SEVENTEEN

I ENCOURAGE EVERYONE TO SIT AROUND THE DINING TABLE AND gesture for Goffery to make drinks and grab some light snacks. I settle in with a drink in one hand and a chocolate-covered fruit wafer biscuit in the other. Milk chocolate. My favourite. Yum.

As I scan the table, I already know trouble is coming the moment Devlain hears the news about Drake.

I reach out with my mind. *'Devlain, I need you to remain calm. Otherwise, I'll have my security detain you. Your choice.'*

He presses against my shields. I let him in. *'Why would I need to be detained, Alexia? What's happened? Where is Drake?'*

'I'm about to address everyone. Sit tight and drink your coffee, Devlain.'

He narrows his eyes at me but lifts his cup and takes a sip anyway.

I glance at Lucy, wink, then tap my knuckles against the tabletop. The room snaps to attention.

"Okay. Down to business," I say. "For the benefit of Devlain and Lucy, it has just come to light that we have a serious situation."

"What has happened?" they ask together.

"This afternoon, four of our people were taken from the school grounds."

They both give me the hurry-up look. Lucy leans forward.

"Who was taken, Alexia? Was Drake one of them? Is that why he hasn't come home yet?"

Smart girl. I nod. "Yes. Drake, Benji, Marcus, and Samual were recorded on the school's surveillance. A van pulls up, five men get out, and head straight for Drake. All nine of them fight. Within minutes, Drake and the guards collapse. They're carried into the van, and it speeds off."

"What are you doing about this? Who has taken my brother?" Devlain demands.

Riley hits play on the laptop, turning the screen so Lucy and Devlain can see.

Lucy's eyes widen. She leans closer, squinting. Recognition hits her like a slap.

"Oh my Goddess, Alexia. I know that van. And I recognise one of those men. These people are most likely from the dark coven. I bet they grabbed Drake, thinking he's Lain."

Oh no. Drake is in serious trouble now. If the coven thinks they have Devlain... they'll kill him. Torture him first, probably. Crap on a stick. We have to stop them.

I look at Riley and see the exact moment he realises the same thing. His jaw tightens.

"Everyone," I say, "as you've probably guessed, Drake is in serious shite. These men will most likely torture and kill him, even though they think they have Devlain."

I turn to Riley, hesitating for a heartbeat. Oh Goddess, what do we do?

The little voice in my head answers instantly. Get him back.

"Riley, contact the castle. We'll need more resources. At least four teams of five men, fully armed and protected from magical wards and spells."

Then I turn to Lucy, meeting her eyes, silently pleading.

"Lucy, we need everything you can give us. Names, addresses, contacts — anything. Make a list of every place they might take Drake. Call your mum and ask if she's heard anything about the coven finding Lain. Use my phone." I head toward the spiral stairs, pausing halfway and look over my shoulder. "I have to go upstairs and feed the twins. Keep working, everyone. We need as much intel as possible, ASAP. We leave in forty minutes."

CHAPTER EIGHTEEN

Sitting comfortably in the nursery rocker, pillows tucked on either side of me supporting both twins, I watch them fight to stay awake while they drink from my exposed breasts.

Damien finally gives in. His little body goes limp, his mouth slackening. I keep my eyes on him until Nanny Sharonia walks over and gently lifts my baby boy. She rests him against her shoulder, waiting for that soft, sleeping burp. I cover my breast with my maternity bra and pull my top back into place. It still amazes me how a baby can stay completely asleep and still manage to burp like a tiny drunk man.

Once he's settled in his cot, I look down at Alley. My daughter is still drinking, eyelids shut, her tiny fingers curled against my skin.

Sensing her presence, I glance upward. Lucy stands in the nursery doorway. I nod to invite her in.

"Hey," I whisper. "What's going on downstairs? Have the boys found anything yet?"

She shakes her head, eyes glued to Alley. "Does that hurt? When the baby drinks? Does she bite?"

My lips lift at the memory of those early days. "At the start, it was uncomfortable. My nipples ached. But I stuck it out, and now I'm fine. I'm comfortable breastfeeding."

Alley's lips go slack as she releases my nipple. Milk dribbles down her chin. I lift her gently, settling her on my shoulder. She finishes her mouthful still asleep, curled into me, while I pat her back and rock us slowly. I cover my breast again.

Lucy sighs. I glance up.

Devlain stands behind her, arms wrapped around her middle, one hand caressing her lower belly. They both watch Alley sleep like they're seeing the future.

Quietly, I say, "This will be you two in seven months." I look down at my daughter. "You'll need to start making arrangements, Lucy. It might be best if you see my doctor — the one who looked after me. He's in Darshia. Once all this mess with Drake is sorted, I'll arrange an appointment."

Nanny Sharonia returns, noticing Alley asleep. I nod for her to take her.

Before she lifts my daughter, I say to Lucy and Devlain, "Can you two meet me downstairs? I'll be there in a minute."

They nod and slip out quietly.

Sitting in the back of one of the SUVs with Lucy and Devlain, we head toward the address Lucy's mother gave her. Four other cars follow behind us, packed with my personal and castle security. We decided Laif would stay with the twins — at least one of my security needs to keep his identity hidden.

Laptops open, headsets on, audio and visual feeds everywhere — my team works nonstop, gathering intel on the area we're heading into and the people we're about to face.

"Lucy, are you sure you should be coming with us? Maybe we

should drop you off. I don't want you getting upset or hurt. They've done enough already."

Lucy shakes her head, determination burning bright. I pity anyone she recognises from that day. She'll make them pay.

"Alexia, I'll be okay. Plus, you need a witch to get you past the magical wards. There will be traps. A witch will spot them long before a Dark One ever will. And I can disable them."

"Are you sure, Lucy? I don't want you getting hurt."

"Ppffftt. Oh, please, Alexia. I'll be fine. Better off than you. At least being a witch, I can enter without being detected. And I've been practising while I've been recuperating. My mother should be proud."

She lifts her hand and wiggles her fingers. Light and sparks dance from her fingertips.

Holy smokes. That's new.

She meets my gaze and winks. "Like I said, Alexia. I've learned a few more things, and I know how to wield them. I'm impressed with myself regarding the charms I've made."

Just as I go to reply, Riley's voice from the front pulls my attention away from Lucy's glowing fingers and stops me from asking more questions regarding the funny-looking magical charms.

"Princess Alexia, we're nearly there. Swan should stay by your side. The three of you should head in on foot and blend in with the other teenagers moving in the same direction."

I nod. We don't need to speak out loud. Before leaving the house, we'd already gone over everything — me, Riley, Laif, and a few others — planning and scheming right up until we walked out the door.

I just hope we covered enough for this plan to work.

I<small>T DOESN</small>'<small>T TAKE LONG BEFORE THE FOUR OF US BLEND IN WITH A</small> group of ten hormonal teenagers, all heading toward a large brick building. A few quick hi's and chin lifts pass between them, and the whole group moves as one.

The hidden charm under my clothes feels heavier with every step. I keep reminding myself not to reach out and touch it in front of the teenagers. Lucy somehow managed to make us magical charms before we left my house — including four more for our people who are captive. Drake included.

So far, the charms are working. These young witches haven't sensed our Dark One status. Our identities stay hidden.

I tap my ear twice, signalling Riley and the team that we're about to walk through the first ward. Not all my security know what I'm capable of; mind-talking isn't always an option. I don't know all the castle guards personally, and Riley wasn't about to vouch for some of them.

Uh-oh. I'm starting to think a few of these men might be influenced by my grandmother — which means they're not to be trusted with my secrets.

I reach out with my mind. *'Riley, so far so good. We're approaching the first set of wards. Lucy's charms seem to be working. Talk soon.'*

'Be safe, Princess. Take care.'

I close my mind to him just as my foot breaks through the first magical ward.

A slight pull tugs at my body, like invisible fingers brushing my skin, but I keep walking. Lucy and Devlain flank me, Swan close behind.

What Lucy and Devlain don't realise is that I'm carrying my sword, my gun, and a few other dark surprises for these unsuspecting witches. No one messes with my family, my friends, or me and gets away with it. I'm wearing one of my armoured chest plates, and I made sure everyone on my security detail has one. No more dusting in my presence unless they're an enemy.

The teenagers don't bat an eye at the three *strangers* among them. All they see are four more magical witches.

So far, so good.

I tap my earpiece again. Static hisses back at me.

Great. No signal.

I try reaching out with my mind. After twenty seconds of silence, worry creeps in. The coven's wards must be blocking our comm units and our mind links. Fantastic. We're on our own for a while. And maybe — hopefully — this is why Drake can't speak with me.

Good thing we had backup plans.

Time for plan B.

I shift my hand just enough to tap out a coded message on my phone.

ME:

Dad. Just catching up on school work.

(Code for: comms are down, blocked by wards. Mind link too.)

A few seconds later, my phone vibrates.

RILEY:

Ok, baby girl. Thanks for letting me know.

(Code for: Yes, we're aware.)

Within ten minutes of passing the last known ward and booby trap, we weave through one of the large multi-storey buildings — this one full of maze-like corridors and levels. By now, we're at least three levels underground.

I brush my hand against Devlain's, tapping my head with a

slight shake. Letting him know I can't mind-talk. He nods. He brushes his temple in return, shaking his head — he can't sense Drake either.

Oh, that is not good.

There have to be more magical wards nearby, or the entire building is protected. Honestly, I think it's both.

The four of us walk casually toward the doorway that will hopefully lead us to Drake and our security men. We've followed Lucy's mother's instructions exactly.

As Lucy reaches for the door, I hold my breath.

Let's hope this isn't a trap — for all our sakes.

CHAPTER NINETEEN

"Hey, you kids. Yes, you girls. What are you doing down here?" a male voice yells from behind us.

Oh shite.

We've been spotted.

And did he just say you girls? He thinks we're all girls. Either he's blind, stupid, or… hmm. What exactly did Lucy ward us with?

As one, we turn casually to face him.

The first thing I see is a creepy-looking man with long, dirty blond hair tied back at the base of his skull. One eyebrow practically stretches across his entire forehead, and a jagged white scar runs from his jaw to his beady dark eyes.

Recognition flashes across his face when he sees Lucy.

Uh-oh.

This is going to be bad.

Real bad, real quick.

"Hey, I know you," he says, grinning. "You're that tasty little chick, and we got to watch thanks to Alistor."

Oh no.

Lucy and Devlain tense beside me — I feel it like a shockwave.

I glance down. Lucy's fingers are glowing.

Scarface — yes, that's his name now — has just signed his own death warrant.

His expression shifts from smug to confused. "Hey, what are you doing here? If you don't leave, you'll be in trouble." Then he pauses, like a genius idea just crawled into his brain. "Hmmm... or maybe I'll take you and your friends into that room over there. Would you like that? I finally get to fuck you. Yes. You and your little friends. We had such a great time last time."

Lucy starts shaking. Not with fear — with rage.

Waves of anger roll off her, thick and hot. My internal senses pulse warnings.

Danger. Danger. Danger.

This idiot doesn't feel it. He just keeps talking.

"Come to think of it, I think a few of the other guys who missed out would like their turn too. What you say? I won't tell anyone if you don't. Shame Alistor and his dog are dead — he knew how to keep the men happy in this coven with all those tasty little morsels of virginal fle—"

He never finishes.

Before Scarface even realises Lucy is moving, she snaps her hands up. Magic flares so fast the air cracks. A burst of blinding light erupts from her fingertips — sharp, focused, furious — and slams into his chest with enough force to lift him off his feet.

He flies backward.

The sound that follows is awful — a heavy, final collision that makes my stomach twist. The crack of his skull echoes down the corridor.

He crumples in a heap. Smoke drifts from the scorched front of his shirt.

He doesn't move.

A cold ripple runs up my arms.

Lucy... what did you just do?

Swan moves fast, searching the body. He finds keys and weapons, hands them to me, then he and Devlain drag the corpse to a nearby door — a cleaning supply cupboard, apparently. They dump him inside and shut the door.

Devlain wraps his arms around Lucy, holding her tight, pressing his lips to her head.

Swan looks at me — then down at my hand.

That's when I realise I've got a death grip on my handgun.

Oops.

Well... I was ready to protect Lucy.

Turns out Lucy can protect herself.

Wow.

I slide the safety back on and tuck the gun away. All three of them stare at me.

"What?" I ask innocently. "I was about to protect Lucy." I glance at her. "But geez, girl, warn me next time. You nearly singed the hairs off my arms."

I wink and step toward her. We both know we need to hold each other — to ground ourselves, to say I'm okay without words.

As I hug her, Scarface's earlier comment hits me.

"Um, Lucy... about something he said — 'all us girls.' Do the guys look like girls to the other witches right now?"

Lucy squeezes me and whispers, "Yes. Anyone wearing my charmed necklaces will appear female to anyone here using magic." She lifts the stone-coloured gem at my neck. "It makes it easier to move around. Girls get more leeway here."

I glance at the boys — their quartz gems are different colours.

Wow. Lucy is good.

"Come on, guys. We gotta move," Swan says, heading toward the doorway we were about to enter before Scarface interrupted.

"Someone's bound to come along any minute. Someone had to have heard him mouthing off."

Lucy stops him before he touches the handle.

"The doors are warded," she warns. "Magic-sensitive. If you touch it, you'll trigger an alarm."

"Hey, what about the cleaning cupboard?" I ask.

"It's only the important doors," Lucy replies. "A cleaning closet doesn't count."

She closes the cupboard door behind us, and we move into another hallway with four doors — two on each side.

Lucy approaches the first door, hand hovering near it, chanting softly. Even with my hearing, I can't make out the words. She shakes her head and moves on.

Second door — chant, hand raised, nothing.

Third door — same result.

Okay. Drake isn't in any of those.

We gather behind her at the last door. Lucy glances over her shoulder at me, then places her hand near the wood.

She chants again — but this time her hand glows with a soft blue light.

Okay, that's new.

Lucy smiles — just a little — then places her hand on the handle. She murmurs a few more words.

I turn the handle slowly.

A soft click echoes in the hallway.

The door releases.

And it begins to open.

CHAPTER TWENTY

WITH THE DOOR FULLY OPEN, ALL FOUR OF US LEAN FORWARD AND peer into the darkened room. It's so pitch-black I can't see a thing beyond the doorway. I try using my ears instead, stretching my senses outward.

There — faint, steady, multiple breaths. More than a few.

Without thinking, I start to step inside, but Lucy's hand snaps out and stops me cold.

I turn my head, confused, but one look at her face tells me everything. She shakes her head — sharp, silent, absolute. Her eyes warn me clearly: do not enter. She lifts her hand again, signalling me to wait.

I give her my best *Geez, are we there yet?* look.

She rolls her eyes.

Hmm. Rude.

Lucy motions for all three of us to step back. We obey instantly.

A split second later, something crackles through the air — an electrical charge slams into the exact spot I was just standing in.

Are we under attack? Booby-trapped door?

What the hell, we were nearly fried…Before I can demand answers, the lights blaze on, nearly blinding me.

In a heartbeat, my gun is in my left hand and my sword in my right. Devlain shoves me beside him, trying to get to Lucy, but my attention snaps forward.

Through the open doorway, my mind and body freeze.

As my vision adjusts, I scan the room — and the breathing I sensed earlier becomes horrifyingly clear. At least twenty-five men stand facing us, weapons raised, all aimed directly at the open door.

Uh-oh.

We might be a little outnumbered here.

My eyes dart past the armed men and land on the group in the centre of the room. Relief slams into me when I finally see him — Drake. And Benji. Marcus. Samual.

The bad news… All four of them are chained by their wrists, suspended from the ceiling, heads hanging forward.

They look battered, bruised, and barely conscious. My senses stretch out, desperate, searching — and finally, finally, I detect their heartbeats.

Thank the Goddess.

They're alive.

But those rope-like things around their necks… what in the world are those? Magical restraints? Wards? Traps?

The urge to run to Drake hits me so hard it nearly knocks me off my feet. But with twenty-plus armed witches between us, I know exactly what I have to do.

Fight my way through every single one of these bastard dark witches and bring them to their knees before I can reach my mate.

In those few precious seconds of taking everything in, Devlain and Swan surge past me and storm into the room. They hit the first wave of witches like a battering ram, taking down anyone stupid enough to get close. Swan moves with brutal precision — one sharp, controlled twist and his opponent drops, unconscious before he hits the floor.

Devlain pushes forward, desperate to reach his brother, but four men block his path, each armed with some kind of baton. They swing fast — but Devlain is faster. He snatches one baton mid-strike, rips it from the witch's grip, and turns it back on him in one smooth, vicious motion. The man collapses instantly in a blood heap.

Lucy stays glued to my side. Her voice snaps my attention back to her.

"Hey, Chicky. You ready for some action? A little one-on-one?"

I flash her a wicked smile. "Oh, yeah. Time to kick some arse and show these boys how us girls get down and dirty." I pull her into a quick, fierce hug and whisper, "Lucy, please be careful." Then I lean back and give her my best bitchy grin. "Now come on — time to kick some Dark Witches' arse. And Lucy? We're here to terminate. Understand?"

She nods, eyes flicking over the room with a hesitation I understand too well. These men were likely in that room with her on that horrible day. They're going to pay for what they did to her — and to my husband.

I flick the safety off my gun and raise it. My finger squeezes the trigger again and again. Three men drop before the others even realise what's happening. I fire three more times, taking down more targets before one shot only grazes the next witch.

Damn.

I holster the gun and I'm already moving, sword in hand, my body slipping into the familiar rhythm of combat. I strike fast, precise, controlled — killing three attackers in seconds, including the one I clipped with the bullet.

Two more rush me. I dodge, pivot, and my blade flashes. One loses his grip on his weapon and stumbles back; the other goes down hard without his head as I spin through them, keeping my focus sharp and my senses wide open.

Lucy can handle herself. Devlain and Swan better keep themselves alive too — because I'm not dragging their arses out of here if they get sloppy.

Another witch lunges at me from behind. I feel the air shift and duck just in time, the attack whistling past my head as air brushes past my cheek — too close.

Oh shite.

Focus, Alexia.

I twist, scanning fast, and spot three big, ugly Dark Witches trying to flank me. Not today, fellas. I flash them a small, taunting smile, wiggle my fingers in a come-on motion, and move. My sword arcs across the first man's chest, forcing him back. I spin, catching the second across his midsection, and the third jumps away just in time, my blade slicing only fabric.

Bugger.

Okay, time for plan B. And increase my Dark One speed. I move faster, dodging and weaving. My sword carving wide arcs through the air. Every strike is deliberate — disabling, disarming, killing anyone stupid enough to get close. If I can't reach their necks, I still make damn sure they can't stand. Adrenaline surges through me as I kick, twist, and block incoming blows, cutting through batons as if they're made of cheap plastic, and continue to spin, and kick another attacker square in the chest, hearing bone crack and break, sending him stumbling. I turn in time to block another's spiked baton, slicing it clean in half, before sending the point of my sword backwards and driving it through another Dark Witch who thought he could sneak up behind me. His body falls near my feet. I stumble for half a second, catching myself before I can fall. My senses warn me, and on instinct, I move my sword. It arcs and slices through more fabric, flesh, and bone. Screams echo in my ears another body lands near my feet.

Frustration burns through me — I don't have time for this. I need to get to Drake — not waste precious minutes fighting every Dark Witch in this damned room.

I look up — and my heart stops.

Across the room, one of the dark witches steps behind Benji. I see the glint of a blade. I see the movement. I see—

No.

Before I can shout, before I can move, the Dark Witch drives the knife into Benji's back and drags it free with a practised flick.

A silent scream tears through me. I pray it stayed in my head.

My hand moves on instinct. Gun. Aim. Fire.

The Dark Witch drops instantly.

There's no satisfaction. No relief. Just a hollow, crushing weight in my chest.

I failed Benji.

I fire again. And again. Two more witches fall before they even realise what's happening. I slam a fresh clip into place, my hands moving automatically.

My gaze snaps to Marcus and Samual. Samual's head hangs at an unnatural angle, and Marcus… Marcus is barely moving, but he is moving. His chest rises — faint, but there. He's alive and that is all that matters.

That's all I need.

I holster my gun, step over another fallen Dark Witch, and move straight toward Drake. My husband hangs limp, unconscious, chained, bloodied and bruised, and everything inside me narrows to a single point.

Get. To. Him.

Needing to get Drake down, I move forward without hesitation.

I release my sword from my back, swing with every ounce of strength I have, and the blade slams into the chain link above him. A burst of bright sparks explodes where metal meets metal.

The chain snaps apart.

Drake's body drops instantly.

Uh-oh.

I did not think this part through.

I lunge forward, catching as much of his weight as I can with one arm. My other hand shoves the sword back into place at my back. Drake's full weight hits me and we both go down, my legs buckling as I pull him close and try to cushion the fall.

I don't care that we land hard. I don't care that the floor is a mess of blood and death. All I care about is Drake.

I reach into another pocket, yank out my small knife, and cut through the rope-like restraint around his neck. It falls away, and I press my trembling hand to his chest.

There — faint, but there.

A heartbeat.

Relief crashes through me so hard my eyes sting. Tears spill down my cheeks before I even realise I'm crying. I made it. I made it in time.

I bring my wrist to my mouth, pierce the skin, and press it to Drake's lips. "Come on, my love," I whisper, working his throat gently, urging him to swallow.

For a terrifying moment, nothing happens.

Then his mouth moves. Slowly. Weakly. He starts to drink before his fangs drop, bites into my wrist, and pulls at my vein.

My breath shudders out of me.

With my free hand, I fumble for my phone. I don't know if the signal will get out, but I have to try. I fire off a text first — anything to punch through the wards — then immediately dial Riley.

"Pick up… pick up…" I mutter.

He answers.

"Princess?"

Relief nearly knocks me sideways. "Riley, we need medical. Drake and Marcus are alive but in bad shape. We need backup now."

He reassures me help is already on the way, but then he asks the question I've been dreading.

"Did we get all four men out?"

My throat tightens. My heart cracks.

"No," I whisper. "Benji and Samual… they're gone. They were tortured. They didn't make it." Saying it out loud feels like breaking.

But I don't have time to fall apart.

Not yet.

Drake is still in my arms.

And I am not losing him.

Movement beside me pulls my attention. Swan and Devlain are working fast, getting Marcus down, removing the chains from his wrists and the rope-like restraint from around his neck.

I force myself to stop focusing on how much blood Drake has taken and gently pull my arm away from his mouth. I seal the punctures with my lips, then shift him enough to rest his head on my lap. He's still unconscious. My blood hasn't woken him.

A flicker of panic rises — I shove it down.

Focus. Get him out. Get him safe.

I glance around the room. Only now does the full picture hit me — every male witch is down. The room is silent. We need to leave before the rest of the coven realises what's happened.

Swan helps me lift Drake. We get his arms over our shoulders and start moving toward the door. Lucy and Devlain do the same with Marcus. With both men unconscious and dragging their feet, it's harder than I expected. Too slow. Too exposed.

We need to get out. Now.

We push through corridors, slipping past danger more than once, until finally — finally — we find an exit leading outside. Cold air hits my face just as Riley and several of his team appear.

Two of the men rush forward, taking Drake from Swan and me. They lift him easily and sprint off in the opposite direction. The moment Riley's arm comes around me, my legs nearly give out. I didn't realise how drained I was until now.

Riley barks orders, sending Swan and a group of guards back inside to retrieve Samual and Benji. Two more guards step in to take Marcus from Devlain and Lucy.

That's when I see it — Lucy slumping in Devlain's arms, completely unconscious.

Oh no.

She's pushed herself too far.

Devlain doesn't hesitate. He scoops her up and takes off after the others, disappearing into the night. My eyes stay locked on his back until he's gone.

Riley's voice pulls me back. He's asking questions, trying to assess the situation. I answer automatically, still staring at the empty space where Devlain vanished.

"Yes, Riley. I have my sword and gun." My voice is flat, exhausted. "Your men will find plenty of witches down there. Some from bullets. Some from blades."

I take a shaky breath and look back at the building — the place I just fought my way out of.

"Gather any evidence. And make sure this place is destroyed."

Riley nods once, sharp and certain.

"And Riley... get me out of here. I need to be with my husband. He'll probably need more of my blood."

I don't get to say anything else.

My knees buckle. The world tilts. My vision blurs.

Oh shite is the last thought I manage before everything goes black.

CHAPTER TWENTY-ONE

In those few precious seconds of taking everything in, Devlain and Swan surge past me and storm into the room. They hit the first wave of witches like a battering ram, taking down anyone stupid enough to get close. Swan moves with brutal precision — one sharp, controlled twist and his opponent drops, unconscious before he hits the floor.

Devlain pushes forward, desperate to reach his brother, but four men block his path, each armed with some kind of baton. They swing fast — but Devlain is faster. He snatches one baton mid-strike, rips it from the witch's grip, and turns it back on him in one smooth, vicious motion. The man collapses instantly in a blood heap.

Lucy stays glued to my side. Her voice snaps my attention back to her.

"Hey, Chicky. You ready for some action? A little one-on-one?"

I flash her a wicked smile. "Oh, yeah. Time to kick some arse and show these boys how us girls get down and dirty." I pull her into a quick, fierce hug and whisper, "Lucy, please be careful."

Then I lean back and give her my best bitchy grin. "Now come on — time to kick some Dark Witches' arse. And Lucy? We're here to terminate. Understand?"

She nods, eyes flicking over the room with a hesitation I understand too well. These men were likely in that room with her on that horrible day. They're going to pay for what they did to her — and to my husband.

I flick the safety off my gun and raise it. My finger squeezes the trigger again and again. Three men drop before the others even realise what's happening. I fire three more times, taking down more targets before one shot only grazes the next witch.

Damn.

I holster the gun and I'm already moving, sword in hand, my body slipping into the familiar rhythm of combat. I strike fast, precise, controlled — killing three attackers in seconds, including the one I clipped with the bullet.

Two more rush me. I dodge, pivot, and my blade flashes. One loses his grip on his weapon and stumbles back; the other goes down hard without his head as I spin through them, keeping my focus sharp and my senses wide open.

Lucy can handle herself. Devlain and Swan better keep themselves alive too — because I'm not dragging their arses out of here if they get sloppy.

Another witch lunges at me from behind. I feel the air shift and duck just in time, the attack whistling past my head as air brushes past my cheek — too close.

Oh shite.

Focus, Alexia.

I twist, scanning fast, and spot three big, ugly Dark Witches trying to flank me. Not today, fellas. I flash them a small, taunting smile, wiggle my fingers in a come-on motion, and move. My sword arcs across the first man's chest, forcing him back. I spin, catching the second across his midsection, and the third jumps away just in time, my blade slicing only fabric.

Bugger.

Okay, time for plan B. And increase my Dark One speed. I move faster, dodging and weaving. My sword carving wide arcs through the air. Every strike is deliberate — disabling, disarming, killing anyone stupid enough to get close. If I can't reach their necks, I still make damn sure they can't stand. Adrenaline surges through me as I kick, twist, and block incoming blows, cutting through batons as if they're made of cheap plastic, and continue to spin, and kick another attacker square in the chest, hearing bone crack and break, sending him stumbling. I turn in time to block another's spiked baton, slicing it clean in half, before sending the point of my sword backwards and driving it through another Dark Witch who thought he could sneak up behind me. His body falls near my feet. I stumble for half a second, catching myself before I can fall. My senses warn me, and on instinct, I move my sword. It arcs and slices through more fabric, flesh, and bone. Screams echo in my ears another body lands near my feet.

Frustration burns through me — I don't have time for this. I need to get to Drake — not waste precious minutes fighting every Dark Witch in this damned room.

I look up — and my heart stops.

Across the room, one of the dark witches steps behind Benji. I see the glint of a blade. I see the movement. I see—

No.

Before I can shout, before I can move, the Dark Witch drives the knife into Benji's back and drags it free bloodied with a practised flick.

A silent scream tears through me. I pray it stayed in my head.

My hand moves on instinct. Gun. Aim. Fire.

The Dark Witch drops instantly.

There's no satisfaction. No relief. Just a hollow, crushing weight in my chest.

I failed Benji.

I fire again. And again. Two more witches fall before they even realise what's happening. I slam a fresh clip into place, my hands moving automatically.

My gaze snaps to Marcus and Samual. Samual's head hangs at an unnatural angle, and Marcus… Marcus is barely moving, but he is moving. His chest rises — faint, but there. He's alive and that is all that matters.

That's all I need.

I holster my gun, step over another fallen Dark Witch, and move straight toward Drake. My husband hangs limp, unconscious, chained, bloodied and bruised, and everything inside me narrows to a single point.

Get. To. Him.

CHAPTER TWENTY-TWO

GET DRAKE DOWN.

Now.

I move forward without hesitation and release my sword from my back, swing with every ounce of strength I have, and the blade slams into the chain link above him. A burst of bright sparks explodes where metal meets metal.

The chain snaps apart.

Drake's naked body drops instantly.

Uh-oh.

I did not think this part through.

I lunge forward, catching as much of his weight as I can with one arm. My other hand shoves the sword back into place at my back. Drake's full weight hits me and we both go down, my legs buckling as I pull him close and try to cushion the fall.

I don't care that we land hard. I don't care that the floor is a mess of blood and death. All I care about is Drake.

I reach into another pocket, yank out my small knife, and cut through the rope-like restraint around his neck. It falls away, and I press my trembling hand to his chest.

There — faint, but there.

A heartbeat.

Relief crashes through me so hard my eyes sting. Tears spill down my cheeks before I even realise I'm crying. I made it. I made it in time.

I bring my wrist to my mouth, pierce the skin, and press it to Drake's lips. "Come on, my love," I whisper, working his throat gently, urging him to swallow.

For a terrifying moment, nothing happens.

Then his mouth moves. Slowly. Weakly. He starts to drink before his fangs drop, bites into my wrist, and pulls at my vein.

My breath shudders out of me.

With my free hand, I fumble for my phone. I don't know if the signal will get out, but I have to try. I fire off a text first — anything to punch through the wards — then immediately dial Riley.

"Pick up… pick up…" I mutter.

He answers.

"Princess?"

Relief nearly knocks me sideways. "Riley, we need medical. Drake and Marcus are alive but in bad shape. We need backup now."

He reassures me help is already on the way, but then he asks the question I've been dreading.

"Did we get all four men out?"

My throat tightens. My heart cracks.

"No," I whisper. "Benji and Samual… they're gone. They were tortured. They didn't make it." Saying it out loud feels like breaking.

But I don't have time to fall apart.

Not yet.

Drake is still in my arms.

And I am not losing him.

Movement beside me pulls my attention. Swan and Devlain are working fast, getting Marcus down, removing the chains from his wrists and the rope-like restraint from around his neck.

I force myself to stop focusing on how much blood Drake has taken and gently pull my arm away from his mouth. I seal the punctures with my lips, then shift him enough to rest his head on my lap. He's still unconscious. My blood hasn't woken him.

A flicker of panic rises — I shove it down.

Focus. Get him out. Get him safe.

I glance around the room. Only now does the full picture hit me — every male Dark Witch is down. The room is silent. We need to leave before the rest of the coven realises what's happened.

Lucy leans over Drake a places one of her charmed necklaces around his neck.

"Thanks, Luce. I forgot about the charms."

"That's why I'm here. Now lets get these boys out of here."

I nod and, with Swan, helps me lift Drake. We get his arms over our shoulders and start moving toward the door. Lucy and Devlain do the same with Marcus. With both men unconscious and dragging their feet, it's harder than I expected. Too slow. Too exposed.

We need to get out. Now.

We push through corridors, slipping past danger more than once, until finally — finally — we find an exit leading outside. Cold air hits my face just as Riley and several of his team appear.

Two of the men rush forward, taking Drake from Swan and me. They lift him easily and sprint off in the opposite direction. The moment Riley's arm comes around me, my legs nearly give out. I didn't realise how drained I was until now.

Riley barks orders, sending Swan and a group of guards back inside to retrieve Samual and Benji. Two more guards step in to take Marcus from Devlain and Lucy.

That's when I see it — Lucy slumping in Devlain's arms, completely unconscious.

Oh no.

She's pushed herself too far.

Devlain doesn't hesitate. He scoops her up and takes off after the others, disappearing into the night. My eyes stay locked on his back until he's gone.

Riley's voice pulls me back. He's asking questions, trying to assess the situation. I answer automatically, still staring at the empty space where Devlain vanished.

"Yes, Riley. I have my sword and gun." My voice is flat, exhausted. "Your men will find plenty of Dark Witches down there. Some from bullets. Some from blades."

I take a shaky breath and look back at the building — the place I just fought my way out of.

"Gather any evidence. And make sure this place is destroyed."

Riley nods once, sharp and certain.

"And Riley... get me out of here. I need to be with my husband. He'll probably need more of my blood."

I don't get to say anything else.

My knees buckle. The world tilts. My vision blurs.

Oh shite is the last thought I manage before everything goes black.

CHAPTER TWENTY-THREE

Waking to the sharp antiseptic sting in my nose is the first sign I'm back in the hospital.

The second sign — the one that matters — is the warm, familiar scent of my husband wrapped around me like a blanket.

Drake is here. He's alive. And he's right here with me.

My senses stir, stretching awake. I lift my head slowly, blinking until my vision clears… and find myself staring straight into Drake's sleeping face. His arms are locked around me, holding me tight against the solid heat of his body. I'm half sprawled across him, legs tangled with his, skin against skin.

It takes me a few seconds to realise we're both completely naked. What the—?

Before panic can take root, something else hits me — a deep, aching pull low in my chest. The need for blood. The need for him.

I lean in, brushing a soft kiss against the warm skin of his neck. His scent curls around me, rich and intoxicating, and I nuzzle under his jaw, breathing him in until my head spins. My teeth descend on instinct, and I sink them gently into his skin.

Warmth floods my mouth. Strength. Connection. Home.

I drink slowly, gratefully, letting the bond settle through me like fire and honey. When I've taken enough, I pull back and seal the marks with a slow sweep of my tongue.

The haze lifts. My body feels steadier. My mind clearer.

I shift to move — but Drake's arms tighten around me.

"Drake," I whisper, but he's already stirring, instinctively pulling me closer, his face buried against my throat. His hands slide over my back, possessive, desperate, as if making sure I'm real.

"Alexia…" His voice is rough, barely awake, but full of emotion that hits me straight in the chest.

He rolls, guiding me beneath him, his body covering mine completely. The heat of him, the weight of him, the way he holds me — it's overwhelming. My breath catches as he presses his forehead to mine, eyes still closed, as if he can't bear to let go.

"You're safe," I whisper, cupping his face. "I've got you."

His breath shudders out, and he kisses me — slow at first, then deeper, urgent, full of everything we've just survived. The bond between us flares, bright and fierce, pulling us together with a force that feels ancient and inevitable.

The world narrows to the two of us — his hands, my heartbeat, the warmth of his skin, the way he clings to me like he's terrified I'll vanish.

We move together instinctively, the connection between us tightening, deepening, pulling us under. The soulmate bond hums through every nerve, every breath, every touch, until thought dissolves and there's only sensation, only us, only the fierce, overwhelming relief of being alive and together. With my legs wrapped around his waist, each one of his powerful thrusts becomes faster, harder.

When the moment crests, it hits like a wave — powerful,

consuming, shattering orgasm — and we cling to each other through it, breathless and shaking.

Content and bursting with love for one another.

Drake collapses against me, holding me as if he'll never let go. I wrap my arms around him, burying my face in his shoulder, feeling his heartbeat against mine.

We're alive.

We're together.

And nothing is pulling us apart again.

"BABE, YOU OKAY?"

Drake's voice pulls me back to reality. His hand glides slowly along my bare back, up and down my spine — a touch I know better than my own heartbeat.

I open my eyes and find his gorgeous ones staring right back at me. I smile, soft and dreamy. "Hey, you. How are you feeling?"

His answering smile nearly melts me. Seeing him alive, warm, right here in front of me… relief floods every fibre of my being.

"Better now," he murmurs. "I notice we're in the hospital. Do you know what's going on?"

I shake my head slightly. "No. The last thing I remember, we'd just saved you and Marcus. We got you both outside, and then… I think I passed out."

Drake stiffens beneath me. "What do you mean you saved Marcus and me and then passed out? One — what were you doing there? And two — where are Benji and Samual?"

Oh no.

This is going to hurt him.

"Baby… Swan, Lucy, and Devlain—"

"What? What was my brother doing with you?"

"Drake, let me finish."

"Alexia," he says, voice stern, "I want to know everything. Start talking."

"Fine." I take a breath. "When you didn't come home, I sent Laif back to the school to find out what happened. I couldn't contact you or sense you or the boys."

"Laif left you and went back to the school? Did you have any security at the house?"

I roll my eyes. "Geez, Drake. Yes, I still had two guards."

"Alexia, you need to be safe. You should be protected at all times."

"Drake, I do know how to protect myself. Now let me continue."

He sighs, frustrated but listening. "Babe, I know you can protect yourself. But I still worry. Don't forget you're carrying our next child."

"Oh, Drake, I love you too." I brush my fingers along his jaw. "Now, the story. Lucy came over like we planned at school — for her to take the pregnancy test. It was positive. We went out back to show her the new pool house, and I sensed someone inside. I left Lucy outside and went to investigate."

"Who would be in the pool house? Where was security? They should have known someone was there. Who was it?" His annoyance spikes — and honestly, he's right. Security should've caught Devlain before I did.

"Let me finish," I say firmly. "I went in, sensed someone sleeping, and found your brother. I woke him up with a swift kick to the bed and confronted him. Then I left Lucy and Devlain to talk. Oh — and by the way — Devlain sensed both pregnancies."

"What? He shouldn't have been able to do that."

"I think it's your twin connection. Anyway, I went inside, and since you still weren't home and no one had heard from you, I had Riley arrange a search party. By the time Laif returned, he'd found out Tabatha had nothing to do with your disappearance — but she does have something planned for me."

Drake groans. "Great. Tabatha. That annoying little human needs her arse kicked. Do you know what she's planning?"

"A little. She's going to try to convince you I'm cheating on you."

"What? That scheming little— just wait until I get my hands on her."

"Drake," I warn, giving him a sharp look, "you will not be putting your hands on her. That's exactly what she wants. Now let me finish."

He grumbles but nods.

"We went through the school footage. One of the boys — Martin — told Laif he saw a strange van and you fighting with five men. The footage showed them overpowering you four and dragging you into the van. When Lucy saw it, she recognised one of the men and the van."

Drake snorts. "The only way they overpowered us was by injecting us with something powerful."

"Oh Goddess, Drake, they could've killed you." I shake my head, still shaken by the thought. "From there, Lucy contacted her mum. She'd heard the coven was bringing in 'Lain' with three others. So we got the address. Lucy made charms for us. Riley sent extra men. And Swan, Devlain, Lucy, and I walked straight into the coven's nest."

Drake frowns. "What do you mean Lucy made charms? What did they do? And why was she with you?"

"Drake, Lucy is a witch. She made charms for all four of us. With her help, we got through the compound without setting off alarms or triggering wards. It wasn't until later I found out Swan and Devlain looked like females."

Drake laughs. "Females? Why do I feel like you're leaving something out?"

"Probably because I am. Now let me continue. A man who had been in the room when Lucy was assaulted caught us near the door to where you were being held. He wanted to take all four of us to a room and have his own private time with us. Yeah, well, that's what he thought — as he was convinced that we were there as females for the coven. He pushed Lucy too far, and she zapped him — killed him instantly."

"What do you mean, she zapped him? With what?"

"Drake, Lucy is a powerful witch coming into her abilities. She can point her fingers, they light up, and lightning shoots out. It's freaky, terrifying, and brilliant all at once."

"Wow. Remind me never to piss Lucy off."

"That's what I said."

We both laugh, but the memory of Scarface flying across the room makes me shiver. Lucy can be extremely dangerous.

"We finally found you chained to the ceiling in a room full of men. There were more than twenty-five of them."

"I wondered how many had been in the room. They rotated people in and out, especially with their questions… and the torture. They didn't want to believe they had the wrong guy. Were Benji and Samual alive or dead by then?"

With a sad face, I nod. "At that stage, all four of you were still alive. But completely unconscious."

"At least Benji and Samual didn't suffer. They were great guys."

"Yes, they were. Benji and Samual were good at their job." I give Drake a small smile. "I had my gun and sword with me and used them against those horrible people. But I wasn't able to stop one of the Dark Witches from killing Samual or Benji. I did stop them from moving on to Marcus… and then you."

"Lucky for me, you were there. Thanks for saving me, baby. This seems to be a repeating pattern — you saving me."

"I just wish I could have prevented that Dark Witch from

killing Samual and Benji. We managed to get you and Marcus outside, met up with Riley and the team, and medical. And that's about all I remember."

"So now we both wake up naked in the same hospital bed. Hmmm. I think I like it when we're in the same bed at the hospital."

I give Drake a small, knowing smile. I like the way he's thinking — both of us naked, alone, and wrapped around each other.

But more than anything, I'm just relieved to have my husband back.

Drake shifts beneath me, warm and solid, and I feel the unmistakable way he responds to me. His nose brushes mine, and then his lips find mine in a long, sensual, toe-curling kiss — the kind that steals my breath and reminds me exactly who we are to each other.

The world narrows to just us — his hands, our pacing heartbeats, the soulmate bond between us — and everything else fades away.

CHAPTER TWENTY-FOUR

Leaving the hospital after getting the all-clear from the doctor, Drake and I end up at his parents' house — or rather, Devlain's house — a couple of hours later. It becomes obvious the moment we arrive that Devlain is now the official owner of the family home, and he's wasted no time making changes. This is going to be… interesting. And maybe a little uncomfortable.

We sit quietly around the dining table — Devlain, Lucy, Mrs Smithlyn, Drake, and me — sharing our first meal together as a family.

We've just finished eating when the front door opens. Riley steps aside to let the twins roll in, tucked safely in their pram, pushed by my mother with my father close behind carrying the nappy bag.

I'm out of my chair in a heartbeat, rushing toward my precious babies and my loving parents, with Drake right behind me. The twins stir awake the moment they sense us.

Mrs Smithlyn leads us to the nursery — the room she's decorated and set up, clearly hoping she'll get to watch over her grandchildren often. There's a comfortable chair perfect for feeding both twins at once, a wide changing table with shelves full of nappies, wipes, and everything else we might need.

Oh wow.

Two matching cots sit side by side, each with a mobile hanging above it. A daybed rests near the big bay window, piled with pillows and a soft throw rug. As I look around, it hits me — this is the room Drake and Devlain slept in as babies, before Drake was sent to the human realm.

After relieving my painfully full breasts and spending some much-needed time with the twins, they drift back to sleep with full bellies. That gives me a moment to give Mum and Dad a brief version of what happened — and to get one of their special hugs. Feeling safe in their arms, I reluctantly pull away so we can rejoin the others in the lounge.

Mum settles beside Dad on the couch, then looks over at Lucy.

"Lucy, it's so good to see you. Alexia mentioned you're a witch. That explains the feeling I kept getting every time you visited. I sensed something changing in you, but I couldn't place it. How are you finding it so far?"

Lucy freezes, eyes wide. She looks like a deer caught in headlights. I jump in.

"Mum, you should see Lucy in action. She's fantastic."

Lucy shoots me a big fake smile and shakes her head slightly. Her violet eyes scream Shut up. And her expression promises payback.

Oops. I'm in trouble.

"Really, Alexia?" Lucy fires back sweetly. "What about you with a gun and a sword? Now that's talent. How many of those men did you take down? I think you'll find you handled more than half of them yourself."

She lifts an eyebrow at me, all innocent.

Okay. Touché. She doesn't want to talk about it.

"What?" my parents screech in unison, nearly making the hairs on my arms stand up. "Alexia, you never said anything about fighting. What were you thinking?"

I roll my eyes and shoot Lucy a look that says I will get you back for this.

Lucy's look says bring it on.

Sensing the tension, Drake and Devlain wisely change the subject.

"Lucy," Devlain says, "didn't you need to call your mother? Let her know you're staying here tonight and at Alexia's tomorrow?"

Lucy blinks, then smiles up at him. "That's right, Lain. I better call her before it gets too late." She turns to my parents and Mrs Smithlyn. "Excuse me, Mr and Mrs Steele, Mrs Smithlyn. I need to speak with my mother."

Mum lifts her wine glass and smiles. "Tell her we said hello, Lucy. And ask her to call me — we should catch up at the coffee house soon."

Lucy gives her a genuine smile. "I'll do that. She'd love to see you again, Mrs Steele." Then she leaves the room with Devlain.

My parents immediately give me the look — the one that says I didn't tell them everything.

Oh great. Here we go.

"Amelia, Brian," Mary says, standing and moving to sit beside me, "you should be extremely proud of your daughter. If she hadn't saved my son when she did, he might be dead. I will always be grateful to her."

She pulls me into a tight embrace. Her voice softens to a whisper in my ear. "Alexia, thank you. You saved me from that horrible man I married. You saved my youngest son from certain death and brought my other son back to me. And now I'm a grandmother to two beautiful twins. Thank you. And welcome to the family."

She releases me and stands, turning to Drake.

"Tell your brother I said goodnight. I'm going back to my parents' home. I'll see him tomorrow — we need to meet with the solicitor."

Drake hugs her. "I'll let Devlain know. Take care, Mum. We'll visit soon with the twins. Say hello to the grandparents for us."

"I will. They'd love to see you — especially with Alexia and the twins."

Mary says goodbye to my parents, then whispers something else to Drake before leaving. I miss whatever it was.

I stand and move toward Drake. "Drake, we should collect the twins and head home. We have school tomorrow."

I turn to Mum. "Thank you both for coming — and for bringing Drake's car. I didn't want to make a big deal out of having a castle driver take us home."

They take the hint and stand. I hug them both tightly, and Drake hugs Mum and shakes Dad's hand.

"Alexia," Mum says, giving me a stern look softened by a smile, "we'll let the details rest for now, but we will be asking for the full story soon. If the twins are still sleeping, consider staying here tonight. You all need rest."

She's right. I nod. "Thanks, Mum. If the twins stay asleep, we'll stay. Hopefully getting a good night's sleep. Drive safe."

We watch them leave, headlights sweeping down the long driveway.

I close the door, press a finger to my lips, and point upstairs. Drake looks confused until I give him the *can't you hear them?* look.

A moment later, his eyes widen.

'Oh. Right. I can sense Devlain now. And that is something I do not need to see.'

'Agreed. I do not need mental images of Lucy and Devlain.'

We slip into the dim nursery. The twins are still asleep — in the same cradle.

Oh no.

Bugger.

We've been trying to get them used to separate beds.

'Alexia,' Drake murmurs in my mind, *'how about we stay here tonight? I don't want to wake them. We'll leave in the morning. We can sleep in the room I used when I visited Mum and Devlain.'*

I nod. We take one more look at our sleeping babies before Drake takes my hand and leads me toward his old childhood bedroom.

CHAPTER TWENTY-FIVE

I'VE NEVER BEEN IN DRAKE'S FAMILY HOME BEFORE TODAY, AND now here we are, standing in his childhood bedroom, surrounded by old photos and a few toys on a shelf. If it weren't for the pictures on the side table and the ones on the wall in matching frames, I'd never guess this had been Drake's room. At least the staff keep it spotless — clean sheets, no dust, and thankfully no stuffy, closed-up smell.

A photo on the bedside table catches my eye. Drake and me, around ten years old, splashing in the shallow end of his pool. I can't believe he used to sneak back into Darshia whenever his father was away on business. His mother would bring him home to spend time with her and Devlain, even taking him to his grandparents' estate.

And now we know the truth — Davelt's obsession with becoming king, creating a "super race," disappearing for days to impregnate women, and slaughtering the innocent babies and mothers who didn't meet his twisted standards.

I turn toward Drake and catch the look on his face — the distant, unfocused expression that tells me he's mind-talking with his twin. Oh, fantastic. Especially considering Devlain and Lucy are currently... occupied... in Devlain's bedroom now that all the parents have left.

We're finally alone, and honestly, christening Drake's childhood room would have been fun — if I weren't so exhausted. That will have to wait.

I glance back at Drake and yawn. He's still mind-locked with his brother. What on earth could they still be talking about? I slip into Drake's mind, expecting to hear their conversation — and instead, I get a front-row seat to Devlain having sex with my Lucy girl.

WHAT THE—

I slam a mental wall between Drake and Devlain so fast I'm surprised sparks don't fly. At the same time, I grab Drake's shoulder to snap him out of it before he sees anything else. He jumps, eyes wide, relief flashing across his face before annoyance settles in. I can already feel it through our bond — he's irritated with his brother.

Why am I not surprised?

"Drake, just what do you think you're doing? What happened to speaking with Devlain? You are not meant to be watching him having sex with Lucy."

Drake blinks, still rattled, then finally gives me an answer I can accept.

"Baby, I tried to speak with Dev. He blocked me at first. Then he held me there in his mind instead of releasing me. I couldn't get out."

What?

That little shit.

How is Devlain even capable of trapping someone in a mind link?

I focus on Devlain, slipping into his mind in seconds — undetected.

'Excuse me, Devlain, stop fucking my friend and listen.'

Devlain pauses long enough to acknowledge me.

'What do you want, Alexia? As you can see, Lucy and I are a little busy right now.'

'Devlain, why did you hold Drake in your mind and not let him leave? He did not need to witness you and my friend having sex.'

'I did not do that.'

'Yes, you did, Devlain. Don't deny it. I helped Drake get out of your mind link.'

I feel the flicker of guilt in him — mixed with smugness. Typical sibling energy. He's annoyed, but also proud he managed to trap his twin.

'As I said before, Alexia... what do you want? You might have noticed I'm a little busy creating new memories for Lucy.'

His tone drips with attitude.

'If you ever try to hold Drake in your mind link again, I will let Lucy know you allowed your twin to witness her naked and having sex. Somehow, I think that's something you don't want her to know. And honestly, she should be aware that we can see what's happening when we're mind-talking.'

'Alexia, if and when I require Lucy to know, I will be the one to inform her, okay? Now, if you're finished?'

'Devlain, you need to be aware — Drake, the twins, and I are spending the night here. The twins are still sleeping, and we don't want to wake them. Drake and I are staying in his old bedroom.'

I reach out to include Lucy in the link.

'We'll see you both in the morning. Good night, guys — and don't forget the twins are sleeping in the nursery. So no sudden loud noises. Night.'

Lucy's voice carries through the mind-link before I can block it out — not directed at me, just loud enough in her thoughts that I catch it.

'What was Alexia doing speaking with us?' she asks Devlain, out loud, confusion colouring every word.

Devlain answers her verbally, but his thoughts brush against mine as he speaks, the link still half-open from our earlier conversation.

'Drake and Alexia are staying here tonight,' he tells her. *'The twins are still fast asleep, so they don't want to wake them.'*

Lucy's worry spikes, her thoughts tumbling over each other, and I feel them as clearly as if she whispered them in my ear.

'Can Alexia hear us? Or... see us?'

Devlain's mind flickers with panic — and then he lies straight through his teeth, both out loud and in his thoughts.
'She can hear us talking, but she can't see anything.'
Little shit.

Lucy is absolutely going to fry him when she finds out the truth.

Turning back to Drake, I catch the look on his face — that wide-eyed what the hell just happened expression he gets when he knows something went sideways but hasn't caught up yet.

I let out a breath and update him on everything: Lucy's confusion, Devlain's half-truths, the lie he fed her about what I can and can't see, and the fact he nearly let Drake watch far more than any brother ever should.

By the time I finish, Drake scrubs a hand over his face and mutters under his breath.

"Yeah... Dev's a little shit."

I nod, crossing my arms. "Finally. Something we agree on."

After a refreshing shower, we climb into his childhood bed — a big canopy queen-sized thing that feels ridiculously cosy after the last twenty-four hours. It's nice to curl up together, legs entwined, finally able to breathe. My head rests on Drake's chest, listening to his heartbeat slow, his breathing deepen. He falls asleep quickly.

I don't.

My mind keeps circling back to how Devlain managed to trap Drake in his head. I slip gently into Drake's mind, searching for any trace Devlain might have left behind. I find small hints — enough to make me curious — so I reach out to Devlain's mind next.

Carefully, I sift through different parts of his memories.

It doesn't take long to find something devastating.

Devlain has suffered at the hands of their father too. Davelt forced his own son into horrific situations, using drugs and coercion to extract what he wanted. The lengths that monster went to in pursuit of his "super race" make my stomach twist.

The memories are awful. No wonder Devlain is still strange around Drake. He genuinely believes Drake was better off in the human realm, protected from their father's cruelty. He tried to shield Drake as much as he could — and paid the price for it.

I pull away from Devlain's mind, shaken.

This family… what they've endured… it's a miracle any of them are sane.

I close my eyes, trying to clear my mind enough to sleep.

Then it hits me — Riley.

Crap on a stick.

I reach out to him mentally.

'Excuse me, Riley. Just letting you know we're staying at Drake's family home tonight. Can you inform the rest of the crew? We'll probably need the castle car to get all six of us back to my house. Oh — and can someone drive Drake's car back tonight?'

'Thank you for notifying me, Princess Alexia. We wondered what was happening since we hadn't heard anything after your parents arrived at the Smithlyn residence. I've been wanting to speak with you alone. I'll have Laif drive Prince Drake's car back shortly.'

'Thank you, Riley. Oh — and whatever happened with the witches' coven? Did—'

He cuts me off. *'Princess Alexia, that is what I wished to speak with you about. As per your instructions and the evidence we collected, the building where Prince Drake and the others were held has been destroyed. We made it appear as a gas explosion. A few surrounding buildings were also affected.'*

My stomach tightens.

'Riley, were any other witches killed or injured?'

'Only the ones who needed to be terminated, along with some of their... animals.'

I don't know whether to feel relieved or sick.

'Riley, did you find evidence of the crimes committed against the female witches?'

'You know what I'm referring to, Princess Alexia?'

My stomach rolls at the memories I saw in Lucy's mind. I swallow hard.

'Yes. The girls tied up. The assaults. That's why I told you to destroy the building. No girl or woman should ever be degraded like that. Their lives are forever changed.'

Riley's mind voice softens. *'If it's any consolation, Princess, we found a young girl in another building, in the process of being assaulted. No male in that room survived. All evidence was destroyed. The girl is in our hospital recovering. If she wishes to return to the coven, she can. Otherwise, we'll help her start a new life with counselling.'*

Tears slip down my cheeks. Riley may be a hardened soldier, but he understands the weight of what happened. All those girls. All those victims. I hope this is the end of it — that they can finally feel safe.

'Thank you, Riley. You don't know how much this means to me — and to Lucy.'

'Princess Alexia... we are aware of Lucy. There was video footage of her. A lot of footage.'

My heart stops.

'Oh my Goddess. Where is it?'

'Once we copied the parts showing the men involved — and the footage of the Dark Witch's death — we destroyed the rest. No one will ever see what happened to your friend. We also collected as much surveillance footage as possible. We need to know which Dark Witches are still alive. We will find them and deal with them accordingly. These acts will never be repeated.'

I wipe my tears and nod, even though he can't see me.

'Thank you, Riley. We'll see you in the morning. Good night.'

'Night, Princess.'

I close my mind to him.

The room is quiet except for Drake's slow, steady breathing. I adjust my head on his chest, feeling the rhythmic thump of his heart beneath my cheek. My eyes grow heavy.

Sleep finally claims me.

CHAPTER TWENTY-SIX

MY BODY WAKES SLOWLY, STRETCHING LIKE A WARM, LAZY CAT after the best sleep I've had in days. A soft sound escapes me as I arch, heat curling through my limbs in slow, delicious waves.

Mmm… yes… that feels good.

Mornings with Drake is always something I look forward to — the way he cherishes me before I'm even fully awake, the way he knows exactly how to unravel me with nothing but his hands, his mouth, his devotion. Even half-asleep, my body recognises him before my mind does.

I blink my eyes open, breath catching as I realise where he is — nestled between my thighs, completely focused on me, on us, on the soulmate bond that pulls us together like gravity.

The sensation of his attention, his tenderness, his deliberate care sends a shiver through me. It's heaven. Pure, blissful heaven. His tongue and fingers are masters in their ministrations.

I sink deeper into the mattress, fingers threading through his hair, letting the moment wash over me — the intimacy, the connection, the way he loves me with every breath. Every stroke of his tongue.

A low sound slips from my throat, my body arching instinctively into the warmth surrounding me. Pleasure hums through me in slow, rising waves, and I can't help the soft, breathy, "Hmmm... yes... right there..."

Sunlight filters softly across the room, but all I feel is Drake — the heat of him, the devotion in every touch, the way he knows my body as if it's an extension of his own. His focus is absolute, patient, maddeningly skilled, and the way he adores me sends sparks racing under my skin.

My breath catches, my fingers curling into the sheets as another shiver rolls through me. Drake's attention is steady, grounding, overwhelming in the best possible way. The bond between us hums, tightening, deepening, pulling me toward him until thought dissolves and there's only sensation, only connection, only him.

When the moment crests, my explosive orgasm hits like a warm, consuming wave — powerful and tender all at once — and I melt beneath him, breathless and boneless.

Drake finally moves up my body, slow and reverent, his lips brushing along my neck, his breath warm against my skin.

"Morning, my beautiful one," he murmurs, voice low and rough. "Glad to see you're back with me."

I smile, still breathless, lifting my hips to meet him. "Morning, my handsome husband. And yes... that was one hell of a wake-up."

He chuckles against my throat, the sound vibrating through me. "Oh, don't thank me yet, Alexia. I'm nowhere near finished."

The promise in his voice sends another warm ripple through me as he lowers his mouth to mine, and the world narrows to just us — heat, breath, love, and the bond that pulls us together like gravity.

Drake positions himself between my thighs, entering me in on thrust of his hips. Each roll of his hips increases the friction, building my senses towards my next orgasm. He moves with a confidence that steals the breath from my lungs, every shift of his body sending a warm rush through mine. The connection between us is deep, consuming, and my body responds instinctively, arching toward him, welcoming him.

His voice drops low, teasing and full of heat. "If you weren't already pregnant, Alexia, I think I'd be accomplishing another conception this morning."

I raise an eyebrow at him, half amused, half overwhelmed by the intensity in his eyes.

But then something changes — he thrusts forward hard, a sudden jolt of discomfort tightens through me, sharp enough to make me flinch. My hand flies to his hip, stopping him instantly.

"Drake… don't," I breathe.

He freezes, concern flooding his face. "Alexia, what is it? Did I hurt the baby? Oh my Goddess — did I hurt our baby?"

I cup his cheek, guiding his gaze back to mine. "Drake. Look at me."

His eyes meet mine, full of guilt and fear.

"The baby is fine," I say softly. "You didn't hurt her. But you could hurt me if you're not careful. My body's changing. Certain angles might feel different now. We just have to learn what works and what doesn't."

He swallows hard, still tense. "I didn't mean to—"

"I know," I whisper, brushing my lips against his. "You didn't do anything wrong. We just need to listen to my body. That's all."

Some of the guilt eases from his expression, replaced by tenderness — that fierce, protective love he carries for me and our child.

I slide my fingers into his hair, drawing him closer. "Drake… make love to me."

His breath catches, and the way he looks at me in that moment — reverent, devoted, completely undone — sends a warm shiver through my entire body.

He lowers his forehead to mine, his voice a soft promise. "Always."

The rest of the world fades away as he gathers me gently into his arms, moving with a care and devotion that makes my heart ache. Every touch is deliberate, every breath shared, every moment threaded with the bond that ties us together so tightly it feels like destiny itself.

He holds me as if I'm precious.

He loves me as if I'm irreplaceable.

I lift my hips, guiding him, showing him I'm okay. Drake hesitates for a heartbeat, searching my face, and when he sees the reassurance there, he begins to move again — slow, deliberate, careful. His body glides against mine in a rhythm that sends warmth curling through my core, building, rising, tightening.

My breath catches. My fingers curl into the sheets. The pleasure builds again, steady and insistent, and Drake's hand finds my hip, then my waist, then the sensitive place he knows so well. His touch sends sparks racing through me, my body responding with a shiver that rolls from my spine to my toes.

The moment crests, sharp and overwhelming, and I cling to him as the world blurs. My second orgasm for the morning is once again earth-shattering. Instinct and our soulmate bond pull me under, my mouth finding his skin, tasting the familiar warmth of him, and I don't wait, my fangs sink into his neck — mouthful after mouthful of his blood fill my mouth and slide down my throat.

Drake's breath stutters against my shoulder, and I feel the answering pull of his mouth at my skin, the soft sweep of his tongue sealing the his bite mark. When the haze finally begins to fade, he lifts his head, eyes full of worry.

"Babe, I'm so sorry. I didn't know I was hurting you. I'll be gentle from now on, I promise."

I cup his cheek, guiding his gaze back to mine. "Drake, you didn't hurt the baby. But you do need to be careful with me. My body's changing. If something feels wrong, we adjust. That's all."

He nods, guilt still lingering in his eyes, but love shining brighter. His hand slides over my lower belly, warm and protective, and I feel the tenderness in every slow stroke of his fingers.

Before either of us can say anything else, a soft knock sounds at the bedroom door.

Drake freezes — still positioned over me — and then quickly reaches for the sheet, pulling it up to cover us both just as the door opens.

Lucy steps inside, holding baby Alley. Devlain follows behind her with a squirming Damien.

"Morning, guys," Lucy says with a grin. "I think these two belong to you."

Drake shifts beside me, settling on the mattress and making sure the sheet covers us properly. I smile at our unexpected visitors.

"Morning, Lucy. Did the twins wake you?"

Lucy laughs. "I was heading downstairs for breakfast when I heard them chatting away. As soon as they saw me, they stopped and gave me those big gummy smiles. And Alley lifted her arms like she expected me to pick her up."

She nuzzles Alley's cheek, and my daughter melts into her before turning her head toward me. The moment her eyes meet mine, her little thoughts brush against my mind.

'Mumum.'

'Morning, my beautiful girl. Were you good for Aunty Lucy and Uncle Devlain?'

Alley looks between Lucy and Devlain, studying him with that intense baby stare that always makes me laugh.

Lucy shifts her weight. "The twins have had their nappies changed — much to Lain's horror. He definitely needs more practice. And I think your daughter might want a feed."

I reach for Alley, and the moment she's in my arms, she's already searching for me. I lower the sheet just enough, and she latches instantly, drinking deeply.

Drake grabs the spare pillows and props them around me. Soon he's settling Damien on the other side, helping him latch as well. Within moments, both twins are feeding contentedly.

Lucy watches, wide-eyed. "I still don't know how you do that. Two at once. It looks impossible."

"It takes practice," I say with a smile. "And you'll be doing it soon enough with your own baby. When he arrives."

"He?" Lucy blinks. "Why do you say he?"

I glance at Devlain, then back to her. I can feel it — the energy, the spark, the truth of it.

"Because you're having a boy, Lucy girl. Just like I'm having another girl."

Oh, crap on a stick.

I said that out loud.

Lucy's eyes go huge. "But... how can you be pregnant again? You only just had twins!"

I look down at my babies, still nursing peacefully. "No mistake. Drake and I are having another baby. And no one knows outside this room. Not even my parents."

Lucy nods slowly, absorbing it.

I grin. "And you better be careful. These Smithlyn men are extremely fertile. Devlain might have you knocked up again before you know it."

Devlain steps behind her, sliding his arms around her waist, his eyes locking with mine.

"If I do, I'll be a happy man," he says. "I want this talented, beautiful woman for the rest of my days. And I'd love for our son to have siblings. Maybe even twins."

Lucy laughs. "Dream on, lover boy. One baby is enough for now. And who says I'm staying here? It's not like you've proposed or anything."

Devlain's expression shifts — a scowl, then determination. He turns her fully toward him and kisses her hard, arms tightening around her. Before she can protest, he scoops her up and carries her out of the room.

I raise an eyebrow at Drake. "He's going to propose. He's not going to do it while he has her pinned to the bed."

Drake snorts. "Alexia, leave them alone. If Lucy didn't want to be here, she wouldn't be. And Dev telling her he loves her? That's huge for him. Let them have their moment."

He glances down at the twins, then back at me. "While they're feeding, I'm going to shower. I'll be back to burp one of them."

Come to think of it, Drake's proposal was just like that. The two of us were in bed, while he was giving me an orgasm.

Before I can comment, he's already halfway to the bathroom — and the last thing I see is his very naked, very muscled backside disappearing behind the door.

CHAPTER TWENTY-SEVEN

WHILE THE CASTLE CAR SLOWLY ADVANCES TOWARD OUR HOME, the hairs on the back of my neck rise in warning, slicing straight through my morning mental checklist.

My inbuilt warning system is screaming.

I look out the window, watching the scenery slide by as my mind reaches outward, searching for the source of the disruption.

It doesn't take long.

Intruders.

Of course, there are. Another day in my hectic life.

And where are they…Parked near our house.

Waiting. Watching.

Armed.

This is not good. No one is going to harm my babies.

My mind snaps to alert. I push a warning to both the driver and Riley. *'Don't go to the front. We have dangerous morning visitors.'*

Riley's response hits instantly — a sharp mental

acknowledgement, followed by the ripple of orders firing through my security team.

"Alexia." Drake's voice cuts through my focus. "What is it? What's going on?"

I look at him, then Lucy, Devlain, the twins. Their expressions shift — shock first, then annoyance — because of course my intruder radar is still catching them off guard.

All three of them talk over each other, demanding to know who's outside and why they're armed.

Before I can answer properly, Drake pushes against my mind shields.

'Let me in.'

I let him through, and he floods me with questions — *'What's really happening, Alexia? What's Riley doing? Why didn't you say something sooner?'*

My eyes meet his determined ones, and I lift my brow.
Impatience thickens the air.

The castle car slows, then turns down a different street.

Lucy leans forward, eyes narrowing. "We're not going to the front."

I shake my head. "Riley's diverting us," I say. "Back entrance."

There…answers answered. Just tension settling over the car as everyone realises the situation is serious.

We pull up behind the house instead of the front, and I notice Riley and several guards are already there, opening the door before the car fully stops. They usher all six of us through the hidden back entrance. Drake and I carry the twins; Lucy has the nappy bag. We slip inside undetected.

Nanny Sharonia appears immediately, relieving me of Damien. Drake heads upstairs with a sleeping Alley. Lucy follows. Devlain stays glued to my side, radiating annoyance and protective instinct.

"Devlain, come on," I say. "Kitchen. Breakfast while we wait for Drake and Lucy."

He doesn't move. "Alexia, now that Lucy isn't here… what's going on?"

"Riley wants us inside. And it's better if it looks like we stayed here last night."

His eyebrow lifts. He knows I'm not saying everything.

"What are you suggesting? Who are those men outside?"

"Put the kettle on," I say, already turning away. "Lucy will want tea before school. And maybe dry toast."

The flicker of hurt in his eyes hits me — he knows I'm holding back — but I don't have time to soothe it.

My mind shifts outward again. Relief floods me as Riley's team has the intruders captured.

Oh, good.

I glance back at Devlain. "They're surrounded. The intruders are on the ground now. I need to grab something upstairs. Be right down."

He's annoyed — very annoyed — but I head upstairs anyway. He needs to remember he's not my keeper, and I'm certainly not obliged to run everything past him first.

Then a thought slams into me.

My parents.

Oh, no. Mum and Dad might be in trouble.

I reach for their home. My mind busy searching. Both cars in the garage. No intruders. Relief washes through me… until I notice the empty kitchen.

That's strange. They're always eating breakfast by now.

Worry builds. I sweep the rest of the house.

Instant regret.

Oh my Gods.

If I could bleach my mind, I would.

My parents. Naked. In bed. Not sleeping.

Busy doing the horizontal tango.

"Ewuuu. My mind. My poor mind," I screech.

No child should ever have to witness that.

At least they're safe — even though they've emotionally and mentally scarred their only child, they are safe.

I scrub the image from my brain as best I can and contact Riley.

'Riley. *My parents are safe.*' I shudder again from the images. *'Keep an eye on them. Not that close of an eye.'* All I hear through our mind link is laughter. '*Not funny, Riley,*' I mumble. The annoying man must know where my parents are.

I RUN TO MY BEDROOM, KICK OFF MY SHOES, YANK OFF MY SOCKS, strip away my clothes, pull on sleep pants and a top, and throw my long winter dressing gown over everything. As I head downstairs, I mess up my hair to complete the "*just rolled out of bed*" look.

At least — within ten minutes of my first warning, castle security has both vehicles secured, and the men restrained. For once, my security is working as a unit.

Outside, I step into the morning air like nothing's wrong. The intruders lie on their fronts, hands cuffed behind their backs, ankles bound with cable ties. I head straight for Riley.

We need answers.

"Morning, Riley. Who are your friends?"

ALL OF THE DETAINED MEN ARE HEAD-TO-TOE BLACK. THREE Caucasian. Two warm milk-coffee skin. Beyond that, nothing. No spark of recognition. No familiar energy.

I study each face anyway.

Still nothing.

Riley brushes the edge of my mind, waiting. I let him in.

'Yes, Riley. What is it? What have you found out?'

'Not much, Princess Alexia. They won't speak, and we can't penetrate their minds. Can you break through their shields?'

'Okay, Riley. Give me a minute.'

Out loud, he shifts into performance mode, voice casual for anyone watching.

"Morning, Alexia. We found these armed men loitering outside your home. Do you know them? Because we don't."

I glance at each one of them, then shake my head. "No."

I look them over again, focusing on the one closest to me — the one radiating I'm in charge energy. Two of the others keep glancing at him.

Leader confirmed.

I raise a brow. "Morning, gentlemen. Any particular reason for your visit? I don't recall scheduling appointments this early. So why are you here, interrupting my morning and my breakfast?"

All five turn their heads just enough to look me over — messy hair, slippers, dressing gown. Good. Let them underestimate me.

While they're busy staring, I slip into their minds.

Their shields crumble like warm butter under a hot knife.

Information slams into me.

They're here to shoot, capture, or kill Devlain — retaliation for his escape from the Dark Witches' coven compound yesterday.

So they're working for witches… but there's no radiating witch magic on them — just a faint trace. If I'm not mistaken, a charm of some description.

I sweep my senses over their bodies.

There.

A magical talon stuck to each of them, masking their minds from my men. Well, think it would mask their thoughts and minds from Dark Ones.

Silly people. As if a little charm is going to stop me when I'm standing right here.

Last night, we learned the rope necklaces around Drake and the others' necks were talons too — ones that prevented Dark Ones from communicating. And yes, we found that out the hard way.

I dig deeper into the men's minds, and the truth hits fast and ugly.

'Riley,' I call out mentally, *'these men are nothing more than hired guns. Humans. They were told a young man had been kidnapped and they're trying to capture one of the supposed kidnappers. They have no idea who they're dealing with.'*

Riley's presence sharpens instantly.

'Humans? Then how are they blocking us?'

'Talons,' I answer. *'Each of them has one stuck to their body. It's masking their minds. Dampening your Dark One abilities.'*

A beat of silence — then Riley's mental voice turns cold, efficient.

'Understood, Princess. I'll have the team search them now.'

Out loud, he barks orders, keeping up the act while maintaining the mental link.

A moment later, his voice brushes my mind again.

'Princess Alexia, you were right. We've located the talons — stuck to their skin under their clothing.'

'Good. Remove them. Once they're off, you should be able to breach their minds without any trouble.'

'Already done,' Riley replies, satisfaction colouring his tone. *'Their shields are collapsing. We'll have answers shortly.'*

Morning crisis handled, I turn and head back toward the house. Time to get ready for school and feed the twins.

AN HOUR LATER, WITH TWO NEW GUARDS REPLACING SAMUAL AND Benji, we're back on the road. Lucy, Drake, and I sit in the back of one castle vehicle while Devlain is escorted separately to Darshia under heavy protection. He made it very clear he is not happy being separated from Lucy and his unborn son.

Yes — his son.

Apparently Smithlyn boys are extremely fertile.

Drake explained to his brother how to communicate with his own child, and Devlain managed it easily. Lucy cried. Devlain cried. It was a whole emotional moment.

Doctor Brean confirmed over the phone this morning that any male Dark One can communicate with a baby he fathered with his mate.

Devlain even tried with our daughter, placing his hand on my lower belly — but Alex wasn't having it. She sensed him, recognised he wasn't her father, and promptly went back to sleep. My daughter is already a genius, even if she's technically still a blob of tissue, cartilage, blood, and veins.

At least this time, I can hear Alex. I can speak with her. This pregnancy is already so different from the twins.

Drake tried to speak with Lucy and Devlain's baby, but it didn't work — confirming what the doctor said. Only the father can communicate with his own child.

What a twenty-four hours. Yesterday morning we were heading to school with textbooks and assignments. Since then, we've lost two guards, gained two more, nearly lost my husband, fought for our lives, and woke up to another ambush attempt.

Thank the Goddess for my Dark One senses. They saved us again.

Before leaving home, Lucy gave me a beautiful rectangular sparkly-stone necklace. As soon as it touched my skin, warmth spread through me, followed by a calming wave.

The pendant belongs to the Smithlyn family. Lucy asked Devlain and Drake if they had anything she could enchant for my protection, and they handed her the gem. She's been busy weaving spells and wards into it.

She told me not to remove it. She also said she's certain I have magic in me — and with the necklace amplifying it, I should be able to perform basic spells. All I need to do is memorise the words she tried to teach me over five minutes ago.

We pull up to the kerb in front of the school. Laif, Jona, and Blade — our undercover student-guards — exit the second car. The six of us walk toward our lockers, ready to face our first class of the day.

CHAPTER TWENTY-EIGHT

By LUNCHTIME, I'VE EXPRESSED MILK TWICE, CHANGED MY TOP and bra once, and squeezed in quick cuddles and kisses with Drake between classes. My school day so far has been surprisingly pleasant. No hassles. Each class has been fun, helpful, and running smoothly. With my last assignment handed in and logged into the school system, today feels like a completely different universe compared to yesterday.

Why do I have the feeling I've spoken too soon?

It's strange for Miss Tabatha the Bitch to be this quiet. Especially after yesterday's threats. I'm sitting with my back to the wall, laughing at a joke Lucy just finished telling our group, when the little hairs on the back of my neck rise.

Uh-oh.

Danger. Trouble. Incoming. Fills my mind.

I casually glance around until I find the source of the brewing storm.

Oh yes. I definitely spoke too soon.

Here comes trouble, prancing into the cafeteria in the form of

Tabatha, flanked by two teenage boys like she's royalty and they're her personal guard dogs.

But beneath that, something else stirs. A strange sensation coils in my gut — something not right. Something bigger than whatever Tabatha thinks she's about to unleash.

We keep our eyes on her as she approaches. Lucy keeps talking, telling another joke, but we're all watching Tabatha and her sidekicks out of the corners of our eyes. The hairs on my neck keep rising, warning me something terrible — something dangerous — is about to happen.

My gaze sweeps the cafeteria. At least three hundred students and a handful of staff are here for lunch. My mind reaches out, brushing against as many minds as possible.

Realisation hits hard.

All these students are innocent. Just chatting, eating, laughing. No threat. No malice.

So what am I sensing?

The unease inside me spikes.

I send a mind message to Laif, sharp and urgent.

'Laif — I feel danger. Something's wrong. Far end of the cafeteria.'

Out of the corner of my eye, I see him stand, one of the new bodyguards rising with him. They talk quietly while scanning the room. Their eyes lock onto something — someone — at the far end.

My eyes follow theirs.

A gasp escapes me.

You have got to be kidding me.

My focus sharpens on the dark figure — or rather, two shadowy figures — and both turn in my direction.

Oh no. This is not good.

What is our now-fired ex-principal doing here?

And why is he talking with my new English teacher — Tabatha's uncle, Mr Stragaft?

Worse, I sense someone else near them.

A familiar presence.

A woman. Maybe?

Hidden in the shadows. I can't see her, but I know she's there.

Then, just as quickly as I sense her, she's gone.

Vanished.

Like she was never there.

I shake my head slightly, clearing the fog, and send a quick message to Drake.

'Drake — ex-principal. Far end. With Stragaft.'

Drake immediately pulls his chair closer and lifts me onto his lap. His arms wrap protectively around my waist as I snuggle into his chest. Lucy hits the punchline of her joke, and we all burst out laughing — right as Tabatha stops in front of our table, twirling her long hair and trying to look smug.

The laughter dies instantly. Everyone turns toward her and her two shadows, waiting for her to speak.

"Drake, the Principal has a message for you. You are required to go to the Principal's office."

Drake stiffens beneath me.

Across the table, I see Laif pull out his phone. He speaks quietly, then his expression twists into something strange. His eyes meet mine, and he gives a tiny shake of his head.

Right.

Laif sends me a mind message. *'I just spoke with Ms Lexington. Tabatha's message is a lie.'*

I update Drake through our mind link.

'She's lying. Ms Lexington didn't send anything. They're trying to separate us.'

It doesn't take a genius to figure out Tabatha is working with her uncle and the ex-principal. They're trying to lure Drake out of the cafeteria.

Drake lifts his chin. "Tabatha, I'm not sure what's going on, but I know for a fact Acting Principal Mrs Hoyt does not have a message for me, and she does not need to see me. So what is really going on?"

Tabatha's smile falters. She glances toward her uncle, then back at Drake.

"Drake, I was given a message to give to you, which I have now done. How am I supposed to know what's going on?"

Under her breath, she mutters, "I tried to warn you."

With a flick of her head, Tabatha sends her hair flying as she spins to walk in the opposite direction. She tries to wiggle her hips in a provocative sway, clearly hoping the boys behind her will drool over her retreating figure.

They don't.

Both boys turn their heads away, unimpressed and uninterested.

Just as I look back toward the cafeteria entrance, I notice Tabatha pause. She glances toward her uncle, something unreadable flickering across her face, before she disappears through the double doors.

The little hairs on the back of my neck stand up again — sharp, insistent.

I do not like this.

Something is about to happen, and I can't work out what it is.

And what did she mean by I tried to warn you?

My eyes flick instinctively toward the entrance again — and that's when I see Mr Smite and Mr Stragaft are still standing there.

Both men are staring directly at our table. And then they smile. Not friendly smiles. Not polite smiles.

No — these are slow, deliberate, evil smiles. The kind that say *we know something you don't, and you're not going to like it.*

A cold shiver races down my spine.

Fantastic. Exactly what I needed today: two grown men grinning like cartoon villains who are about to press the big red button that blows everything to hell.

Their eyes linger on Drake, then slide to me, and the malice sharpens. It's like they want me to see it. Like they're daring me to react.

My stomach twists.

Before I can warn the others, both men turn in unison and slip through the double doors, disappearing from sight as if they were never there.

The moment they vanish, the pressure in the air spikes. My Dark One senses flare so sharply it almost hurts.

Whatever they're planning… it's already in motion.

I send a mind message to both Drake and Lucy, my thoughts sharp and urgent.

'Drake. Lucy. Something's wrong. Can you feel that?'

Their eyes snap to mine. Both give a slight nod.

Oh, crap on a stick.

Whatever this is, the intensity is rising fast.

That's it — I'm sending for Riley.

With my mind, I reach out, contacting him instantly.

'Riley, get to the school. Bring the team. Something's wrong —

very wrong. I want royal security on alert. I am not doing another abduction today.'

Warning. Leave. Warning. Spin through my mind.

"Hey guys, can you feel something is wrong here?" I ask aloud, my voice low but firm. Maybe the students near our table might overhear as well. "Something is warning me we need to leave this building. NOW."

Drake, Lucy, and the rest of our group stand immediately, glancing around the cafeteria. Concern etches their faces as they instinctively move around me. Something is pushing us to get out — to evacuate.

Time to do something serious before it's too late.

I reach out with my mind. *'Ms Lexington, something is very wrong here at the school. I don't know what it is, but it's bad.'*

Her response is instant, sharp with concern. *'Alexia, what's happening? What are you sensing?'*

'Mr Stragaft and the ex-principal,' I tell her, my mental voice tight. *'They were just inside the cafeteria watching us. Their expressions were... wrong.'*

'That does not mean there's something wrong. But, I did see them on the cameras earlier,' she replies, unease bleeding through her tone. *'I didn't like the way they were moving around the school. Places the staff do not enter.'*

I glance back to where the men had been standing...what are they up to? Why did they take off?

My internal alarms explode.

'Ms Lexington, check the security screens. Are they showing up anywhere? They should be on surveillance unless—'

'Alexia,' she cuts in, *'I'm sending all video feeds to your security team now. I don't know what's happening, but—'*

I cut her off, the spike of danger hitting me so hard it steals my breath. *'We need to evacuate the school. Now. Get everyone out of the building.'*

'Alexia, someone should go and...'

'Pull the fire alarm — NOW,' I shout through the link. *'And get out of the building before it's too late.'*

The fire alarm pierces the air, shrieking its warning to evacuate, followed by the voice message: "This is not a drill."

Just as I begin to walk through the exit, I turn to see students looking around, trying to decide if this might be a false alarm.

Stupid idiots.

When you hear this is not a drill, you should be moving your arse.

The recorded message blares repeatedly through the overhead speakers along with the evacuation alarm: "This is not a drill. Exit the building immediately. This is not a drill. Exit the building immediately."

Instantly, I yell out to everyone in the room, as loud as I can, "Come on! We need to get out. Get out, now!" Waving my arm in the air, I motion for them to follow. "This way. Quickly!"

Drake and Lucy also shout to leave, waving their arms about.

I turn and exit the building, our group right behind me.

Instead of heading toward the interior cafeteria doors, the

students follow us through the exterior doorway and out of the building. Walking at a fast pace, we head toward the football field.

Doom hangs heavy in the air.

Whatever time we had remaining… has just run out.

Before we know it, everyone starts to run. Panic spreads like wildfire — one person bolts, then another, and suddenly the entire cafeteria erupts into a stampede. Shoes slap against tiles, trays crash to the floor, chairs scrape and topple. The air fills with shouts, gasps, and the frantic rustle of bodies pushing toward the exits.

Glancing back over my shoulder, I see the students nearest us break into a sprint too, their faces pale with confusion and fear.

I send a sharp message to Riley, my mental voice cutting like a blade. *'Riley — get your arse to the school boundary. Now.'*

We're barely halfway across the football oval when the world detonates behind us.

A deep, violent BOOM tears through the air — not just sound, but force. A shockwave slams into my back like a giant invisible fist. The ground bucks beneath us, throwing everyone off their feet. I hit the grass hard, the breath punched out of my lungs, my ears ringing so loudly I can't hear my own gasp.

Another explosion follows — louder, closer — and the ground heaves again. Students scream as they tumble, arms flailing, legs tangling. Some roll across the grass, others curl into balls, shielding their heads.

I try to push myself up, but the earth vibrates like it's alive, like something monstrous is clawing its way out from underneath. I drop to my hands and knees as burning debris rains down around us — chunks of metal, shattered tiles, flaming scraps of roof insulation. One piece lands so close the heat sears my cheek.

I whip my head around.

The cafeteria — the place we were sitting in minutes ago — is gone.

Gone.

A roaring inferno devours what remains of the structure. Flames shoot high into the sky, thick black smoke billowing upward in a choking column. Windows from nearby buildings shatter outward, spraying glass across the oval like glittering knives.

Students scream. Some cry. Some stand frozen in shock. Others try to run back toward the destruction, shouting names, searching for friends.

"Oh, my Goddess… no." The words barely leave my lips.

Drake's arms wrap around me from behind, pulling me tight against him. His body curls protectively over mine, his hands covering my lower belly. He's shielding our child with everything he has.

My heart hammers painfully.

If I hadn't felt the warnings…

If I hadn't pushed Ms Lexington…

If we'd stayed even thirty seconds longer…

We'd be dead.

The thought hits me like another explosion.

Sirens wail in the distance — multiple vehicles, multiple directions — the sound growing louder with every passing second. Relief floods me, but it's tangled with guilt, fear, and the sickening knowledge that not everyone made it out.

Seconds or minutes pass as I feel my phone vibrating in my pocket. My hands shake as I pull it free. Mum's name flashes on the screen.

I answer, my voice trembling. "Hello."

"Alexia. Oh, thank Goddess you're okay. I just heard your school is on fire — it's on the radio. What has happened?"

Tears sting my eyes. The adrenaline crashes hard, leaving me raw and shaking. "Mum… you won't believe it. I felt something was about to happen. I got Ms Lexington to pull the fire alarm. I just hope everyone got out."

"Where were you when you felt it?"

"In the cafeteria. Mum, the hairs on my neck stood up. Drake and Lucy felt it too. And then I saw Mr Stragaft and the ex-principal watching us. They were staring straight at me. That's when I knew we had to get out."

"Are you all okay? Drake? Lucy? Your security?"

"We're together, but we have to move. There are still explosions happening. We'd just reached the oval when the first blast hit."

"I'm just glad you're alive. Come home as soon as you can."

"We will, Mum. But we're still on the ground where we landed."

"Alexia, please stay safe."

"I'll try. Love you."

I end the call and turn to Drake. His face is tight with fear and relief.

"Alexia… if you hadn't warned us…"

He pulls me closer, kissing the top of my head.

"Drake," I whisper, "Tabatha tried to get you out of the building. And she said, 'I tried to warn you.'"

"I know. I heard her."

I scan the oval. Students are scattered everywhere — some crying, some limping, some helping others to their feet. Smoke rolls across the field like a dark fog. The air tastes like ash and burning chemicals.

Then I spot Lucy curled on the ground.

Oh no. Lucy.

I scramble out of Drake's arms and rush to her. "Lucy, are you okay?" My hand trembles as I touch her shoulder. She moves — thank the Goddess.

"Oh shit, Alexia… what bullshit are we in this time?" she croaks, turning her head. Her eyes widen as she looks past me. "Holy shit — look at the school."

We all turn.

What's left of the school is collapsing in on itself. Flames roar. Another explosion erupts, sending a fireball into the sky. More debris rains down — twisted metal, burning wood, chunks of concrete. We duck instinctively, though it won't help much if something big hits us.

My senses scream — move.

I grab Lucy's hand. "Come on, everyone — we gotta move. We have to get out of here, it is not s—"

The ground shakes violently again, cutting me off. A fissure cracks open nearby, widening with each rumble. The earth splits like a jagged mouth.

"Oh, shite. Quick. Move. Run!" I yell, dragging Lucy away from the destruction.

Drake appears beside me. "Lift Lucy!" I shout. "She's slowing us down!"

He scoops her into his arms, and the rest of us sprint, using our Dark One abilities.

Within minutes, Riley's vehicles screech to a stop at the boundary. Drake and two guards reach the fence first. Riley jumps out, flinging open a car door.

I push myself harder — but a sharp pain stabs my side.

Oh no. Not now.

I clutch my side, breath hitching. I still have twelve metres to go. I see Drake placing Lucy inside the car. He turns back toward me—

Another explosion detonates.

The ground bucks violently. My feet fly out from under me. I stumble, trip, and fall hard. A new fissure tears open right beside me.

Uh-oh.

I'm falling.

I look up at Drake — and the truth hits me like a punch.

I didn't make it.

CHAPTER TWENTY-NINE

FALLING INTO NOTHING BUT AIR IS NOT ON MY TO-DO LIST TODAY.

The ground disappears beneath my feet, the world tilts, and for one horrifying heartbeat I'm weightless — suspended over a widening crevice, wind rushing past my ears, my stomach lurching into my throat.

Then something big slams into me from behind.

Something grips my waist. A shove. Hard. Unexpected. My body flies upwards.

My arms fling forward on instinct, reaching for anything — anyone — and Riley's hand clamps around my wrist. His grip is iron. He yanks me toward him with so much force my shoulder screams, but I don't care. I'm moving toward the car instead of the abyss.

The world blurs.

Before my body even lands, another pair of hands grabs me — someone hauling me, throwing me, shoving me into the back seat of the vehicle.

I hit the leather seats face-first, my cheek smacking the

upholstery, my ribs slamming into the edge. The impact knocks the air out of my lungs in a brutal whoosh.

I barely have time to gasp before a massive weight crashes down on top of me.

A full-body slam.

A wall of muscle.

A human boulder.

I'm crushed into the seat, unable to breathe, my chest pinned, my spine bending awkwardly. Panic flares hot and sharp. I wiggle, clawing at whatever is on top of me, desperate for air.

My head finally tilts enough for a breath to squeeze in — a ragged, burning inhale.

I twist, trying to see what the hell flattened me.

It's Drake.

Of course it's Drake.

"Drake — get off me," I wheeze. "Having trouble breathing down here."

"Oh shit — sorry, babe." He scrambles off me, landing beside me on the seat. "I just wanted to make sure Laif is okay after he saved you. I thought he was going to be a goner — fall straight down that massive crevice and never be seen again."

Air floods my lungs again, sweet and painful. Blood tingles back into my arms and legs. Drake helps me sit up, but his words hit me harder than the fall.

"Laif? What about him?"

"Alexia… Laif saved you." Drake's voice cracks. "He grabbed you and threw you toward Riley and me. If he hadn't been right behind you, you'd be gone. I don't even want to think about it. I could've lost you. Both of you."

His hand slides to my lower stomach, protective and trembling. I feel him reach out mentally to baby Alex, checking she's okay.

The car swerves sharply, taking a corner fast. The interior jolts.

I look around, scanning for Lucy — and find her pressed against Riley, his arms wrapped tightly around her.

Oh, hell no.

If Devlain sees that, Riley will be a dead man walking.

I clear my throat loudly.

Riley's head snaps toward me. His mind brushes mine.

'Yes, Princess Alexia?'

'Riley, move your arms. Slowly. Lucy is engaged to Devlain — Drake's brother — and she's carrying Devlain's child. If my brother-in-law sees you holding his fiancée like that, he will kill you. Do you understand me?'

'Yes, Princess. I was only offering comfort.'

'I know. And thank you. But if Drake mind-talks with Devlain, Devlain will know exactly what's happening in this car...'

Riley leans down and whispers something to Lucy. She nods, and he gently releases her, sitting back stiffly like he's trying not to breathe too loudly.

I turn to Drake — and see the distant look in his eyes.

He's mind-talking.

Of course he is.

I reach out, tapping into the link.

'Drake, I just heard. How is Lucy? I cannot sense her. Is she with you?' Devlain's voice is sharp, frantic.

Whew. That was close. Riley's safe to live another day.

'Yes, Dev,' Drake answers. *'Lucy is with Alexia, Riley, and me in one of the royal cars. But it was too close. We could have lost them, bro. This attack almost got us.'*

There's a pause — then a dangerous edge enters Devlain's tone.

'Riley? Why is Riley in your car?'

Drake smirks. *'Aww, my brother sounds a little jealous.'*

Drake, do not piss me off. Devlain's voice drops to a lethal growl. *'Lucy is my fiancée and carrying my child. I am extremely concerned about both of them. Now tell me how she is. You've only said she's with you — not how she is.'*

Okay, time to stop this before Drake pushes him too far.
I cut into their link, my mental voice firm and slicing through the tension.

'Hi, Devlain. How are you going?'

I make sure Drake is looped in so he hears everything.

'Alexia, how are you? Can you tell me how Lucy is, please? My brother seems to think it's funny not to update me on her status.'

I nearly roll my eyes. *'Devlain, stop fussing. Lucy is fine. We've all had a massive shock. Nearly dying and getting swallowed by the ground tends to do that to you. And you should be thanking your brother — Drake picked Lucy up when we ran for our lives. He saved your fiancée, made sure she got into the car safely...*

and left me behind. If it weren't for Laif, I'd be dead. So shut up, Devlain, and start being nice to Drake.'

'What...? Drake saved my Lucy?'

'Yes, Devlain. Drake saved Lucy and your unborn child from being swallowed by the ground.'

'But why did Drake leave you behind?'

'Because I told him to pick Lucy up and run. She was slowing us down. It was the only way to save all of us. Lucy doesn't have our Dark One speed.'

'Drake, why did you listen to Alexia? You should have had one of the others pick Lucy up.'

Drake doesn't hesitate. *'Devlain, when your wife tells you to do something, you do it. I was closest to Lucy. Alexia nearly made it, but another explosion hit. Laif saved my wife and my unborn child. When we arrive, I'm shaking his hand. He saved my family today.'*

There's a pause, then Devlain asks, *'Drake, where are you going? Back to your house or here to Darshia?'*

'I'm not sure...' Drake says, glancing at me.

I answer for us. *'We're going back to our house, collecting the twins, then heading to Darshia. We'll see you later this afternoon, Devlain.'*

'Alexia, can you look at Lucy? Please. I need to see her.'

I turn to Lucy. "I'm speaking with Devlain."

Her eyes widen. "Alexia, can he hear me through you? I'd love to see him."

I take her hand. "Let me try to include you in the link."

"Really? You think you can?"

"I can only try."

I focus, weaving the connection carefully until I feel the link expand.

'Devlain, can you hear us? Can you see Lucy?'

Lucy gasps — a sharp inhale — meaning she sees him.

'Lain, can you hear me, babe?'

'Lucy. My Lucy. It's so good to hear your voice. Can you see me?'

'Oh, wow — yes, Lain, I can see you. This is fantastic.'

'Lucy, how are you? Are you okay? How's the baby? Should I have Alexia take you straight to the hospital?'

'No, I'm okay. Alexia should be the one seeing a doctor. After the way she entered the car, I'm amazed she's conscious.'

'My love, I'm relieved you're safe. I can't wait until you're back in my arms.'

'I love you, Lain.'

Oh boy. It'll be a relief when Devlain can do this without me acting as the magical telepathic switchboard.

I glance out the window — we're pulling up to Drake's house. Our house.

'Excuse me, lovebirds. We're about to arrive. Say your goodbyes.'

'Alexia, you and Drake are welcome to stay at my house,' Devlain adds.

'Thank you, Devlain. I'll let Drake know. Bye.'

I let the two of them finish privately. A moment later, Lucy touches my leg — her signal she's done. I disconnect the link and smile at her.

A guard opens the door, letting Drake out first.

"Come on, Lucy girl," I say, stretching my sore ribs. "Time to go. I need a shower."

"A shower sounds amazing. And a cup of hot chocolate with marshmallows. Oh yes... melted chocolate..." Lucy rubs her belly like she's summoning dessert spirits.

"Oooh, yes. Chocolate. And maybe some of Mum's apple pie."

"Ooh! I love your mum's apple pie. Do you think she has any?"

"Only one way to find out. We'll have to call her."

"Phone her, Alexia. It is way beyond apple-pie time. Hmmm mmm." Lucy pats her flat belly again, already dreaming of sugar.

Lucy and I are still laughing as I climb out of the car. I turn, reaching a hand back to help her out — when every hair on the back of my neck snaps upright.

Danger.

My eyes lift instinctively, searching for the source—

A sharp, burning pain explodes through my shoulder.

The force of it jerks me sideways. I nearly stumble backward off the driveway.

For a split second, I don't understand what just happened.

Then instinct takes over.

I duck hard and shove Lucy back into the car with all the strength I have left. "Stay down!" I bark, even as my own knees threaten to buckle.

The realisation hits me like another blow.

I've been shot.

My hand flies to my shoulder. The moment my fingers brush the wound, white-hot pain lances through me. I hiss and pull my hand away — and freeze when I see it.

Blood.

Wet. Dark. Spreading fast across my palm.

Uh-oh.

I slap my hand back over the wound, trying to stem the flow, but warm liquid seeps through my fingers almost immediately. It's too fast. Far too fast.

"Crap on a stick... no," I whisper, staring at the blood soaking through my top, blooming outward like a nightmare flower.

Lucy's scream tears through the air.

"HELP! Someone help! Alexia's been shot!" Her voice is raw, panicked, echoing off the driveway and the stone walls of the house. Doors slam. Footsteps thunder. Voices shout.

But everything around me starts to blur. My head swims. The world tilts. Dark spots flicker at the edges of my vision like someone dimming the lights.

Not today.

Not after everything.

"Well... crap on a stick... not again," I mumble, my voice slurring as my knees give way.

The last thing I feel is my eyes rolling back — and the world collapses into black.

CHAPTER THIRTY

WAKING TO THE FAMILIAR ODOUR OF ANTISEPTIC HAS MY NOSE twitching as my senses adjust to being back in the hospital again.

Damn.

What is it this time?

I search my mind, trying to remember how and why I'm back in here again. Before I open my eyes, I push out with my senses to see who and what is around me.

The only person in the room is Riley.

Hmm.

Where is Drake?

Reaching out further, I can't sense or feel Drake anywhere in the hospital.

Okay, I do not like this.

Where is Drake?

Where is my husband?

It doesn't take me long to check each section of my body with my mind, working out what's been damaged this time.

Ouch… my shoulder.

And then it rushes back to me.

I was shot getting out of the car.

My eyes snap open and lock straight onto Riley. I require answers, and I want them now.

"Princess Alexia, it is good to see you awake. Would you like me to call the doctor?"

"In a minute, Riley. First, I want to know if Drake is alright. And where is he? Why is he not here?"

Riley nods — but he hesitates.

Delaying.

Avoiding.

Stalling.

My brain is still fogged, thoughts dragging like they're wading through mud, but one thing pulses beneath the haze: the bond. The thread that is Drake. It's faint... muted... but still there.

Still, panic spikes hard enough to override logic.

I try to push myself up — a stupid instinct — and pain detonates through my shoulder. A sharp, white-hot bolt that rips a gasp out of me. My body flinches before I can stop it, and the movement sends another wave of agony rolling through my chest.

"Riley," I manage, breath tight, "is Drake alive?"

He nods again before speaking. "Oh yes, Princess Alexia. Drake is alive, and no, he was not injured."

Relief hits so fast it's dizzying. Of course, he's alive — I would feel it if he wasn't. Even half-drugged, half-dead, half-conscious, that bond would tear itself apart if he were gone. But the fear still clings, sticky and stubborn.

"Then why is he not here? Where is he?"

"Ah, I should w—"

"Riley, either you start talking, or I take a walk through your mind. Your choice."

He straightens in the hospital chair, nodding again.

"Princess Alexia, when you were exiting the car, you were shot in the chest. Somehow, you managed to push Lucy back into the car, out of harm's way. You protected your friend. You saved her. If you hadn't pushed her back into the car and out of the path of the flying bullets, she would have taken a bullet to the head."

Oh shite.

"Riley, was it another assassination attempt on my life or Lucy's?"

He glances down at the floor, avoiding my eyes.

Okay, so it was mine — but he's hiding something.

"Riley... tell me."

He grows visibly nervous. What is going on?

"Riley," I repeat.

Finally, he meets my eyes. And I already know I'm not going to like what comes next.

"Um, Princess Alexia... it was another attempt on your life."

Oh, crap on a stick.

Not again.

"Who? Did you capture them?"

"Yes, we did."

"Are you going to tell me, or do I need to breach your mind?"

He shakes his head, discomfort rolling off him. "Princess Alexia... the person who shot you is my cousin."

What—

Oh, crap on a stick. Am I in trouble with my own guard?

My eyes instantly scan the room for weapons or guards. Nothing. Just a bag beside Riley's chair. Damn it. No one else is here, and I have nothing to defend myself with.

I take a deep breath and look straight at him. "Are you here to finish what your cousin started, Riley?"

He shoots to his feet, knocking the chair backward. Shock floods his face as he shakes his head.

"What— no. Never, Princess Alexia. I would never hurt you. I am here to protect you. You are the next Queen of Darshia."

I sense the truth in him, and relief loosens the tension in my chest.

"Who is your cousin, Riley? What is their name?"

"My cousin's name is Zeeland. Zeel—"

You've got to be joking. Alexettia's toy boy.

"Zeeland Courtlandt. The queen's lover."

Shock freezes Riley's expression. "How did you know?"

He's not going to like what I have to say. "My grandmother was with him the night the castle was under attack. He was also with her when I was attacked in the hospital. He was with her the night of my joining and marriage to Drake."

Speaking of Drake…

"Riley, where is my husband?" I ask again.

With a sigh, Riley replies, "Prince Drake is back at the castle, interrogating my cousin."

Okay. That explains why Drake isn't here.

"Riley, does Drake know the shooter is Zeeland — the queen's lover?"

"I don't know. He knows the shooter's name is Zeeland. Anything beyond that, I'm not sure, my Princess."

Oh, crap on a stick.

Drake might be connecting the dots.

"Riley, where is the queen right now?"

"I'm not sure, Princess Alexia."

That is not a good answer.

I reach out with my mind, searching for Drake in the royal castle.

Danger fills my mind.

Danger.

Danger.

Finally feeling him — that familiar pull, that unmistakable presence — I breach his mind.

'Drake, get out of the castle now. Get out.'

'What? Alexia, you're awake. How are you, baby?'

His relief washes through the link, warm and overwhelming, but I don't have time for it.

'Drake, get your arse out of the castle now.'

Through the bond, I sense him moving — the echo of his footsteps, the shift of air as he steps through a doorway. He's alert now, tension sharpening his thoughts.

'Why? What is going on?'

'Drake, is Grandma Ma there with you? Was she in the interrogation room?'

'How did you know? She was. She had to do something and left. One of the guards said she's on her way back down here. She should be here any minute.'

Oh Goddess, no.
It might already—

'Drake, get out of there now, before it is too late.'

'Okay, Alexia. I'm on my way out. I'll be back at the hospital shortly.'

'Drake, let me know once you're outside the castle.'

'Okay, Alexia. I'm relieved you're finally awake. I can't wait to hold you in my arms again. I love you.'

'I love you too. Now go. Quickly.'

The moment the link quiets, I look back at Riley.

"Drake is leaving the castle and heading here, but something is telling me I need to get dressed. ASAP."

My gaze drops to the bag at Riley's feet. I narrow my eyes.

"Riley, did Drake bring me clean clothes to wear?"

He gives a small shake of his head. "Actually, Princess Alexia, Lucy gave me this bag to give to you."

He picks up the bag and steps toward me.

Hmm. Okay. Thank the Goddess for Lucy.

As I sit up, the hospital gown drags heavily against my chest, and my breasts throb in protest — tight, full, demanding attention. The skin stretches uncomfortably with the weight of the milk.

Yep. I need to express before I explode.

"Riley, where are my twins? Who is looking after them?"

"They're with your parents and your nanny at their home. I have five guards stationed around the property and the usual security at your home for backup if required."

Good. My parents and babies are safe. Guarded. Protected.

"Riley, can you inform the nursing staff I require the breast pump and bottles, please? It's time I expressed before I start leaking everywhere."

Riley practically bolts from the room.

Before the door even closes, I feel him brush against my mind.

'Yes, Riley?'

'Princess Alexia, just let me know when you are ready to leave, and I will escort you.'

'Thank you, Riley.'

WHILE I WAIT FOR THE NURSING STAFF TO ARRIVE WITH THE equipment, I decide I'd better go to the bathroom and relieve my bladder, taking Lucy's bag with me. And since I'm already up, I figure I may as well shower before I get dressed.

After washing and drying my hands, I pick the bag up off the bathroom floor and unzip it.

My eyes and mouth fall open the moment I look inside.

Oh, my Goddess.

What has Lucy packed?

I open the bag wider and start pulling things out. First, my heavy-duty combat boots with their secret compartments — and clean socks tucked inside. Then my stretchy, comfortable, snug-fitted black jeans. A clean maternity bra and nursing pads. Oh, thank the Goddess, I need a dry bra. A pair of my lacy hi-cut barely-there black undies. Next comes a long, snug-fitting black singlet and a long-sleeve black t-shirt.

And then — oh, perfect — my new protective black chest plate, my leg rig, and a handgun with four extra clips of ammo resting on a black jumper. My toiletries bag. And last but absolutely not least — my sword in its sheath holster.

What does Lucy think I'm walking into?

Then again… I'm grateful.

It doesn't take me long to shower and get dressed, leaving the chest plate and sword off until after I've finished expressing.

Once the equipment arrives, it doesn't take me long to fill six large bottles. Relief floods through me as my breasts finally feel lighter. With each lid screwed on tight, I place the bottles into an insulated bag, ready to be taken to the twins for feeding.

I secure the protective chest plate under my long-sleeve t-shirt and adjust the harness with my sword at my back. I almost feel ready to leave when I notice the charmed necklace Lucy gave me is missing.

Taking one last look in the mirror — making sure the sword handle doesn't stand out, my hair pulled into a neat ponytail, a touch of makeup to hide how pale I really am — I pack my toiletries away, zip the carry bag closed, and reach out with my mind to inform Riley that I'm ready. And that someone trusted needs to take the insulated milk bag to my parents' house for the twins.

Walking back toward my hospital bed with my bag, making sure I haven't left anything behind, a glint of light catches my eye. There, sitting on the little side table beside the bed, is the charmed necklace. Relief washes through me as I pick up the gold chain and place it around my neck once more. The calming sensation rolls over my body instantly, warmth blooming from the stone.

With my bag in hand, I turn toward the door.

Not hearing back from Drake has my stomach tightening.

He should have been here by now.

Something has happened — and I don't need anyone to tell me otherwise.

After several attempts, I can no longer sense or feel him at all.

Walking down the hallway, Riley catches up to me, his long strides matching mine before he offers his hand for the carry bag.

"And where are we off to, Princess?"

I give him a quick smile and nod, passing him the bag in thanks.

"If you would like to escort me up to the castle, that would be great, Riley. I think my husband might require my assistance."

"What... Prince Drake has not contacted you?"

"No. Not yet. And I can feel it — deep inside — something is wrong. I can no longer feel or sense Drake. It's as if someone is blocking our connection. It's time to go to the castle and find out exactly what is happening."

CHAPTER THIRTY-ONE

BEFORE WE REACH THE ROYAL CASTLE, I OPEN A MIND-LINK TO MY mother. The moment the necklace warms against my skin, my magic sharpens — stronger, clearer, more controlled. The charm always amplifies my Dark One abilities, but right now it feels like someone turned the volume up on my power.

'Mum, I'm okay, I say quickly, before she can spiral. Yes, I survived another attempt on my life. No, I'm not bleeding out. Yes, I'm being careful.'

Her voice rushes through the link, sharp with fear. *'Alexia, sweetheart, are you sure you're alright?'*

'I'm fine,' I insist, *'even though my shoulder throbs. I'm on my way to the castle to find Drake.'*

As I speak, the necklace pulses again — a soft, steady thrum.

My mother must sense it too, because she suddenly calls out, her voice muffled through the link, *'Hold my hand.'*

There's a shuffle, a breath, and then —
My father's presence flickers into the connection.
The necklace flares warm against my chest, stabilising the link, just like when I allowed Lucy to speak with Lain. My mother's touch acts as the bridge, letting my magic pull my father into the mind-link.

His voice comes through, firm and steady. *'We'll keep guarding the babies. Don't worry about them. Just focus on finding your husband.'*

Relief loosens something tight in my chest. *'Good. Please tell them their mummy and daddy love them.'*

'We will,' Mum replies softly. *'And Alexia... be extra careful. We love you.'*

'I love you both,' I whisper, before closing the link and letting the warmth of the necklace fade back to a gentle hum.

One thing I know is that I have the best parents in the world.
I recheck my handgun, ensuring it is fully loaded and ready, before sliding it back into my leg rig. My foot taps against the floor, and that's when it hits me — I'm more worried and stressed than I first realised. My instincts already sense something bad has happened to Drake. My belly knots tighter with every passing second. Now it's just a waiting game to find out what has befallen him.

Watching Riley drive around to a different area of the castle, it becomes clear we're entering through the security personnel entrance. At least this way, no one will expect me to come through the staff access, keeping my presence secret — well, low-key anyway.

Because of my dark clothing, I blend easily with Riley and the other security personnel. Riley hands me a security vest, allowing me to walk freely among the castle staff. He quickly pulls one on over his jumper as well. Several people acknowledge Riley as we move through the hallways.

At first, I don't mind the staff not noticing me. But the more I think about it, the more wrong it feels. They should be more attentive, more alert — especially with someone fully armed walking through the castle. Something else to speak with Riley about later. Right now, I need to go where Drake was last seen. I need to follow his previous footsteps and discover what happened to him.

With my mind, I speak to Riley. *'Riley, we require Drake's surveillance footage collected from when he first entered the castle to when he left. Alternatively, the last images recorded of Drake. Can you organise that, please?'*

'I'll get right on that, Princess.'

'Thank you, Riley. We have to find him.'

'I'll contact Freddi. He is the head of the surveillance department. He seems to be fitting in since our last man was killed in the attack. More security has been put into place.'

That is something else I do not need to hear right now — another member of staff lost their life the night of the attack. When will I stop hearing that another person in Darshia has died because of Drake's stupid father and his idea of the world — okay, Darshia domination?

Oh, Drake, where are you? …fills my mind, and my heart aches for the missing man I love. And then there are the events of the last seventy-two hours. When will this end?

Concentrating again, I try to focus on Drake. I feel and sense the section of the castle we're standing in.

…Nothing.

Next, my mind touches the Dark Ones in my vicinity, breaching their thoughts. I search each one quickly, moving from one to the next. If someone has seen Drake, I follow the thread until that person can no longer see or hear him.

So far, nothing to follow up on. No leads.

Bugger…

RILEY'S VOICE CUTS THROUGH MY ANNOYANCE AND disappointment. "Princess, come with me quickly. We might have a lead. Freddi owes me a few favours."

I look back at Riley, relief flickering through me, but the reality settles hard — we still might not find Drake. This is only a long shot.

With the information we have, it's time to check the different locations on video surveillance. It's time to see Freddi. Personally, I'll feel better if I can scan the footage myself.

Entering the medium-sized room, I stop short. Two walls are covered in screens — one wall showing every angle of the castle, the other covering Darshia. I've never seen this place before. Several desks are lined with monitors, at least ten computers, each with multiple screens.

How can anyone keep up with all this footage at any given minute? More manpower is definitely required here, especially if this room is supposed to be the first place alerted when trouble starts in Darshia.

After scanning the monitors, I sit at one of the workstations. The sheer amount of information presses in on me, but I remind myself why I'm here — to find Drake. I glance at the multi-monitor setup; each computer has three large screens. I cross my fingers. Hopefully, I remember enough from my old computer sessions back at school to get through this. Riley stands beside me and demonstrates how to use the software and bring up the different footage.

Okay. So far, so good. I might actually understand this.

With a bit of practice and searching, it doesn't take long before I find Drake — from the moment he arrived at the castle all the way down to the holding cells to question Zeeland.

I can even tell when we were mind-speaking — the worried look on Drake's face, followed by relief, ending in his trademark panty-dropping smile. Continuing to scan the footage, I watch him turn and make his way out of the questioning area, away from Zeeland.

I keep my eyes on the video clock, especially the seconds. Something clicks in my mind — a memory from school about video editing, special effects, and splicing footage. Something isn't right with the time counter. Drake is in one corridor, and then suddenly he's in the next.

The footage flickers slightly before Drake reappears in the following corridor. The camera shows him walking, but as soon as he turns a corner, the next camera doesn't pick him up.

Drake is gone.

"Riley, where exactly is this corridor? And what rooms and secret corridors are in that area?" Riley steps closer, looking over my shoulder at the three screens. I have footage of Drake right up until he disappears — vanishes.

Something else is wrong with this footage. I rewatch it,

keeping a close eye on the time counter. On the workstation beside mine, I have Freddi bring up the same footage with Grandma Ma. By the time she reaches the same corridor Drake had been in, she also disappears.

I point out the time frame and the missing seconds. On the next workstation, I have Freddi bring up the footage of Zeeland in the holding cells. After a moment, it hits me.

We're watching the same footage.

It's looping.

Unless you watch the time frames and the counter, you'd never notice.

"Look here and pause. On the next screen, play it... now watch. See... now pause. On the next screen, watch and now... pause. What do you see? Boys, if you haven't worked it out by now — we're watching the same footage on a loop."

"What... no. You must be mistaken."

"Watch again," I murmur. Thank the Goddess for school computer and media lessons. I never would have noticed the difference otherwise.

After a few more minutes of watching the repeated footage — fast-forwarding, rewinding, time-lapse, checking the timer sequence, skipping to the next location and camera feeds — we continue to watch three workstations and all their monitors: first Drake, then Grandma Ma, and finally Zeeland.

"Sorry, Freddi, but your surveillance system has been hacked."

Damn... now what are we going to do?

After another minute, I decide it's time to do something in real time, in person.

"Riley, we require two holding-cell guards. If I'm right, we'll see the staff members appear on loop footage. Make sure one holds a sign and the other a book. I want to see for myself what the surveillance shows when they reach Zeeland's cell door."

Within minutes, one guard walks through the corridors holding a book. Two minutes later, the second appears with a banner tucked under his arm, the word hello written in big letters.

Sure enough, on the footage, the first guard appears with the book. Two corridors later, the screen flickers — and the book is gone. When the second guard reaches the same spot, the screen flickers again — and the sign disappears.

"See, Freddi? I was right. You've been hacked," I say, pointing at the screens. "You need someone to check every feed, cable, and camera in this place."

Freddi's face drains of colour as he stares at the looping footage. Without a word, he snatches up the phone and starts dialling.

I turn to Riley. "Come on, Riley. We need backup. Something is wrong, and we need to go down there now. I can feel it — Drake's life is in danger."

"Certainly, Princess. I've contacted some of my team. They'll meet us on level two. Let's go."

CHAPTER THIRTY-TWO

ON OUR WAY DOWN TO LEVEL TWO, RILEY POINTS OUT AND explains the servants' secret walkways and hidden passages. He gestures upward, showing me the narrow platforms high above — the "secret" walkways I somehow never noticed before. Then he taps the walls, pointing out the different panels and explaining how to spot the release buttons that open the hidden passageways.

I shake my head at the thought of so many secret routes throughout the castle — places anyone could slip into and hide. Even though the primary purpose of most of these passages is to let staff move unseen while doing their jobs, there are hundreds of them. Most hidden. Some obvious. All of them a security nightmare. No wonder the castle was attacked the way it was... and no wonder Riley took so long to reach my bedroom that night.

Finally, we reach the corridor where we're sure Drake and Grandma Ma disappeared. Riley points out two different secret panels in the walls. As I study them, something catches my eye. I lean closer.

Fabric. Embedded in the wall...

Then it clicks. A piece of ripped fabric caught in the panel.

"Riley, did you see this? I wonder who it might belong to?"

Riley steps closer. With one hand, he gently holds the fabric. With the other, he presses a section of the wall. A soft click echoes as the secret door releases.

He lifts the fabric to his face, inhaling deeply. His eyes close as he sniffs, and after a second, they snap open.

"What is it? What can you smell?"

"The fabric belongs to the Queen. It has her scent on it."

"Are you sure?"

"Yes. I'm convinced. I know that scent anywhere."

"The question is… was the Queen here alone, or was she forced and taken?"

"Yes. That is the question."

I look into the dark opening. Only then do I notice the dim lighting along the floor. I turn to Riley. "Riley, my next question is — where does this tunnel lead?"

Anywhere. That is the problem. But there are a few storage rooms I think we should check out first."

With low LCD lights lining the floor, the tunnels stretch ahead in long, dark corridors. I keep my senses sharp, watching for any unexpected visitors.

After ten, maybe twenty metres, I reach out with my mind and say, *'Riley, keep our conversation strictly through the mind link, careful not to alert anyone to our presence.'*

He nods and takes the lead, relying on his nose and Dark One senses to follow the Queen's scent. But my mind keeps circling the same fear… is Grandma Ma with Drake? Or are we following a dead end?

After a few more turns, muffled voices echo from ahead. I slow my pace to match Riley's.

'Riley, can you make out the voices? Do you know who they are?'

'No. Not yet.'

We listen for another minute. The main voice becomes clear —
Zeeland.

But who is he speaking with?

CHAPTER THIRTY-THREE

LISTENING AND WAITING, THE ANNOYING PART OF STANDING HERE IS not being able to understand half the words spoken. What language are they speaking in? I look back at Riley, noticing the strain tightening his face.

'What do you think? Can you hear the woman's voice clearly enough to know who she is? Because she does not sound like Grandma Ma to me. Also, what language is she speaking? I don't understand a word.'

'Princess Alexia, I am not sure who the woman is. The language is from the old Darshia tongue. Some of the old ones still speak it. I have not spoken it for many decades. Listening to her, I can make out a few of the ancient words she is pronouncing. Maybe something for you to look at in the future — to make sure our young never forget their heritage.'

'I think that is an excellent idea. I'd like to learn the old language myself — to prove to the old ones I'm not just a pretty face.'

I tilt my head toward Riley, flash him a big happy smile, and wink. But the question remains… who is behind this door?

With my senses, I reach out, trying to distinguish how many are in the next room — and who.

The who is stull a mystery apart from Zeeland, the how many… six, seven, eight.

Uh-oh.

'Riley, we need more men…'

I<small>T ISN'T LONG BEFORE TEN ARMED MEN ARRIVE</small>. W<small>ITH</small> L<small>AIF</small> taking up the rear, I somehow end up at the very back of the group.

Hmmm.

Men… really?

Do they think I cannot handle myself?

I feel Laif brushing the edge of my mind, and I allow him into the link.

'What is it, Laif? I didn't know you would be joining us here.'

'Sorry, Princess Alexia. I had to come. I cannot stay behind knowing you are walking into danger. It is my job to protect you, and yet here you are, protecting others. Fighting to save your soulmate.'

'Laif, have you ever learnt the old language?'

'Old language, Princess?'

'Yes, Laif — the old language of the Dark Ones.'

'I used to speak it with my great-grandparents, but it has been many years. Why? Why do you ask?'

'Because the people behind the door are speaking it.'

'Are you sure, Princess? Not many speak the old language.'

'Exactly. That's probably why they're using it — because not many young Dark Ones would understand them.'

'Do you really think so, Princess? Maybe whoever is behind the door is part of the old ones.'

'We'll soon find out, Laif. Come on. It's time to go.'

'What? Where?'

Moving forward, I reach out to the surface thoughts of the men ahead of me. Their minds are loud, unguarded. Half of them don't want me here — assuming I'm an annoying little girl. The other half are relieved I'm backing them.

Within moments, I slide into all their minds.

'Okay, gentlemen, how are we all today? If any of you feel you cannot work with me, you can leave — and you will say goodbye to your position here at the castle.'

I watch them closely, meeting each gaze. One man starts to turn away, taking a step. His buddy smacks his arm, giving him a warning look. A quick read of their thoughts tells me everything — they're only here to keep their jobs. They'll listen to Riley, not to some *"little girl."*

Hmm.

Okay.

If that's how they want to play it.

'So, gentlemen, for those of you thinking I am only a little girl and you refuse to follow my orders — you may leave. Hand your weapons and ID badges in, and you may go.'

I lock eyes with the two men. Both glare at me, annoyed.

By the time they turn and take two steps, I've already read their memories. Lovers of Alexettia. Loyal to her. Worried about Grandma Ma's disappearance.

I breach their mind shields.

'You know… there is every chance Queen Alexettia is in there.'

Their reactions hit instantly. I knew before they moved — they want their Queen back. Safe.

'If you can continue to work with me and have my back, just as I would have yours, then you can stay. What do you say, gentlemen?'

Both men nod.

Hmm.

Time will tell with these two.

I might be the Princess and the new kid on the block, but I am still royalty. Chances are, they'll be finding new employment soon.

With Riley as my point of contact in security, I send him my thoughts and concerns about the two men. He agrees. It might be time for them to move on.

'We will have your back, Princess Alexia.'

I nod.

'That is good to hear, gentlemen. Now let us get back to why we are here.'

CHAPTER THIRTY-FOUR

It is times like this I would have appreciated Lucy being here with us, right by my side. Using her magical talents. Checking for traps and wards. Because with everything going on lately, I have a feeling we are still dealing with witchcraft and Dark Magic.

Thank the Goddess I'm wearing the charmed necklace Lucy made for me. I replay everything she explained and demonstrated before we left this morning, making sure I copy her movements and use her exact words.

Walking back up to the locked door, I grip the charm around my neck with one hand. With my other hand, I reach toward the door and the frame, repeating the words Lucy drilled into me.

With far too much concentration, I start to feel something — an energy force with a faint buzzing sensation.

A barrier. A magical ward covering the doorway. Now I understand exactly what Lucy meant. Feeling the magic as my hand hovers over it again. The door is definitely protected.

Hmm. Now, how do I break it?

Apprehension hits hard. I am no witch, even though Lucy

insists she can sense magic deep within me. That had been a surprise — me, having magic? I'll believe it when I see it.

I sense along the doorframe, chanting the words Lucy demanded, repeating and believing as much as I can. Something in me shifts — a small instinctive nudge — and I change the words slightly. I don't know why. It just feels right.

A moment later, the ward I first sensed around the door... disappears.

Oh, wow.

It's gone.

The magical ward is actually gone.

I give myself a mental high-five, excitement bubbling at the edges of my nerves — until reality slaps me. Oops. We're here to rescue Drake, not celebrate my new talents.

Reaching out with my mind, I sense no one near the door on the other side. I touch Riley's arm.

'Riley, how many can you sense on the other side of the door? Because at the moment, I can sense eight people. One of them is Grandma Ma.' And — relief floods me. I finally detect Drake on the far side of the room. *'Drake is in there.'*

His presence is faint. He's definitely unconscious. But alive. My heart aches, but at least it's still beating for a reason.

Then I sense Zeeland for the first time. His thoughts stand out from the others — sharp, bitter, twisted. A quick skim of his surface thoughts shows he would enjoy killing Drake and Devlain. Zeeland believes he is the rightful Prince, not the twins.

What?

What is Zeeland going on about?

Digging deeper, I hit something startling — Zeeland is the older half-brother to Devlain and Drake. Same father. Different mother.

Oh, my Goddess.

No.

What had Davelt done?

'Riley, can you gain access to anyone's mind behind the door?'

He shakes his head, frustration tightening his jaw.

'No, Princess Alexia. I can only sense, just like you. Eight people are behind the door, and I cannot distinguish Prince Drake either.'

'Riley, who is Zeeland's father?'

'Why? What is going on, Princess? What does my cousin's father have to do with any of this?'

I decide to cut straight to the chase.

'Riley... do you know Zeeland's father was Davelt Smithlyn?'

His denial is instant. *'What— no. That cannot be right. We were told Zeeland's father was a human one-night stand.'*

'Riley, I just looked into Zeeland's mind. According to his thoughts and memories, Devlain and Drake are his younger half-brothers — and he wants them dead. I've never met Zeeland, so I don't know what he looks like. But if he has the red-ringed iris like Devlain and Drake, then he might be related to Davelt — a Royal Red.'

'No. That cannot be true. Surely I would have recognised the eyes belonging to a member of the Royal Red family.'

I dive back into Zeeland's memories, searching deeper, pulling up the earliest ones. And there he is — Zeeland, spending years with Davelt.

I reach for Riley's hand, pulling him into the memory stream.

Together, we watch Davelt speaking to Zeeland, telling him that one day he will be a Prince of the Royal Red family — because he is Davelt's son. Davelt's voice echoes through Zeeland's memories, warning him never to reveal his true parentage.

Riley jerks back, ripping free of the memory, his voice dragging me out of the dim passageway.

'Princess Alexia... as much as Zeeland is my family, he is also determined to destroy the Royal Blue family — the family I have pledged my life to protect — and the residents of Darshia. It hurts to say, but I cannot allow Zeeland to continue his quest. He must be stopped.'

I nod and look over the men in my new group. I reach out to each of them with my mind — all at once.

'Okay, men. For those of you who didn't know, this door had a magical ward placed on it. Yes — a magical ward. I am certain I have removed it.'

Several men make disbelief noises in their minds, shaking their heads. A few wonder what game I'm playing. Several others look at me with awe.

'It is not the point whether you believe me or not. In today's technology and mixed races of Paranormal Entities, it has become clear — especially in the last forty-eight hours — that witches'

wards and talons have been used extensively. Used against Dark Ones. Specifically used against us.'

I lift the warm charm hanging from my neck, letting them see it.

Reaching out again, I confirm all eight people are still inside — and that none of them have detected the missing ward or the group of Dark Ones waiting outside.

But something feels... off.

Eight people.

No — nine.

Someone else is in there.

'Riley, do you sense anything different? Something is happening. I'm sure someone else is in that room... someone familiar.'

He shakes his head. *"I'm having trouble detecting the exact number.'*

Okay then...I look back at the group. *'Okay, guys. I need you to reach out with your minds. We need to know if anyone can work out what's happening behind that door.'*

Riley gives me a look. *'What are you doing?'*

I frown. *'Riley, what is it?'*

'Princess Alexia, if you want the men to work with you, you really need a better strategy.'

'Riley, I don't know these people. I want to know if any of them have hidden abilities the others don't know about. If one of them

can pick up more than me, then we'll find out who has hidden talents.'

I feel two of the men press against my mind shields. I look toward them, touching Riley's arm to include him in the conversation.

MY GAZE LANDS FIRST ON RITCHY — SIX FOOT SEVEN, A SOLID wall of muscle, short buzz-cut red-and-blond hair, and sharp brown eyes that look like they miss nothing.
'Yes, Ritchy, do you have something to bring to my attention?'
Ritchy's mind brushes mine, steady and controlled.

'Princess Alexia, I first sensed eight Dark Ones beyond the door — one is the Queen. And yet I can detect another Dark One — they're blocked somehow. I'm sure they are male. But there is... a ninth presence I cannot identify. I...'

'Thank you, Ritchy. I've detected eight people too, but there is someone else in there. I wanted to know if anyone else could sense the unknown person. As you know, I'm still new to the world of Dark Ones.'

I turn toward the second man — Saimni. Six foot three, lean, built for speed. A fighter who uses agility as a weapon.

'Yes, Saimni, do you have something to add?'

His mind-voice is blunt, edged with impatience.

'Princess Alexia, what exactly do you expect from us?'

'Saimni, I expect the men working with me to have skills I can rely on. Talents we can all benefit from — and have each other's backs.'

He exhales sharply. 'What do you want me to say? I know exactly how many people are in that room. I can sense a witch hiding in the shadows, cloaking themselves from the other Dark Ones. Whether they're good or bad, I don't know. The Queen is tied to a chair with a gag in her mouth — preventing her from speaking clearly, which I find amusing. I can also sense the Queen is unable to communicate via her mind. And there is another Dark One in the room who seems to be blocked from us.'

'Thanks, Saimni,' I say with a smile and nod.

I cut the connection with Saimni and turn my thoughts to Riley.

'Riley, did you know about Saimni? Do you know his talents?'

'I know a few. As leader of my men, I keep their confidence. If they want their fellow guards to know what they can do, it is up to them.'

'Did you know about the witch before Saimni mentioned them?'

'No. Not until he said it. Then I searched the room myself. Only then did I detect the person hiding. Otherwise, no — I did not know there might be a witch in there.'

I glance back at Saimni and nod.

'Thank you, Saimni. It's good to know someone else can verify the person hiding in the shadows.'

I look over the line of men in the darkened passageway. It's time to move. Drake is still unconscious — I can feel the dead weight of his mind. Grandma Ma is still going off through her gag, her muffled fury vibrating through the room. Zeeland moves toward her, irritation spiking through his thoughts.

Then I feel it — the sharp crack of impact.

Zeeland hits her.

A hot flare of anger snaps through me.

'Are you ready, men? We are here to rescue Drake and release the Queen. There are eight Dark Ones and someone in the shadows. Be extremely careful; we don't know what other wards might be waiting for us. Weapons up.'

Riley and Saimni burst through the door first, their movements a blur of speed and precision. The rest of us flood in behind them, fanning out across the room.

Chaos erupts instantly.

I dive into the minds of the six Dark Ones — traitors to Darshia. Their thoughts flash like a spinning disco ball:

Two loyal to the Queen.

Two loyal to Zeeland.

One woman speaking the old language.

And one more — the one hiding in the shadows — aligned with something supernatural.

Whoever she is…

Wait.

The presence in the shadows — female.

Familiar.

My hand flies up and back on instinct, sword sliding free with a metallic whisper just in time to block a long blade arcing toward my throat. The impact jolts down my arm. I grunt, twist, and slam my boot into the attacker's chest, forcing him back.

He recovers fast.

Steel clashes against steel as he drives me backward, his strikes relentless. I pivot, duck, parry — my sword a blur as I block each thrust and counter with my own. Sparks fly. My muscles burn. The air tastes like metal and adrenaline.

He pushes me toward the shadows.

No.

Absolutely not.

A quick breach of his mind shows his intent — kill me or trap me in a ward.

Yeah, no thanks.

I block another strike, twist my body, and with my free hand, yank my handgun from its holster. I don't hesitate. I fire point-blank.

The bullet hits dead centre.

He turns to dust mid-step, collapsing into nothing. His weapon clatters to the floor.

I spin toward Drake. He's still unconscious — too still — and fear claws at my ribs.

Movement flickers in the shadows.

I dodge right, spin, and bring my sword up just in time to block another attack from behind. My senses catch up — Zeeland. He lunges again, only to be intercepted by Riley. Ritchy barrels in, taking over the fight with a roar.

I pivot back toward the shadows, gun raised, sword ready — and stagger as a wave of magic slams into me.

It hits like a hammer to the skull.

My vision blurs. Pain detonates behind my eyes. Someone is attacking my mind — hard.

I force my shields up, layer after layer, gritting my teeth as the assault intensifies. The buzzing becomes a scream inside my skull.

Through the haze, I see her — the woman in the shadows — hand raised, magic pouring from her like a storm.

I shove my sword into its holster and grab my charm. Lucy's chant burns through my memory. I whisper it, then say it louder, then shout it inside my mind. The counterspell pulses through me, pushing back against the magic tearing at my shields.

Slowly — painfully — the pressure eases.

I suck in a breath and look around. My men have dusted or subdued the Dark Ones. Grandma Ma is free from her ropes. Zeeland lies face-down, hands bound, still breathing — unfortunately.

My gaze snaps back to the woman in the shadows.

I raise my gun. "Move out of the shadows with your hands where we can see them. And do not try to cast another spell. Or I will shoot you where you stand."

Another mental attack slams into my shields — weaker this time — followed by Grandma Ma's frantic mind-voice.

'What is it, Grandma Ma?' I ask, keeping my gun trained on the woman.

'Alexia, put your weapon down right now.'

'Why, Grandma Ma? Because I do not appreciate being attacked by her magic. This chick will be taken into custody alongside Zeeland.'

'No, Alexia. You will not be taking — as you put it — "this chick" anywhere. There is no woma—'

She stops abruptly as the woman steps back, deeper into the shadows, hiding her face.

What the hell?

Out loud I say, "I think you better start talking, Grandma Ma, because right now this woman will be placed in custody. And you will be questioned and have a complete medical check-up."

"I am the Queen. I will not be questioned and do not require a medical check-up."

"Grandma Ma, we are not going to argue about this. Do I need Mum to come down here and speak with you?"

She lifts her chin in a pathetic attempt at authority. Honestly, it's like dealing with a sulky teenager. I nearly laugh.

"Your mother does not scare me, Alexia."

"Oh, Grandma Ma. You have not seen the other side of Mum when she goes into mum mode. That is something you do not want to witness firsthand."

She tries to stand — and her legs give out. She drops back into the chair with a very un-Queen-like thud.

"Grandma Ma, you will be having a medical check-up."

My attention snaps back to the woman in the shadows. Whoever she is, Grandma Ma is protecting her. Why?

Ritchy moves into my peripheral vision, approaching slowly from the left. I move with him, keeping the woman's attention on me while he circles in.

"Grandma Ma, why are you trying to prevent us from discovering who this woman is?"

"I do not know what you speak of, Alexia."

"Grandma Ma, the group of men I arrived with — we can all see the woman hiding in the shadows." My annoyance spikes. What is she hiding? Who is this woman? "And do not pretend you do not know about the woman hiding here, Grandma."

I raise my gun again, steady and aimed at the woman's chest. She feels familiar — too familiar.

"Move out of the shadows. Now. Or I will shoot. The choice is yours."

She doesn't move.

I push into her mind — and slam into a wall. Thick. Layered. Reinforced. A magical talon blocks me.

Fine.

I grip my charm, focus, and push harder. I feel the layers, the weaves, the knots. I peel them apart one by one, faster and faster, until—

There.

A weak point.

Gotchya.

I slip through.

A flood of thoughts and memories crashes into me, nearly knocking me out of her mind. I breathe through it, steady myself, and push deeper.

Images.

Voices.

Faces.

And then—

Oh.

My.

Goddess.

You have GOT to be kidding me.

My head snaps toward Grandma Ma.

CHAPTER THIRTY-FIVE

Accessing as much information as possible, I don't know whether to be relieved I've found another family member… or furious that Grandma Ma has kept this woman hidden from me.

"Grandma Ma, have you got something to tell me regarding the woman in the shadows, or should I just shoot her now and see if she turns to dust? Yes, Alexettia, I know this woman is half Witch and also half Dark One."

The worried look that washes over Grandma Ma's face is instant. Her eyes flick from the woman in the shadows back to me, wide and unsettled.

"Alexia…"

I shift my gaze to the men, calculating who I can trust with what's about to be revealed.

'Riley, who do you trust with top-secret information? Choose two quickly and have them stay. Then have the rest escort Zeeland and the other captured people to the holding cells.'

Riley brushes my mind shields. *'Yes, straight away, Princess.'*

'Riley, I need you to move over here and have your gun trained on the woman in the shadows. I have to go and check on Drake.'

Within a minute, the room is cleared. Only Riley, Laif, and Ritchy remain. Riley steps beside me, gun raised, eyes locked on the hidden woman.

Still watching the shadows, I ask again, "Grandma Ma, are you going to introduce your daughter to me?"

Her sharp intake of breath tells me everything — she knows I've just revealed more of my Dark One abilities than she expected. I move toward Drake.

"After all, it would be nice to meet another family member. Even better, I'd prefer not to be attacked," I add dryly.

I drop to my knees beside Drake. My hands skim over his body, searching for a pulse. Relief loosens my chest when I find it — slow, but steady. My fingers move quickly, finding the talon on his chest. I rip it free, then untie the ropes binding him to the chair.

The moment the talon is gone, I sense him again through our mate bond — faint, but it's there. My Drake.

I lean in and kiss him, piercing my tongue against my sharp tooth. Blood wells instantly. I swipe it across his lips, then slip my tongue into his mouth.

He responds almost immediately, kissing me back, suckling at the wound to draw more blood, pulling strength from me.

'Hello, babe, glad to have you back.'

'What? ...What do you mean?' His mind voice is sluggish, confused.

'Drake, you had been captured — again. Also, heads up, we're about to speak with my great-aunt. Alexettia has another daughter — Alivia.'

I kiss him once more and rise, turning toward the woman in the shadows — my aunt. The cut on my tongue seals quickly. I run my tongue across my lip, clearing the last trace of blood.

As I step closer, questions slam through me. Why is she still hiding? Is she glamoured? Is she the presence I sensed at the witch's coven? Near my house? In the school cafeteria with the ex-principal and the new English teacher?

Was she involved in blowing up my school?

"Move out of the shadows, now — Aunty," I demand.

Alexettia's voice snaps across the room. "Alexia, you have no right to order anyone around. This is not—"

"This is not what, Grandma Ma?" I turn, locking eyes with her. "At the moment, I am still in the process of rescuing my husband. Can you explain why both you and Drake were tied to chairs and held against your will?"

I take another step toward my aunt, senses razor-sharp, ready for another spell.

"Are you able to speak, Aunty? Or do you only cast spells against your family members?"

A double attack slams into me — a mind assault and a magical strike. Pain detonates behind my eyes. I shove my shields higher, chanting the counter-spell Lucy drilled into me until the pressure eases.

"Riley, if you think I am in trouble from a cast spell, I want you to shoot this person. Do you understand me, Riley? Shoot her."

"NO!" Grandma Ma shouts. "No one is killing anyone."

She whips her head toward the shadows. "Alivia, stop it. Alexia will shoot you if you keep attacking her. She has a habit of shooting people in her family. Just ask her husband — Drake. She dusted his father, after all," she adds dryly.

A soft, firm voice drifts from the shadows. It freezes me.

"Oh, Mother, just shut up. Alexia is not going to shoot me."

Alivia steps forward — slowly, deliberately — her presence cold and confident.

"You are not going to shoot me, will you, Alexia?" she purrs. "Otherwise, I will end the life of your beloved."

My mind screams. *'What...?'*

"**D**ON'T PUSH YOUR LUCK, ALIVIA. NOW MOVE OUT INTO THE light so we can see one another properly. It's time for the two of us to be properly introduced. Then you can explain why you've been trying to attack me, why you seem to appear wherever trouble erupts, and why you were at my school. Did you have something to do with the explosions? Why were you with Mr Smite and Mr Stragaft?"

Drake rises and is instantly at my side, his body still unsteady but his presence fierce. His voice cracks with barely contained rage. "What in the hell, lady?"

His anger rolls off him in waves — hot, sharp, protective. His thoughts race so fast they scrape against my mind. The anguish of nearly losing me and our unborn child, nearly losing Devlain's partner and their unborn child, is still raw and bleeding inside him. He's wondering why I'm standing here talking instead of putting this chick on her arse or dusting her where she stands.

'Babe, I need you to calm down a little. You're extremely upset. It wasn't that long ago you were unconscious. Please, let me handle this. Just remember, I love you.'

'Alexia, this bitch has tried to hurt you far too many times. She needs to be stopped at all costs.'

'She will be stopped, Drake.'

Alivia laughs — a cold, sharp sound that slices through the room — and then she speaks.

"Oh yes. Drake. Drake Smithlyn, the handsome one. The one Mother wants for her own bed. Isn't that right, Mummy? If Alexia wasn't around, do you think Drake would turn to you? If that's what you think, you're fooling only yourself. Anyone watching these two would know they love one another only. He would never turn to you, …Mother."

Her words drip venom, but her tone is almost bored — like she's commenting on the weather.

Then she steps forward.

Out of the shadows.

Into the light.

And the last of her words hang in the air as she emerges fully.

Oh.

My.

Shite.

My mouth falls open. My breath catches. My heart stutters.

The vision before me is… Impossible. Unbelievable even. And yet she's standing right there.

CHAPTER THIRTY-SIX

Oh my Gods.

I try — really try — to hide my shock, but my eyes and mouth betray me, wide open like an idiot.

No. No, it can't be…?

Standing before me is a replica of my mother.

A younger version of Mum — same bone structure, same eyes — only with long, straight dark hair that falls like a curtain down her back.

This has to be a joke. A cruel one.

Alivia stands there with a smug little smirk, flicking her gaze toward her mother before stepping forward again.

"What's the matter, Alexia?" she says, her tone dripping with annoyance.

My eyes drag from her head to her toes and back up again. My head shakes slowly, disbelief twisting through me. I turn to Grandma Ma.

"Alexettia, is this something that happens throughout the generations in this family? One person resembling another? Because Alivia is the spitting image of my mother. Why did you not inform us you have another daughter?"

I look at Alivia again. Mum is going to freak.

I guess now she'll understand how I felt the first time I saw Alexettia — staring into the face of someone who looks like you.

I sense Drake lifting his phone. He snaps a few photos of my long-lost great aunt. Thank the Gods one of us is thinking clearly enough to gather proof.

"Alexia, I do not have to inform anyone regarding my daughter. Especially you. Now get out of my sight."

Whoa.

Wow.

Grandma Ma sounds... rattled. Scared, even.

"Grandma Ma, you had been tied to a chair and gagged. You are not about to change the subject and palm me off." My spine straightens, shoulders pulling back. I'm not letting her bulldoze me. She's hiding something. "I am here with the royal security guard. We found both you and my husband Drake held against your will, bound and gagged. At present, your daughter is a traitor. Working alongside your lover Zeeland—"

"No." Grandma Ma tries to stand, fails, and drops back into the chair with a thud. "My daughter is no traitor."

"You sure about that, Grandma Ma? Because after all, she is here in the room where you were held. And Alivia was also at my school before it exploded."

"You have it completely wrong, Alexia." Grandma Ma shakes her head hard.

"Tell me. Explain it to me then, Grandma Ma." My eyes narrow, sharp as blades.

I glare straight into her eyes, waiting.

"Alexia, my daughter was at your school to protect you. Alivia snuck in here to save me but instead got herself caught in one of the warded traps."

Protect me.

Save her.

Right.

I bite my tongue, forcing myself to stay silent long enough to hear the rest. She better hurry.

"Imprisoning herself until you set her free," Alexettia adds.

What?

How did I set Alivia free?

I glance back at Alivia, still half-hidden in the shadows, while Grandma Ma continues.

"We had suspected Zeeland for a while now of being a traitor to the Dark Ones and the residents of Darshia."

What?

I whip my head back toward Grandma Ma.

"So you're telling me you kept sleeping with Zeeland to fool him into a false sense of security with your false trust!"

Her eyes fly wide.

Oops.

Maybe I said too much.

"How did you know I had been sleeping with Zeeland?"

I ignore the question. "Do you know who Zeeland's birth father was?"

Her eyes narrow. Her thoughts spike — sharp, defensive, panicked.

"I am not going to answer the question."

But she's rattled.

And she knows I know it.

I HEAR HER THOUGHTS AS CLEARLY AS IF SHE'D SPOKEN THEM aloud.

'Hmm, Alexia is hiding something. How did she know...? I wonder if she has her own spies in the castle? What is Alexia saying regarding Zeeland's father? He is human. That is what I had been told.'

Well then.

Grandma Ma has absolutely no idea who Zeeland's birth father is.

For someone who is the Queen — someone who can slip into nearly anyone's mind without effort — it's almost laughable she never bothered to dig into Zeeland's memories. Never checked. Never questioned.

Or maybe she didn't want to know.

My gaze flicks to Alivia.

Does she know?

Her shields are strong. Too strong. And the way she watches me — calculating, guarded, almost daring me — tells me she's hiding far more than Grandma Ma ever has.

Fine.

If Grandma Ma won't give me answers, I'll take them myself.

I steady my breathing, tighten my mental grip, and focus on the woman who has been lurking in shadows, casting spells, and threatening my family.

Time to dig deeper.

Time to break through Alivia's mind.

Time to find out exactly what she knows — and what she's hiding.

CHAPTER THIRTY-SEVEN

DRAKE, THANKFULLY, PULLS THE ATTENTION AWAY FROM ME. HE shifts his weight, moves around the room, firing off questions with that barely-restrained fury simmering under his skin. His distraction gives me the opening I need — the space to slip deeper into both Grandma Ma's and Alivia's minds.

And what I find…

Grandma Ma feels wrong.

Off.

Naïve in a way she has never been. Her thoughts are softer, slower, almost fogged. This is not the woman who raised a kingdom. It's as if something in her has changed since before the attack — something fundamental.

What happened to her?

As for Alivia, on the other hand, she's nearly a locked vault of shadows. Every memory I breach is wrapped in another layer of darkness. But what I can reach confirms what I suspected — she's half Witch, half Dark One, hiding from the Dark Witches who betrayed her father's side of the family.

I push harder, slipping through another layer of her shields — and then I see it.

Oh no.

Not her cousin too.

Alivia's memories slam into me: her cousin — a girl barely older than a child — used, abused, terrified, and finally killed. Brutally. Viciously. At the hands of Alisitor — Lucy's vile, demented step-uncle. The same monster who tortured innocent girls under the guise of "testing innocence." The same monster who enjoyed every second of their suffering.

Alivia has been hunting vengeance for twenty-two years.

My stomach twists. My chest tightens. Rage, grief, disgust — all of it hits me at once.

Why would a coven allow this?

Why would any witch stand by and let such atrocities happen?

And how in the hell did Grandma Ma get tangled up with a witch in the first place?

My window into Alivia's mind starts to close. I grab what I can, but it's not enough. Not nearly enough.

I keep my mouth shut while Drake continues speaking — demanding answers, pushing for clarity. Through our mind link, he updates me on what I missed, guiding me toward the question Alivia just asked.

"What do you think, Alexia? Should we stage a war against the Witches Coven?"

Oh, crap on a stick.

We've officially left the boundaries of Darshia.

I slide my hand across Drake's back, fingers curling around his waist in a slow, grounding caress. I take my time answering.

"Alivia, not all witches are dark. After this week, you should find quite a few less of them."

Her eyes narrow, sharp and assessing. She realises I'm hinting at something.

"After what the Dark Witches did to Drake — and the atrocities they performed — I know what kind of evil lurks among them. But then hearing that some of their buildings were destroyed in the gas explosion a couple of days ago... with many men and animals perishing... it is a sad day. Yes, a sad day for the Witches Coven."

Her brow raises. A particular look appears in her eyes as she asks, "What do you know of this explosion, Alexia?"

Now she takes notice, and I reply, "Only what was mentioned to me yesterday. Why?"

Her body stiffens. Shoulders tighten. My hearing and eyes detect as her pulse spikes.

She's hiding something. Maybe something to do with her cousin... "Oh, nothing. I wondered if you might have had something to do with it."

I shake my head. "Sadly, no. I was in the hospital with Drake — recovering."

"Who is your friend, the witch?" Alivia asks, eyebrow arching high.

"Oh, do you mean Lucy?" I keep my tone light, careful. "Lucy and I grew up together. We're best friends. She'd been away for over a month and only recently returned. That's when everything came out — discovering — she's a witch, and I'm a Dark One."

She shakes her head, I just about expect her to tsk tsk at the same time. "Yes, that does seem a little odd. For the two of you to be such good friends. And yet... neither of you knew what the other truly was. Amazing how life throws a curveball."

"Yes, life can be full of surprises. That is for sure." I glance at Alivia, then back at Alexettia. "And yet here I stand — in a world I never knew existed. Dark Ones are real, and I now drink the blood of my beloved soulmate. Yes, life can indeed be full of surprises. Many Dark Surprises."

She stares at my hand. Directly at the royal rings. "It amazes me how you come to be wearing the royal wedding rings, Alexia. Where did you get them from?"

I expected this.

"Good question," I casually say as I glance down at my rings, then back at my new relation. "Well, Alivia — after your sister Allasett left Darshia to marry her beloved in the human realm, she hid the rings in a safe place. For the day one of her family — one of her daughters, a descendant — would wear the family rings on their wedding day. Marking them a Dark One of the royal family."

"Yes, I know. My sister stole the rings and took off. How did you end up wearing them?" her voice rises, and her tone a bitchy.

"I married my beloved soulmate, of course. Drake and I completed the Joining Ceremony."

"No. I would have known?" Grandma Ma snaps, cutting in.

I turn to her, keeping my voice steady. "Grandma Ma, not everything in this kingdom has to be run by your desk. After all... I am a Royal Blue Princess of Darshia."

"No, you are not," she spits, her voice sharp enough to cut stone.

The room stills.

Drake's fury spikes so fast it scorches through our mind link.

But I don't move.

I don't flinch.

I just look at her.

"Excuse me?" My voice is quiet — too quiet — the kind of quiet that makes grown men rethink their life choices.

Grandma Ma lifts her chin, trying to reclaim authority she lost the moment we walked into this room. "You are not a Royal Blue Princess. You are not—"

"Careful," Drake growls, stepping forward, placing himself half in front of me. "Choose your next words wisely." His voice is low, lethal. His eyes burn red around the edges — the warning glow of the Royal Red Dark Ones.

Alivia watches us with unsettling interest, like she's observing a chess match she already knows the outcome of.

I place a hand on Drake's arm, grounding him. *'Babe, breathe. Let me handle her.'*

He doesn't like it — not one bit — but he steps back half a pace, still close enough to strike if needed.

I turn back to Grandma Ma. "You don't get to decide who I am," I say, my voice steady, my power humming under my skin. "The rings chose me. The Joining Ceremony bound me. The bloodline recognises me. Whether you like it or not."

Her eyes flash — anger, fear, something else I can't name.

"You are not ready," she snaps. "You are reckless. Emotional. You act without thinking. You—"

"Oh, that's rich," I cut in. "Coming from the woman who slept with a traitor for months and didn't even realise he was plotting against her kingdom."

Her mouth opens.

Closes.

Opens again.

She has no comeback.

Alivia lets out a soft, amused hum. "She has you there, Mother."

Grandma Ma shoots her a glare sharp enough to peel paint.

I take a step forward, closing the distance between us.

I pause, choosing my words carefully. "Why do you say…that I'm not ready? If you did your homework, you would know my birth was registered here in Darshia. Just like my mother and her mother before her and so on. So you should also know, once these rings are placed on my finger, they cannot come off until my daughter is ready to marry her Beloved soulmate and take over the throne."

The tension spikes instantly.

The fine hairs on the back of my neck rise.

Grandma Ma shakes her head and waves her hand about as if she can spell me. "No. That cannot be true. You are a human. Only a true Dark One can wear the rings. Those rings are mine. Take them off right now. I demand it."

My blood pressure surges — not good. I force myself to breathe, to stay calm. I am not risking this pregnancy. Not again.

Before I can say a word, my aunt steps forward. "Oh, shut up, Alexettia. Grow up. The rings can only be passed on to the first-born daughter. And you know it," Alivia hisses.

Her voice drops lower, quieter, as she leans toward Grandma Ma.

Damn it. I can't hear the words, but I can see the tension in their shoulders, the sharp flick of their eyes. They're arguing. Whispering. Plotting.

Enough.

"These rings will only release my finger when my first-born daughter Alley, is ready to become queen and marry — and not before. So back off, Grandma Ma."

Drake presses against my side, his warmth grounding me, his arms wrapping around me in silent support. His presence steadies my heartbeat.

Alivia's gaze snaps to Drake — to the matching rings on his hand.

"How did you manage to get your hands on the rings, Alexia? I see Drake is also wearing the royal rings. You still have not explained how you obtained them. Who gave them to you?" Her voice rises, sharp and demanding.

My muscles tense. This is about to get ugly.

"Alivia, listen — and listen very carefully. As previously

mentioned. Your sister Allasett took the rings when she left Darshia, but she never sold them. She made sure each new generation of daughters knew about the Dark Ones. The first-born daughter was told about the rings — rings that belong only to the rightful princess of Darshia. Rings that can only be worn by the princess next in line for the throne. She made it very clear that whoever wears these rings acknowledges they will be the next rightful Queen of Darshia."

Alivia shakes her head, disbelief twisting her features.

The hairs on my arms rise again — a warning.

I shove Drake away from me with a mental push. *'Move. Now.'*

He obeys instantly, stepping back just as the air around Alivia begins to crackle.

Power builds around her — thick, electric, dangerous.

No wonder the rings were hidden.

No wonder they were kept far away from Alexettia and now Alivia.

If they'd stayed in Darshia, they would've been stolen, corrupted, or destroyed.

I feel the surge before she releases it.

My hand clamps over the charm at my neck. I start chanting one of Lucy's counter-spells, the words tumbling out fast and sharp, it builds a barrier, and something hits it and bounces off before the barrier disintegrates around me.

"Alivia, stop it! You are family — and family does not treat one another like this!"

My plea hits the air as if I'm speaking to a brick wall, as hse sends another spell my way.

Her magic grazes my skin — a burning, prickling sensation — but something inside me rises to meet it. A strange power, unfamiliar but fierce, coils in my chest and spreads through my limbs.

I don't know what it is.

But it's protecting me.

"Alivia, why have you been following me? Did you have anything to do with Drake being taken from school? Were you working with Mr Stragaft and Mr Smite? What was going on? Is this how you think you're helping your cousin?"

Her eyes snap to mine.

And for the first time, I see it — the grief.

The rage.

The wound that never healed.

A sad, broken light flickers in her gaze at the mention of her cousin — her dead witch cousin.

And the room shifts from her emotions.

Alivia's voice trembles. "What do you know of my cousin, Alexia?"

The pressure of her power finally eases off my skin, and I breathe again. Good. She's listening. She's reachable. Now comes the hard part.

"I know enough," I say softly. "What happened to your cousin was barbaric. What happened to all those innocent girls was barbaric. No female should ever have been treated that way. And yes, Alivia — I know about the dogs too."

The words hit her like a physical blow.

Alivia's knees buckle. She collapses onto the cold stone floor, her power flickering out like a dying flame. A broken sob escapes her lips — raw, wounded, human. The pain in her eyes is unmistakable.

Oh Gods…

Why didn't Alexettia protect her own daughter?

"Alivia," I whisper, stepping toward her trembling form. "Alivia, please look at me."

I glance up at Drake and send the message through our link. *'Drake, take Riley, Laif, and Ritchy out of here. Quietly.'*

'Alexia, I will not leave you alone with that woman.'

'Drake. Please. For me.'

'Alexia...'

His eyes soften with love before pain clouds them. He knows I'm putting myself in danger. He hates it. But he also knows I need to do this.

'I love you too, Drake. Now go.'

His emotions brush against mine — fear, anger, protectiveness — before he pulls away. The warmth of his body leaves me instantly, replaced by a cold emptiness. I keep my eyes on Alivia as Drake and the others slip out of the room.

Silence settles.

Then Alexettia ruins it.

"Alivia, what are you and Alexia speaking of? What bastards and their dogs? What is going on?"

Anger flares hot in my chest. Betrayal. Disgust. How could she not know? How could she not see?

"Grandma Ma," I sigh, "I think you need to keep quiet for a little while."

"Alexia, do not tell me what to do. I am the Queen—"

"Right this minute, Grandma Ma, you are not," I snap, cutting her off. "Be quiet. Can't you see how much pain your daughter is in?"

"If someone bothered to explain what is happening, maybe I could help."

"Grandma Ma, you are a little late in the helping department. You should have been there for Alivia. Instead, horrific things happened to your daughter, and you did nothing to prevent it. Nothing to stop it. Nothing to make sure it never happened again. So tell me — where were you while your daughter was repeatedly hurt and raped?"

Alivia brushes the edge of my mind shields — hesitant, fragile.

'Alexia... please tell me. Did your friend Lucy suffer as well? What happened and when?'

My heart cracks for her. For all of them.

'Alivia... you cannot repeat this. To anyone. I am breaking my friend's confidence.'

'Yes, Alexia. I understand. I will not repeat it.'

'Lucy was held against her will. Restrained. Blindfolded. Gagged. And yes... she was assaulted. A dog was in the room. Devlain — her soulmate — saved her.'

Alivia's eyes fill with tears. Her voice breaks. "No... When will this madness end? I am so sorry for your friend, Alexia."

I nod, swallowing the lump in my throat.

'Devlain killed the dog first. And Lucy's step-uncle... he died during the rescue.'

"Thank goodness," Alivia whispers outloud. "At least justice was served."

"It was more self-defence than anything else," I say quietly.

"Whichever way you look at it, Devlain succeeded where others failed. He should be honoured for his bravery."

It takes me a moment to realise I'm nodding.

"I'm forever grateful he saved her. The sad part is… in the chaos, Alisitor fell. He hit his head. Broke his neck. Technically, Devlain isn't responsible for his death."

"Alexia," Alivia says gently, "that man can no longer hurt anyone else. Now tell me what happened with Drake this week."

I inhale slowly, the memory clawing at me.

"When Drake and three of our security team were captured and tortured by the Dark Witches… Lucy, Devlain, one of my guards, and I went in to rescue him. Only one of the three guards survived. The other two were killed before we could reach them."

Alivia's face crumples. "Oh no… that is devastating."

"Yes. It's been a rough week."

"What happened after the rescue?"

I meet her eyes. She deserves the truth.

"Before I was taken to the hospital, I ordered evidence to be collected. The building Drake was held in needed to be destroyed. There were too many bodies — too much to cover up. We didn't need a war starting. The Dark Witches were already trying to start one."

"Why do I feel you're leaving something out?"

"Because I am," I admit. "My security men found several cases of stored video footage."

Alivia's power spikes — sharp, electric. The hairs on my neck rise.

Her voice fills my mind. *'What kind of footage? Please don't say they filmed the assaults.'*

I shake my head. *'I'm sorry, Alivia. They did. They filmed everything. Turned it into short movies. Sold them. Made money off them.'*

My stomach twists. My skin crawls. I never want to see those images again.

'With the footage collected, we now have the identities of the men involved. My guards are hunting the Dark Witches who escaped. All of them are on a wanted list. No other innocent girl will be hurt like that again.'

Alivia nods, tears streaking her cheeks. *'The footage... what they did to those girls... it was horrific. Your people did the right thing destroying everything. The dogs. The equipment. The recordings. The buildings.'* She wipes her face, voice trembling. *'Thank you, Alexia. I am sorry for my behaviour today. You will be a great Queen one day.'*

Grandma Ma's voice slices through the air, dragging our attention back to her.

"What... no. I would have known." Her head shakes violently, denial twisting her features. "Raped... no." She tries to stand, legs trembling. "Alivia, baby girl... please tell me what Alexia says isn't true. Surely that did not happen to you."

Alivia lifts her chin, eyes swollen and raw. "It's a bit late now, Mother. Your granddaughter is the one who finished my justice. Something that should have been done years ago."

"What are you both talking about? What justice? Where?"

Alivia lets out a bitter, broken laugh. "Oh, Mother. You were so wrapped up in your perfect little world, there was no room for me. You left me with my father. And that pathetic coven of witches. They hurt us, Mother. They hurt many girls." Her breath shudders. Tears spill again. "Those men hurt us repeatedly. And where were you while it happened? Where?"

"No," Grandma Ma whispers. "No, I would have known. I would have felt it if you were hurt."

"Face facts, Mother." Alivia's voice sharpens. "You were a useless parent. No wonder Allasett left. How could she rule Darshia with you hovering over her shoulder? I hope she found peace with her husband — far away from you."

Alivia rises slowly, turning her back on her mother before speaking again, voice steady but trembling at the edges.

"Mother… do you know what those Dark Witches did to us? To the innocent girls? Lucky for you, you're already sitting down."

She turns back around — and the pain in her eyes is a storm. Magic fills the air. A strange kind of power. A power, I think, I never want to know about.

"They restrained us. They violated our bodies. They treated us like objects. And when they were done, they let their animals loose on us."

Grandma Ma screams — a raw, guttural sound that rips through the room. I spin toward her as she clutches her head.

"No. Gods, no. Stop. I don't want to hear anymore," she wails. "Please stop. Stop the visions." Tears streak down her cheeks. "Why didn't you tell me? Why?" Feeling sick to my stomach, now I know what that power is. Alivia is forcing images into Alexettia's mind.

"Why?" Alivia's voice cracks with fury. "You are the Queen of Dark Ones, Mother. You should have known. My father loved you — and look what happened to him." Her breathing becomes ragged. "He tried to protect me. The first time. They punished him for it. They broke him. And you… you weren't there."

Alivia steps closer, her presence chilling the air.

"For a week, they dragged him in every time they dragged me in. They hurt him to punish me. They hurt me to punish him. I can still hear his screams."

Grandma Ma sobs, shaking uncontrollably.

Alivia's voice drops to a deadly calm. "They tortured us both until the end. And when they were done with him... they let the animals finish what they started. They didn't stop. Not even when he stopped screaming."

The room goes silent.

Heavy.

Suffocating.

Alivia turns to me, tears streaming down her face. She wipes them away with the back of her hand, trying to regain control.

"Alexia... you've proven you are a true Royal Blue Dark One princess. You will protect Darshia. You will be a better Queen than my mother ever was. I'm only sorry we didn't have more time."

Oh no. Why do I feel she is about to do something drastic? Something bad...

My head shakes. "Alivia. Please don't."

She steps forward and wraps her arms around me. Her warmth hits me like a wave — strong, fierce, heartbreaking.

"Thank you for stopping the Dark Witches. For protecting the innocent. You've done more than my mother ever did. I'm sorry I attacked you. My nature clouded my judgment. Raise your daughter to be strong. Treat your children equally."

"Alivia..." I try again, but she presses on.

"When you can, go to my father's family home."

I blink, confused. She gives me a small, knowing smile.

"Don't worry, Alexia. I'll leave you the address. Check your pocket. There are things I want you to collect — and answers to questions you haven't asked yet." Her smile fades. Her face hardens. "Now... you need to leave the room. Mother and I need to speak privately."

I shake my head. "Alivia, no. I should stay."

But she's already speaking — and the moment her words hit the air, something shifts.

A pressure builds.

A hum.
A darkness creeping at the edges of my vision.
My stomach drops.
No.
No, no, no—
The room tilts.
The shadows thicken.
My knees buckle.
And the world goes dark.

CHAPTER THIRTY-EIGHT

ONE OF THE MOST ANNOYING THINGS IN MY YOUNG LIFE IS WAKING up in a strange bed — knowing immediately that it wasn't mine — because it feels different from the start.

My body fights my consciousness, tugging me back toward sleep while my mind claws upward. The first thing I register — the only thing that matters — is Drake beside me. His hand strokes slowly along my back, warm and steady.

"Hey, baby. Good to see you're back with us. How are you feeling?"

I stretch, a slow, instinctive movement, until his words finally sink in.

Back with us.

Where have I been, and how long was I asleep?

My eyes snap open. I turn my head, blinking at the unfamiliar room. I'm lying in Drake's arms, but this isn't our room. The bed is too big, the walls too ornate, the air too still. It feels like the castle — but not our wing. Someone's bedroom. Someone important.

I look up at Drake.

Sadness sits in his eyes like a shadow.

My stomach drops.

"What has happened?" My voice is almost a whisper. "Drake, what's going on? Where have I been? Where are we? What happened?"

He hesitates — and that alone terrifies me. Drake never hesitates with me.

"Um, baby… I have some bad news."

My hand flies to my lower belly. I reach inward with my senses — and relief floods me. My baby girl is safe. Strong. Present.

I sit up quickly. Drake lets me go, giving me space, but his eyes stay locked on me. When he closes them briefly, I take the chance to scan the room again, searching for anything familiar. Anything that explains why I'm here.

"Drake, what is going on? Why are we here?" And where are we, keeps repeating within my mind?

He inhales slowly, chest rising with a heavy breath. He's stalling. Whatever he's about to say, it must be bad.

"Come on, Drake. Just say it. What has been happening, and why am I in this room?"

He glances around the room, and I follow his gaze until it lands on the large mirror opposite the bed. Our reflections stare back — and Drake's eyes aren't on me. They're on my chest.

No — on the necklace.

Lucy's charm.

My fingers rise to touch it. The moment my skin brushes the stone, a pulse of energy rolls through me — warm, powerful, ancient. The magic inside it feels… different. Stronger. Familiar in a way that makes my breath hitch.

"Drake… what is going on? Why does my necklace feel different? And—" I pause, really feeling myself for the first time. "I feel different. I can sense magic inside me. Why? What happened?"

Drake's voice softens. "Alexia, baby… we don't know how, but your Aunt transferred her powers through you to the baby. Our baby girl is now a Dark One with magic."

My mind blanks.

"What? How?"

"Alexia, let me explain first." Drake slips from the bed, crosses to a side table, pours two glasses of water, and hands me one before sitting beside me again. "I'll start by saying… you've been in this room since yesterday."

My head shakes before I can stop it. "No."

A heavy dread settles in my chest. My throat tightens. I can't force the words out, so I send them through our link.

'Ah… no. That can't be right.'

Drake nods, confirming he heard me. His eyes meet mine — warm, steady, but full of something I don't want to name.

He exhales slowly. "Alexia… you… once again came to my rescue. You saved me from Zeeland — my half-brother."

Oh.

Right.

'Yeah… I remember. Zeeland was working with the Dark Witches. He wanted to destroy the Royal Blue family. Finish what his father started.'

Drake nods. "While you and the team took control of the room, you sensed your Aunt. It turns out she was there to help, not harm. She'd been trapped in a magical ward."

'Yeah… that took me a while to figure out. I was sure Alivia was there to hurt us.'

"You asked Riley, Laif, Ritchy, and me to leave the chamber so you could speak with your Aunt and Alexettia. You refused to let me stay. And then… something happened. We don't know what. Your Aunt sent me a message telling me to return to the chamber and look after you. I didn't know what she meant, but I ran back."

His jaw tightens.

"I found you unconscious on the floor."

My breath catches.

'What? Why? What happened?'

Drake's expression shifts — something tightens behind his eyes — and I know the words coming next will break something inside me.

"I don't know how to say this, so I'll come straight out with it." His voice cracks. "We found your Grandma Ma on the floor, Alexia. Alexettia is gone. We found her dead."

The world tilts.

'No. No, that cannot be. Grandma Ma was alive when I last saw her. What about Alivia? Is she okay?'

Drake swallows hard. "Alexia… when we entered the last part of the chamber looking for Alivia, we arrived just in time to see her —" He hesitates, pain flickering across his face, "—stake herself."

My breath leaves me in a violent rush. I shake my head, refusing the words, refusing the truth.

"No. No, Drake. No."

"Alexia… we all saw it. Alivia turned to dust. There's no mistaking it. She dusted herself."

My chest tightens. My throat burns. No. Why would she do that? Why would she—

Drake continues, voice low. "We also found a USB. Full of information, photos, documents. Evidence against the Dark Witches. Names. Faces. A list of the innocent girls... especially the ones who didn't survive."

My voice barely works. "Why would Alivia do it? Why would she kill her mother?"

Drake exhales slowly. "According to the information she left behind — and the autopsy — your grandmother was terminally ill. And Alivia... she carried the same illness. Doctor Brean can't figure out how Alexettia survived this long. She should have died over a hundred years ago. The doctors think her being Queen somehow prolonged her life. But her mind... we've all seen the decline."

A cold dread slides through me.

What about Mum?

What about me?

What about my babies?

My voice finally breaks free. "How did this happen? Have I been tested? Do I have this illness?"

Drake shakes his head immediately. "No, Alexia. You and your mum were tested. Even baby Alley. None of you carry the gene Alexettia and Alivia had. You're all healthy."

Relief crashes through me so hard I almost sag into him. "Drake... does Doctor Brean know where this gene came from? Could my grandmother Allasett have had it? Did she know?"

"No one knows, Alexia. I'm sorry. There are too many unanswered questions. Maybe we'll find more in Alivia's files."

My mind spins — too many thoughts, too many emotions — until one horrifying realisation slams into me.

"Um... Drake. Who is running Darshia right now?"

He gives me a sad, almost apologetic smile. "Good question. At the moment, your security team and the Council. Now that you're awake… you're technically in charge of Darshia, my Queen."

My heart stops.

Say… what?

"How — why — what… Queen?" The word feels foreign in my mouth. Wrong. Too big. Too heavy. "No. I can't be the Queen. I'm — I'm too young."

Drake reaches for my hand, his voice soft but steady. "Alexia… everything has changed. But you're not alone in this. Your mother is here. And our daughters — all of our children — they carry the Royal Blue bloodline."

The breath I didn't realise I was holding escapes in a shaky rush.

Right.

The Royal Blue line isn't ending.

It's expanding.

I'm not the last.

Not even close.

Thanks to my mother, I am here. Thanks to Drake, we have our twins.

Now, within me — my unborn daughter — as scary as it sounds, is now carrying Alivia's magic.

Drake squeezes my hand gently. "Darshia isn't without a future. Alley will be Queen after you one day. And our new little girl… she's already powerful. Strong. Protected."

A tremor runs through me — fear, awe, responsibility all tangled together.

"I'm not ready," I whisper.

"You're more ready than you think," Drake says, brushing his thumb across my knuckles. "You're not stepping into this alone. You have me. You have your parents. You have your children. And you have an entire kingdom that already sees you as their Princess."

His words settle over me like a cloak — heavy, warm, terrifying.

Alexettia was not the last Royal Blue Dark One ruler. Darshia and its people aren't left without a queen, now that their long-reigning queen is dead — this isn't the end of Darshia and the Royal Blue Dark Ones. It's only the beginning.

Things are changing. Because I'm changing. I'm no longer the heartbroken teenager from the human realm. I arrived here as a human and became Darshia's new princess of the Royal Blue Dark Ones.

And now, with Grandma Ma's untimely death — I am the first in over a hundred years to become the new Queen of Darshia.

CHAPTER THIRTY-NINE

I SCROLL BACK THROUGH THE EMAIL I RECEIVED FIVE DAYS AGO, the words still hitting like a punch to the chest.

The school is officially closed down. Until further notice.

My stomach twists. Ninety-eight percent of the school gone — blown apart, burned, reduced to rubble and ash. There's no "until further notice" about it. That place is never coming back. Nothing will ever be built on those grounds again. The land feels cursed now. Haunted.

I keep reading.

All year twelve students will receive a pass based on completed work and will be awarded their official graduation certificate. Final exams for university entry will be held at the town library.

A shaky breath escapes me.

At least my education didn't go up in flames with the rest of the building.

Then the next part hits harder.

A memorial will be held for the twenty staff and students who perished in the explosions.

My chest tightens.

Twenty lives.

Twenty people who didn't make it out in time.

Faces flash through my mind — teachers, students, people I passed in hallways every day. Gone.

The email praises Ms Lexington for pulling the fire alarm and announcing the evacuation. If she hadn't acted when she did, the death toll would have been catastrophic. Her name appears again in the list of staff who survived. Thank the goddess.

The list of those who didn't...

I can't bring myself to read it again.

When I spoke to Ms Lexington on the phone, she told me all the security footage and office files had been uploaded to the cloud before the explosions. The teachers' records too. That's the only reason the year twelves can graduate. All those hours of work over the break — not wasted.

Small mercies.

As for Mr Smite — the ex-Principal — and Mr Stragaft, the English teacher... their bodies were pulled from the debris. The fire didn't leave much behind, but enough to confirm they didn't escape.

Tabatha and some of her friends were found in the destroyed car park.

The idiot should have run.

Instead, she tried to get to her car.

Three hundred students followed us out of the building that day — running, screaming, stumbling — but alive. Thirty staff and students were injured trying to go back inside to help others. Brave. Stupid. Heartbreaking.

My security team reviewed the footage they recovered. They traced the explosives. The deliveries. The planning.

It all pointed to one person.

Mr Smite.

Phone taps, surveillance, hacked files — all of it confirmed he orchestrated the entire thing. He wanted revenge for losing his job. Revenge for losing his "side business." He wanted everyone to pay.

If he hadn't blown up the school, my royal security would have detained him and dragged him to Darshia for sentencing. He would've rotted behind bars for a very long time.

Instead… he chose destruction.

My English teacher, Ms Lallown, is still in the hospital. The doctors say she'll recover fully. The police found evidence her car crash wasn't an accident. The damage matched another vehicle — Mr Stragaft's second car. The one he hid. The one with the dents and scratched paint work, that matched hers.

He wanted her job.

He wanted her gone.

He wanted in on Smite's little empire, part of his business.

THE ROYAL FUNERAL STILL LINGERS IN MY MIND LIKE A HEAVY fog. Two days ago, the entire kingdom lined the streets as Grandma Ma's coffin passed by — a carved hardwood carriage pulled by midnight-black horses, gold flowers draped across the polished surface. The air smelled of incense and rain. The streets were silent except for the rhythmic clop of hooves on stone.

Dark Ones from every kingdom came. Vampires from distant districts. Even a few from overseas. They didn't just come to honour Alexettia's life — they came to see the new Queen.

Me.

Drake stood on my right, solid and steady. Mum stood on my left, her hand brushing mine every so often, grounding me. Somehow, between the grief and the pressure and the eyes of thousands watching, I managed to hold myself together. To look like a royal. To act like one.

A couple of the Old Ones even praised me — my behaviour, my composure, my "strength of spirit."

Yay me.

Cue the internal eye-roll.

Riley stayed close, murmuring names and titles in my mind each time someone approached. Dark Ones of every rank stopped to speak with us. Most offered condolences. Some requested meetings. A few looked disappointed when they realised I was already married and joined with Drake.

For a funeral, it was surprisingly political.

And I learned fast.

One old saying echoed in my mind all day:

Not all Dark Ones can be trusted.

The official story of Grandma Ma's death followed the truth — mostly. She died of illness. Her heart stopped. Her organs failed. That's what the autopsy will show. Only a handful of us know the real reason. Only a handful ever will.

Even though I'm technically in charge, the Council and the Old Ones refuse to swear me in. Not until I turn eighteen. Not until *"I'm officially a Dark One."*

With my birthday — and Drake's — less than two weeks away, preparations are already underway. A double celebration. My eighteenth. My full transformation. And the coronation.

The moment I become Queen of Darshia.

Unofficially, I already am.

And the workload proves it.

Meetings. Decisions. Reports. Security briefings. Endless questions. Endless expectations. And every day, I discover another thing Alexettia never taught me. Another responsibility she never explained. Another gap in my training.

It's like stepping into a role I was born for…but never prepared for.

And Darshia doesn't wait.

Life still continues.

MOVING BACK INTO THE ROYAL CASTLE FEELS LIKE STEPPING INTO someone else's life. For the first time, I'm choosing my own bedroom instead of being assigned one. Every corridor opens into another enormous room, each one bigger or grander or more ridiculous than the last. Too many choices. Too much space. Too much responsibility pressing down on my shoulders.

Finding Alivia's room is another story entirely.

No staff member can get through the door — not one. The wards reject them instantly. But Mum and I? We walk straight in. No resistance. No warning. Just a quiet click as the door swings open, like the room has been waiting for us.

The air inside feels heavy. Still.

Like Alivia's presence lingers in the walls.

We move slowly, careful not to disturb anything. Her belongings sit exactly where she left them — clothes folded neatly, books stacked in strange, precise patterns, trinkets arranged with intention. It feels like trespassing. It feels like grief.

Then we find the hidden panels.

Secret compartments tucked behind carved woodwork. Concealed drawers under the bed frame. False backs in wardrobes. Each one reveals something new — journals, letters, photographs. Pieces of a life no one ever got to know.

Mum freezes when she finds the first photo — Alivia smiling, her face a mirror of Mum's own. The resemblance is so strong it steals the breath from both of us.

"I wish I'd met her," Mum whispers.

I swallow hard. "Me too."

Thank the goddess Drake also had taken photos in the chamber. I have two precious images now — one of Grandma Ma, Alivia, and me... and one of just Alivia and me. Proof she existed. Proof she mattered. Proof she was family.

We keep searching.

Alivia's notes are meticulous. Detailed. Painful. She documents everything — including the defective Dark One gene. Where she believes it came from. How far back it goes.

Five hundred years of royal inbreeding.

Uncles marrying nieces. Cousins marrying cousins. Even siblings.

Darshia once locked its borders so tightly that the royal bloodline twisted in on itself.

By the time Alexettia was born, she was only the second generation with outside blood. Allasett — my grandmother — was the first. And now we know the truth: Mum, Alley, and I are clear of the gene. Safe.

But Allasett...

Her journal says she was cremated.

Mum and I both suspect the truth — she arranged to be staked, dusted, to hide the evidence of the disease. To protect the line. To protect us.

Maybe that was her final act of love.

With Drake and the guards' help, we gathered Alivia's ashes and placed them in an urn. She now rests beside Grandma Ma. Mum retrieved Allasett's urn too, placing all three women together — mother and daughters reunited at last.

Then I find it.

A journal dated forty-plus years ago.

A photo tucked between the pages — Alivia holding a baby. She looks so young. So hopeful. So proud.

My heart cracks.

The entry explains everything.

The baby was her son.

Conceived through violence.

Killed before his first birthday by the same monsters who hurt her.

A cold fury coils inside me.

If any of those Dark Witches are still alive…

They won't be for long.

I look up at Mum. She's flipping through another journal, unaware of the storm she's about to walk into.

"Mum," I say quietly, "I need to fill you in on a few ghastly details before you read too much."

She frowns. "What do you mean, Alexia?"

Our eyes meet. I gesture for her to sit. "Please. What I'm about to tell you… it's not pleasant. But you need to know."

"Okay, Alexia. You're starting to worry me. What can—"

She sits, and I hand her the photo of Alivia holding her baby.

"Here. Look at this."

"Oh my. What a little cutie," Mum says, smiling warmly.

"Mum… that photo was taken forty years ago."

Her smile widens — then freezes.

She looks up sharply, the colour draining from her face.

"Alexia… what are you not telling me?"

I inhale slowly. The words stick in my throat. I force them out.

"Mum… the baby didn't make it to his first birthday."

Her hand flies to her mouth. "What? No. That's… that's heartbreaking."

"The thing is, Mum… the baby was conceived by rape."

Mum stands abruptly, shaking her head. "No. No, that's — that's horrific."

"I know." I close the journal gently. "Hopefully, as we go through these, we'll find out why Alivia lived with her father — a witch — instead of her mother."

"Her father was a witch?" Mum asks, stunned.

"Yep. His name was Hayes. And he was killed by Dark Witches."

"Hayes sounds like a surname," she mutters. "And Dark Witches? Really? I've never heard of them. Who are they?"

I exhale. "Mum… this is the part you're not going to like."

"Alexia, I don't like anything you've told me so far. So out with it. Who are the Dark Witches? And does this have anything to do with Alivia's baby?"

CHAPTER FORTY

Mum sits frozen for a moment, the weight of everything I've told her settling like a storm behind her eyes. Shock flickers across her face — wide, stunned, disbelieving — but it doesn't last long.

Her expression hardens.

Her jaw tightens.

Her eyes sharpen with fury.

"Alexia, if what you say is true…" Her voice trails off as her mind races ahead of her words. I can practically feel the gears turning, the anger building. "Alexia, I need to follow up on a few things. First — Alivia's birth. Second — I'm going to contact Lucy's mother. It's time the atrocities of the Dark Witches are exposed. And prevented. Permanently."

My stomach drops.

Oh, fantastic.

Mum is about to dive headfirst into a nest of Dark Witch politics with nothing but righteous fury and a mobile phone.

"Mum…" I start, but she's already pacing, already planning, already ten steps ahead.

She's going to open a can of worms so big it'll swallow her whole.

But the thing is…

She's not wrong.

Something does need to be done.

Someone needs to speak for the girls who never got justice.

Someone needs to speak for Alivia — who died without closure, without peace, without anyone fighting for her when she needed it most.

A heaviness settles in my chest.

Alivia never got justice.

Not truly.

Not fully.

And now Mum wants to take up that fight.

Part of me wants to stop her.

Part of me wants to protect her from the darkness she's about to step into.

But another part — the part that carries Alivia's last words, her last tears, her last plea — knows this is the beginning of something bigger.

Something necessary.

Something dangerous.

And something long overdue.

A FEW DAYS PASS BEFORE THE MEMORY FINALLY HITS ME — Alivia's last words, faint and echoing in the back of my mind.

Make sure to check your pocket.

Her voice feels like a ghost brushing past my ear.

I shoot upright, heart thudding. My jeans. The ones I wore in the chamber. The ones I had on when I last saw her alive.

Panic flares for a moment — what if they were washed? What if someone tossed them into the laundry without thinking?

I tear through my wardrobe, pushing aside dresses and jackets until I spot them. Folded neatly on a shelf. Untouched. Unwashed. Relief floods me so hard my knees almost buckle.

I grab the jeans and dig through the pockets, fingers searching, fumbling, desperate. Then — there. Something small. Something stiff. Something folded tight.

My breath catches.

I pull out a tiny square of paper, creased and worn from being hidden. My hands tremble as I unfold it.

Alivia's handwriting stares back at me.

My throat tightens.

It's a note — short, rushed, but unmistakably hers. Addressed to me. And tucked inside is exactly what she promised:

The address to her father's family home.

A place I've never heard of.

A place she clearly didn't want anyone else to know about.

Her message is brief, but the urgency bleeds through every stroke of ink.

She wants me to collect the chest.

And the journals.

Before it's too late.

Too late for what?

A chill runs down my spine.

Alivia knew something.

Something she didn't have time to say out loud.

And now it's up to me to find out what she left behind — and why she was so desperate for me to get there.

MUM MOVES LIKE A WOMAN POSSESSED ONCE SHE GETS information from the Witches Council. When she's determined, she becomes a storm — fast, loud, unstoppable — and before I can blink, she's dragging Drake and me into the car for the trip to Hayes Reinhold's family home.

Hayes Reinhold.

Alivia's father.

A man we never met.

A man who somehow feels like he's always been part of us.

The Council confirmed it: this house belonged to Hayes, and after his death, it passed directly to Alivia. She never sold it. Never let anyone else inside. She kept it exactly as her father left it — protected behind wards only blood relatives could bypass.

And now that Alivia is gone…the house is no longer hers.

It's mine.

Not because I claimed it — but because she chose me. Trusted me. Left me the address and the responsibility to collect what she couldn't protect anymore.

Only Drake, Riley and my mother know about the note. Something deep inside me urged me to remain vigilant and silent, so that the wrong people don't get wind of what we are up to. But somehow, with my mother's pursuit of information regarding Alivia and her father, I think it did open up a can of worms. I just hope we are not too late.

So when we pull up to the cottage — a beautiful brick home tucked deep in the bushland near my hometown — I feel it. A pull. A whisper of Alivia's magic brushing against my skin.

This place belonged to her.

Now it belongs to me.

And whatever secrets she hid inside… they're waiting.

I step out of the car and take a few photos of the house, the lake, the trees. The air feels thick with memory. With warning.

My senses tingle.

Wards. Strong ones.

My fingers find the stone pendant at my neck. I whisper the incantations Lucy taught me, feeling the magic shift and part. The front door unlocks with a soft click.

We step inside.

"I still can't believe family lived this close," Mum murmurs, her voice tight. "All this time… and we never knew."

The air inside is stale, heavy with dust and something else — something wrong. My nose twitches. My instincts flare.

Danger.

I freeze.

"Mum. Drake." My voice drops. "Something's off."

They stop instantly. They've learned to trust my warnings.

I reach out through the mind link, my thoughts sharp and urgent. Riley, and my team — be ready. Something's coming. Get here ASAP.

A ripple of acknowledgement hits back immediately, tense and alert.

'Roger that.'

Then I turn to Mum and Drake and send another message through our link, fast and clipped. 'Take photos. Everything you can lay your hands on. Paintings, portraits, books — all of it. Go. Move fast. Go.'

We move fast.

I check behind frames, under shelves, inside cupboards. My phone camera clicks nonstop. Every instinct screams at me to hurry.

Drake and my mother race back and forth, removing objects and taking them to the car.

Down a long, dark hallway, something pulls at me — a

wrongness in the wall. I press my hand against the panelling. The energy shifts beneath my palm.

"Mum. Drake. Here."

The panel groans and swings open, revealing a hidden chamber.

Before I can even process the weight of the hidden journals and the dark jewelled chest, Drake is already moving — fast. Too fast. Like a man on a mission.

The moment I pull the first stack of journals from the safe, he's there, scooping them out of my hands with one arm while grabbing framed photos off the nearby shelves with the other. He doesn't even look at what he's taking — he just moves, efficient and relentless, as if every second counts.

"Drake, careful—"

"No time," he snaps, already halfway down the hallway, arms overflowing with books, frames, and a carved wooden box he must've grabbed from a side table. His footsteps thunder across the floorboards, and then he's gone — out the front door, racing toward the car.

Mum isn't far behind him.

She darts from room to room, snatching up portraits, loose papers, and anything that looks remotely important. Her arms fill so quickly she wedges a large framed painting under her chin just to keep everything from spilling.

"Alexia, this is unbelievable," she mutters breathlessly, juggling a stack of leather-bound journals and a portrait of Hayes Reinhold. "All this time... all this history..."

"Keep moving, Mum," I urge, my senses prickling with that familiar warning. "We don't have long."

She doesn't question me — not this time. She hurries toward the door, nearly tripping over a rug as she goes. Drake meets her halfway, relieving her of half the load before sprinting back outside.

He moves like a blur.

In. Out.

In. Out.

Each time carrying more than any person should be able to.

By the time I reach into the back of the safe and pull out the heavy, hidden books wedged deep inside, Drake is already returning for another load, sweat beading at his temples, chest rising and falling with sharp breaths.

"Give them here," he says, voice tight.

I hand him the stack, with another box, and he turns on his heel, muscles straining as he carries the weight like it's nothing. Mum adds two more framed portraits to the pile in his arms before he disappears again.

The urgency in my chest spikes.

I shove the last of the items from the hidden safe into Mum's arms. "Take these. Go. Now."

She doesn't argue. She rushes toward the door, clutching the books and frames to her chest.

Drake comes racing back in, grabs the last items from the floor beneath the hidden safe and a nearby bookshelf, and bolts outside again.

Mum, red-faced and panting, rushes back in and scoops up another pile of items.

Then it hits me.

Danger.

Danger.

GO.

Leave.

Escape before we're dead.

The warning slams into me so hard I stumble. It isn't a thought — it's a command, a primal scream ripping through my mind.

Another violent surge follows, dread and urgency slamming along my spine, nearly knocking me to my knees.

"Mum!" My voice cracks like a whip. "Move! Don't look back!"

Her eyes widen. She doesn't question me — she bolts, books and frames clutched to her chest.

I send a mental scream to Drake, sharp and urgent enough to burn.
'Start the car. Back it up. NOW.'

Outside, the engine roars to life — the exact sound I need to hear right now.

Mum and I sprint toward the exit, arms full, hearts pounding. We burst through the doorway just as a deep rumble shakes the ground beneath our feet.

A split second later —

BOOM.

The back of the house erupts in a fireball, flames shooting into the sky. The shockwave slams into us, nearly knocking me off my feet. The explosion rolls forward like a living thing, devouring the walls, the roof, everything.

"Get in!" Drake yells, leaning across the front seat to throw the back door open.

We dive inside. Books and frames spill everywhere. I shove them toward Mum, desperate to clear the doorway. Drake slams the car into gear, tyres spinning, dirt and stones flying as the car fishtails and rockets forward.

My door slams shut from the force.

I twist in my seat just in time to see the house explode again — a massive burst of fire and debris shooting into the air like a volcanic eruption.

Mum gasps, voice trembling. "Oh my goddess, Alexia... how did you know?"

I swallow hard, staring at the inferno behind us.

"That warning sensation I get before something bad happens?

Yeah… that was it."

I look down at the items in my lap — still clutching a piece of Alivia's past.

"I just wish we could've saved more," I whisper. "All that family history… gone."

Mum places her hand over mine, grounding me. "We managed to grab a lot, sweetheart. More than I expected. And all those books from the safe? That's a treasure trove on its own." Her gaze drops to the pile in my lap, then to the ornate box wedged between the journals. "But that jewelled-encrusted box… I can't stop wondering what's inside it."

The flames reflect in the rear window as we speed away, the house collapsing behind us in a storm of fire and ash. Nearby bush catches fire and begins to burn.

And deep in my chest, something cold settles.

Someone didn't want us to find those journals.

Someone didn't want Alivia's truth to survive.

And now they know we have it.

CHAPTER FORTY-ONE

FIRE ERUPTS INTO A LARGE FIREBALL ROCKET. HIGH ABOVE THE trees. The earth continues to shake.

We're lucky. Ridiculously, impossibly lucky.

Watching the house behind us erupt into a massive fireball, flames clawing at the sky, is unbelievable. Scary and shocking, and somehow we're still alive.

Drake keeps the car steady, knuckles white on the steering wheel, shock tightening his jaw. Mum sits rigid beside me, chest heaving, books and frames still clutched in her lap like she's afraid to let go.

My heart slams against my ribs. My mind finally kicks back into gear.

I reach out through the mind link, my thoughts sharp and shaking. *'Riley — the Reinhold house is on fire. Multiple explosions. It's still going.'*

His response hits instantly, clipped and tense. *'Local Fire Brigade is already on the way. Get out of there. Drive to safety.'*

The last part of Riley's command I share with Drake. He doesn't need telling twice. He pushes the car harder, gravel spitting behind us as the burning house disappears through the rear-window.

But my focus shifts.

Pulls.

Tightens.

The castle.

My twins.

The need hits me like a physical ache — sharp, overwhelming, primal. I need to see them. Hold them. Smell them. Make sure they're safe with my own eyes after the morning we've just survived.

And my body reminds me with a heavy, throbbing ache across my chest — it's time to feed them. My breasts feel full, tight, almost painful. The twins will be hungry. They'll be fussing. They'll be wondering where I am.

A wave of guilt crashes over me.

I press a hand to my chest, breathing through the ache. "Drake… faster."

He glances at me, reads everything in a heartbeat, and nods. The car surges forward.

Thankful for the local portal, we drive directly to Darshia, and soon the castle towers rise in the distance, and relief floods me so hard my eyes sting.

I'm coming, my babies.

Mummy's coming.

EMOTIONS SWIRL INSIDE ME AS I STARE AT THE ITEMS SPREAD across the long wooden table. The exquisitely crafted chest — dark timber, metal hinges shaped like vines — sits open and empty, its purpose fulfilled. The large variety of books we rescued from Alivia's father's home are stacked in uneven piles, some of their worn spines and faded lettering whispering age and secrets. The whole table gleams beneath them, polished timber reflecting the chaos of our morning.

Shock still clings to me like smoke.

Shock… and disbelief that we managed to save this much.

Drake, in his frantic rush out of the burning house, somehow grabbed framed photos and paintings off the walls. I don't know how he did it — how he carried so much, how he moved so fast — but the evidence is right here. Portraits. So many, I am amazed to see the variety of images through the decades and centuries. Family moments frozen in time. All of it saved by sheer instinct.

We stand there, the three of us, staring down at the collection: family jewels, old photographs, coins, gold bars, documents, bundles of paper money tied with brittle string. Mum looks like she's about to drool. Her eyes shine with a hunger I've never seen — not greed, but fascination. History. Legacy. Answers.

She's desperate to learn everything she can about this family. And from what we've seen so far, one thing is obvious: they weren't poor. Not even close. But they didn't flaunt it. They hid it — tucked it away behind wards, walls, and secrets.

One of the dark leather-bound books pulls at me. Thick. Heavy. Old. The family Witch Spell and Enchantment book. The moment my fingers brush the cover, my senses flare. Magic hums beneath my skin, eager and restless. My fingertips itch to open it, to turn every page, to drink in every word.

My unborn daughter reacts too — a soft flutter of magic inside me, like she's leaning closer. Learning. Listening.

It still amazes me that she absorbs knowledge when I read. Doctor Brean explained it during my last antenatal check-up, his excitement barely contained. When he learned that Alivia transferred her witch powers to the baby through me, he nearly vibrated out of his chair. My own witch abilities — faint and inconsistent before — have grown stronger because of it.

And thank goodness to Lucy's charmed necklace — I never would've sensed or disarmed the wards protecting the house without it. I never would've survived the magical attacks thrown my way.

And then Mum's research uncovered the truth. We do have witch blood in our line.

My mother's great-grandmother, Annette, married a witch named Alistair Owens. They had two daughters — Anita and Augusta — before Alistair died in a workplace accident. Annette remarried a human man, Thomas Edwards, and swore never to return to the Witch's Coven. When neither daughter showed any magical talent, she hid everything connected to the coven and buried the truth.

Only a brief paragraph in an old family journal revealed the truth: the girls' birth father had been a male witch from a local coven. Neither daughter displayed powers, so the family assumed the magic had died with him.

But that wasn't the only surprise.

My father's side carried witch blood too — three generations back, a woman named Elizbith. Her child, and then her grandchild, showed no powers, so everyone assumed the magic ended with her.

Maybe it did.

Maybe it didn't.

Because here I am — a Dark One with witch magic.

And my unborn daughter?

She's something else entirely.

ONCE EVERYTHING IS LAID OUT — THE ITEMS FROM SEVERAL chests, the pieces we pulled from the hidden wall panel, the things Drake and Mum grabbed in the chaos — the sheer scale of it hits me.

Coins. Paper money. Gold bars.

The numbers are staggering.

The coins and notes alone total $1,959,000.

The gold bars? Easily worth another $2.5 million.

All up, the value sitting on this table climbs to well over $4 million.

And that's not even counting the house.

Before the fire, the property and land were valued at over $1.2 million. The photos we took on our phones show the heirlooms and antiques that were still inside — proof for the insurance claim. Thankfully for Alivia, the house and contents were covered under a $1.9 million insurance package.

But the family jewels…that's a different story entirely.

Magic hums from them — faint but unmistakable. My fingers tingle as I hover over the collection, drawn to one piece in particular.

A gold ring.

Intricate.

Delicate.

Three blue sapphires set in a pattern that feels familiar, like something I've seen in a dream.

Something inside me urges me to pick it up.

To slide it onto my finger.

Before I can talk myself out of it, I do.

The fit is perfect.

Too perfect.

A warm sensation blooms beneath the metal, spreading from my finger up my hand, then racing through my arm and into the rest of my body. It's not painful — just… claiming. Recognising. Binding.

I lift my hand, watching the sapphires catch the light, glittering like tiny captured stars.

"Okay… that's pretty," I murmur.

Then reality kicks in.

I should take it off.

I should.

I pinch the band and tug.

Nothing.

I try again. Harder.

Still nothing.

"Oh, crap on a stick," I mutter under my breath, giving it one last determined yank. The ring doesn't budge. Not even a millimetre.

Fantastic.

Just fantastic.

Looks like I've got another family ring that's decided it wants to stay exactly where it is.

CHAPTER FORTY-TWO

"Ah… Mum, I have a little problem."

I lift my hand, fingers spread, the sapphire ring glittering like it's proud of itself.

Mum's eyes narrow. "Oh, Alexia. What have you done now?"

"The ring is beautiful, Mum. I had to try it on." I wiggle my hand, annoyed. "And now it refuses to come off."

It does look incredible on my finger — annoyingly perfect — but still.

Mum sighs, half exasperated, half amused. "Alexia, you're fortunate. This jewellery belongs to our family."

"Yep. Lucky for sure." I roll my eyes so hard I'm surprised they don't fall out.

A knock hits the door — firm, familiar.

I sense the presence instantly.

"Enter, Riley," I call out.

The door opens slowly, and Riley steps inside. One look at his face and my stomach drops. Something's wrong. Something's happening outside this room.

"Yes, Riley?" My voice tightens.

"Princess Alexia," he says, formal and tense, "your presence is required in the main conference room. The Old Ones and most of the Council are here. They wish to speak with you regarding the Coronation and the Crowning Ceremony."

A cold ripple slides down my spine.

So that's the unease. The warning.

"Oh, crap on a stick. No. Not the Old Ones." I turn to Mum. "You're coming with me. I'm not facing that pack of vultures alone. And Riley — don't even think about disappearing. You're coming too."

"Princess, you can handle—"

"No, Riley." I cut him off sharply. "You will be right by my side. Along with my mum."

He bows his head slightly. "Yes, Princess. But we must leave soon. The Council cannot be kept waiting."

Bugger.

I glance back at the table — the jewels, the documents, the gold, the photos — all of it gleaming like bait for the wrong kind of attention.

"We can't leave this sitting here," I mutter.

Mum nods toward the door. "Alexia, can you place one of those magical ward thingies on the room? Stop anyone from entering while we're gone?"

Hmm.

She might actually be onto something.

My gaze flicks between the table and the door. Images flash through my mind — symbols, colours, words I don't recognise but somehow understand. Magic stirs inside me, eager, ready.

That's it.

Found one.

My lips widen and form a smile.

Riley is already heading out, knowing to leave before I do anything silly. Mum follows, watching my face over her shoulder, like she's waiting for me to sprout wings. I keep my thoughts steady. I can do this.

Once they're both outside, I focus.

Slow steps toward the door.

Magic rising like warm air under my skin. I lift my hands. Close my eyes. Strange words slip from my mouth — soft, ancient, nothing I consciously know. But they feel right. They feel protective.

The door swings shut on its own behind me.

A brilliant blue light flares around the frame, wrapping it in shimmering energy before fading into a single glowing hieroglyph etched into the wood. My magic settles, satisfied.

The room is sealed.

I turn to Riley. "Can you see anything on the door? Or open it?"

He gives me a look — part curiosity, part concern — and reaches for the handle.

The door hisses. A deep growl vibrates through the wood. Riley jerks his hand back with a sharp inhale, shaking it out.

Oops.

Yeah… that's definitely pain.

"Um — sorry about that, Riley."

He flexes his fingers, wincing. "Princess, I think you've succeeded. The door is protected. Very protected. Next time, warn me before I test your wards."

Despite the sting in his hand, he gives me a small smile — no hard feelings.

'My hand will recover, Princess Alexia. Come — we must go.'

With the room secured, the three of us turn toward the main conference hall. The air feels heavier with every step — like the castle itself knows what's coming.

Before we get too far, I pause.

I need to update Drake.

He deserves to know what storm we're walking into.

I reach out through the mind link, gathering my thoughts, bracing myself for whatever comes next.

CHAPTER FORTY-THREE

Two whole hours of questions, and I'm one breath away from flipping this entire conference table.

I sit there, spine straight, jaw tight, pretending I'm not dying of frustrated boredom inside. It feels like I've been dragged back into high school — oral exams, pop quizzes, teachers staring at me like I'm about to fail spectacularly.

Test after test.

Question after question.

Necessary for them? Maybe.

Necessary for me? Absolutely not.

Still, I hold my ground. I answer everything they throw at me, weaving my Dark One instincts through each response — planning, strategising, calculating how I'd handle every scenario they toss at me. And somehow, I surprise myself. Apparently, I have been paying attention during training with Riley and the instructors.

Every time Riley gives a tiny approving nod, something warm

settles in my chest. At least someone in this room believes I'm not a complete disaster.

One of the Council members finally speaks. "Princess Alexia, we understand you are prepared to fight for the rights of others and protect the residents of Darshia. Your actions since the attack on the royal castle have shown strength, skill, and respect — the qualities of a ruler."

Their faces all carry the same expression — something unreadable, something layered.

Something that makes my stomach twist.

Double meaning. Most likely a hidden agenda.

Fantastic. With a huge side of sarcasm.

Another Council member clears his throat. "Princess Alexia, we understand you are married and joined with your husband."

"Yes. Yes, I am. Very happily married," I say, louder than necessary.

Where is he going with this? The air shifts — wrong, heavy.

"Usually, you would have been requested to marry a Dark One from outside Darshia. But that is no longer possible, given your two children... and the one you are now carrying—"

Mum stiffens beside me. Gasps.

Oh, crap on a stick.

I was going to tell her myself — not have some pompous Dark One blurt it out like he's announcing the weather.

Mum turns toward me, eyes wide, hurt and disbelief swirling together. "Alexia... is this true? Are you pregnant again?" Her voice is tight, clipped. "Why didn't you tell me?"

Before I can answer, I watch the moment she puts the pieces together. Her face drops. "The Joining Ceremony... that was to make you pregnant again, wasn't it?"

Heat crawls up my neck. I force my shoulders back, chin up, but it doesn't stop the shame from burning through me. I feel like a child being scolded.

"Something like that — Yes, Mum. Part of the Joining Ceremony means the female Dark One *can* become pregnant. In my case, I needed to conceive for my powers to fully activate. That's why Drake and I had to stay in the Ceremonial suite. I wasn't allowed to leave until I conceived."

Her disappointment hits harder than any Council interrogation.

"Alexia... why didn't you tell me?"

"Mum... that look on your face right now. That's why."

She steps forward and pulls me into her arms, her voice soft near my ear. "Oh, honey. Yes, I'm disappointed — but only because I hoped you'd go to university. With Alexettia gone... that future to enjoy your young adult lives at university and furthering your education is gone too."

Her hug tightens, her hand rubbing slow circles on my back. "But I know you. You'll put Darshia first. You'll be a great Queen, Alexia. I'm proud of you."

Tears slip down my cheeks before I even realise I'm crying.

"Thanks, Mum," I whisper. "And... before you ask... I'm only having one baby this time." A shaky laugh escapes me. "She's healthy. A little girl. Drake and I already named her. Alex."

"Alex?" Mum pulls back slightly. "Are you sure?"

"Yes. It's her shortened name. Like Alley."

Mum blinks. "My precious granddaughter... what about Alley? Are you telling me Alley isn't her full name?"

I shake my head. "No, Mum. Alley is her shortened name. It always has been. Alexettia warned me — I have to be careful with the names I give my children. Especially the next Queen of Darshia."

Before I can explain further, someone behind us clears their throat.

Right.

Audience.

Fantastic.

"Princess Alexia, Amelia," an older woman says, "we did not mean to reveal the unborn babe."

Her tone is polite. Her eyes are not.

Noted.

I mentally file her face away. Some of these people are not to be trusted. Something is off in this room — the air feels wrong, thick with hidden intentions.

Another Council member catches my eye — dark, beady eyes, a quick sneer before he wipes it away. My skin crawls. My stomach flips.

Fine.

Let's see what you're hiding.

I slip into his mind. The surface thoughts hit first — then the memories.

My knees nearly buckle.

Oh my Gods. No.

No, no, no.

I force my face blank and move to the next mind. And the next. And the next.

Rotten.

Corrupt.

Dangerous.

I send a sharp mental message to Mum. *'Start talking. Ask questions. Keep them busy. And strengthen your shields.'*

'Alexia, what happened?'

'Something is very wrong. I need to read more minds. Keep them distracted.'

'Okay. Be careful.'

I reach out to Drake next. He feels me instantly. *'Hi, babe. What are you doing? The twins—'*

'Drake, listen. Get your brother and Lucy. Take the twins and go somewhere safe. Now.'

'Alexia, what's going on? Where are you?' He's panicking — I feel it through the bond.

'I don't have time to explain. Riley and Mum are with me. We're still in the meeting with the Old Ones and the Council.'

'Still? It started over two hours ago.'

'I know. And it hasn't stopped. Please — take the twins, the registered paperwork, the family journal, all our birth records, and go. Protect the twins. Especially Alley.'

A long pause.
Fear.
Acceptance.

'Okay, Alexia. I've made contact. My brother and Lucy are meeting me in a couple of minutes. But keep yourself safe.'

'I will. I love you. Hug the twins for me. Tell them Mummy loves them.'

'We love you too. Please... be careful.'

With the number of traitors in front of me, I am not going to risk the lives of my family.

I close my mind to Drake and let out a slow breath. Then,

casually — so casually no one would ever suspect — I lift my hand and brush my fingers against Riley's. Just a light touch against his leg, nothing noticeable.

But the moment our skin connects, I snap the link open.

Riley's mind floods into mine, steady and disciplined, and I push the information straight across. Five minds breached. Five traitors. High-ranking. Dangerous.

His shock hits me like a jolt. His disgust follows, sharp and bitter. Through our joined link, I see what he sees — each of the five council members, their faces calm and composed while their thoughts reek of betrayal.

Riley's gaze sweeps the room, slow and deliberate, weighing options, calculating risks. The traitors sit there like they own the place, completely unaware that we now know exactly what they are.

'Riley,' I send, my mental voice low and urgent, *'I need you to organise as many loyal palace guards and security as possible. Quietly. Get them summoned here. If we're walking out of this conference room alive, we're going to need numbers.'*

Riley's mind tightens, a hard knot of anger and disbelief. *'Traitors. Council members. Old Ones. People sworn to protect Darshia.'*

He mentally shakes his head, the weight of it hitting both of us. I cannot believe this. Among the Council… Among the Old Ones. They have to be stopped.

Riley's disgust nearly knocks me over. I can sense he wants to reach for his gun and shoot them.

I keep my expression neutral, my posture calm, but inside, my pulse is hammering.

This room is a nest of vipers. Ready to attack.

And now that I'm becoming the next Queen. They want to control me or not allow me to become queen of the people. Queen of Darshia.

We need backup. We need a solid plan. And we need it fast.

With Riley beside me, he understands that better than anyone.

CHAPTER FORTY-FOUR

WITHIN A SHORT AMOUNT OF TIME, RILEY AND I HAVE SORTED THE room full of Dark Ones into two categories. Group A—innocent. Group B—traitors.

My beautiful and very talented mother manages to keep the room of Council members and Old Ones entertained and captivated with her wit and charm. Ha. She more or less confuses them with her legal spill. With a few brief words to Mum, keeping her up to date, she now knows traitors, amongst the innocent, surround us. Just like myself, Mum is not surprised by that piece of information.

A sharp ripple hits my mind. Someone attempts to breach my shields. My eyes snap across the room, hunting for the source. My mind pushes back, brushing against every shield in the room, sensing, testing, searching. The intrusion presses harder, threading into my thoughts. Whoever this is… they're the only one here in Darshia strong enough to break through.

It doesn't take long before I find her — a woman I somehow haven't noticed until now. Interesting. Very interesting. Especially when she looks strikingly similar to my great-grandmother. Hmm.

Who is this woman? I break eye contact and glance at Riley, reinforcing my shields. Riley is already scanning the room, assessing everyone with that razor-sharp focus of his.

I look back at the woman and slip into her thoughts, easing past her surface mind. Hmm. She's watching how I handle today's meeting. My eyes lock onto hers. Oh, my goddess.

'Alexia, you have succeeded. Well done. Bravo, bravo, young one.'

What the…?

How has this woman breached my shields? I give myself a quick mental shake and ask, *'Who are you? And what do you want with me?'*

'Oh, my dear young one. I am so proud of you. You have passed. You also have found the traitors amongst us. Well done.'

'Who are you?' I ask again, watching her lips curl into a coy smile.

'Dear, dear young one. I have been waiting so long for you to arrive and take over from Alexettia.'

'What is your name and who are you exactly?'

I study her face, her expressions, her eyes. She looks around forty, but I can feel the truth beneath her skin — easily over three hundred, maybe closer to four hundred years old. This woman… I don't know how, but I sense she is one of the Old Ones. One of the powerful Old Ones.

'You are correct, Alexia, for I am one of the Old Ones. I am not too fond of that term. Do I look old to you?' Was that a twitch of her lips forming a smile, or is she trying to pout?

'Thank you for the confirmation. However, you have still avoided the part where you tell me your name and who you actually are.' I ask her again. She doesn't answer. She just smiles at me, silent and infuriatingly patient.

With no response, she leaves me with little choice. I breach her mind shields and slip deeper, moving through her thoughts and surface memories before pushing further.

Oh, my goddess.

This woman is a relation of mine — a cousin of Alexettia. My mind floods with her memories and thoughts.

THE FEELING OF A HAND ON MY SIDE SNAPS MY ATTENTION BACK to Riley. In seconds, a ripple of nervous energy rolls through several Old Ones and Council members. I reach out with my mind and brush against clusters of men stationed outside every exit of the chamber. Breaching Riley's shields, I catch the tail end of his mind-talk — he's coordinating with the guards outside. His security. Or, as he keeps reminding me — my security. The royal security I requested.

Interrupting his conversation, I say, *'Riley, ready your guards. Start with two men entering each doorway. It is time to detain the traitors.'*

'Yes, Princess. Everyone is ready and waiting for your signal.'

'Thank you, Riley. It is time to start this party. Let's go.'

Through the mind link, I hear the guards confirm their orders a heartbeat before every door bursts open. Security floods the chamber, surrounding and detaining the traitors so fast no one has time to understand what's happening.

That strange woman presses against my mind shields again. When my eyes meet hers, I let her in.

'Well done, Alexia. You have super-seeded all our expectations. You will be a fantastic Queen for Darshia.'

I lift an eyebrow. Did I hear her correctly? Seriously…

'Are you going to tell me who you are and what your name is, Cousin?' I ask, watching shock flicker across her beautiful features before she smooths it away.

'Oh, my. You are more powerful than I imagined. Just think, with the proper training… you will be a force to be reckoned with.'

Enough time wasted, I dive straight into her mind, searching until I find what I need. Her name is Augusta — Alexettia's older cousin, technically Alexettia's great-aunty. The joys of inter-family breeding. Augusta's parents were the last to marry within the family before the Dark One community finally realised their species would die out if they didn't change their way of life and joining. Miscarriages, stillbirths, birth defects, infertility — all rampant. Just like Augusta — The poor woman cannot conceive.

Screaming, yelling, and a colourful variety of language erupts around me. I turn to face the crowd of Council members and Dark Ones.

Okay. My time to shine and take back control of the room. I whistle sharply, as one does, actually it is more high-pitched, and just for the sake of it, I whistle again, several times in fact, cutting through the noise. My guards have already separated the traitors from the innocent.

Hands fly to ears. Eyes swing to me. The captured Dark Ones glare with pure venom.

"Now that I have everyone's attention, I will explain what is happening."

My gaze sweeps the room. When I meet my mother's eyes, I smile and tilt my head, signalling her to move back to my side. I call Riley over as well — I need him close so he can see everything I show him through the link.

Multiple voices crash over me at once, sharp and vicious.

"What is the meaning of this!"

"Release us immediately!"

"You have no right to treat us this way!"

I stand tall, shoulders braced, chin lifted. "My guards are here to take several of you into custody for treason to Darshia." My eyes sweep the furious crowd. "It has come to my attention that we do indeed have traitors amongst us."

A voice spits from the back, "What proof do you have? Half-breed."

Gasps ripple through the room — even from those who dislike me.

I focus on the man who spoke. Breaching his shields, like a hot knife slicing through butter, I gather what I need. Something captures my attention and I delve deeper. Much deeper. The man is vile.

"Good question. Now, regarding proof... let me start there, shall I, Marcist? It is Marcist, correct? I believe you are an Old One and also on the Council. Is that also correct?"

The thirty-ish looking man — tall, balding, grey, beady eyes — gives me a smug nod.

"Now, Marcist. You are not married. You were once engaged to your younger cousin, who broke the engagement when Darshia changed the rules preventing marriage between family members. Your cousin married someone outside Darshia. Is that not correct?"

His eyes narrow. Another stiff nod.

"Okay, Marcist. You would prefer the old ways."

He nods. "Many of us would prefer to go back to the old ways. Why? What does that have to do with being accused of being a traitor?"

"Marcist, with you, it has everything to do with being a traitor. Especially when everyone here finds out how you didn't like being cheated out of the marriage — and the wealth that would have come with it. You murdered your younger cousin and her new husband on their wedding night. But not before you raped her in front of her dying husband and slashed her throat. Then you staked the husband. You dusted him."

Marcist's face drains of colour. A vein throbs at his temple. His thoughts turn vicious. I keep one hand on Riley's arm so he sees and hears everything through our shared mind link.

"You have no proof!" Marcist screams.

I shake my head. "You see, Marcist, that is where you are very wrong. My head of security has just seen your thoughts and memories. And one of your fellow Old Ones — whom you may find has now shared that knowledge with several others."

"No. No one can breach our shields. Alexettia thought she might have been able to do it once. We put a stop to that." His smugness returns as he scans his little group.

"Oh, really. And how exactly did you prevent Alexettia from breaching one's mind shields?" I ask casually, though I've already seen what he and the others did to her. Disgust twists in my stomach. I look to Samini and nod.

'Take him away before I shoot him. And make sure you take his little friends with him. Keep them separate, chain them, and place witch wards on them to prevent them from using their Dark One abilities.'

Samini nods and shoves Marcist toward the door. Ten guards follow, escorting five struggling traitors.

Four traitors remain.

Riley and I turn to them. Before continuing, I sweep my mind across the rest of the crowd. I wait as ten more guards arrive to escort the remaining traitors.

"Now, ladies and gentlemen, the threat of traitors is serious. We cannot sit by and allow men and women to act and behave in this manner. We, the residents of Darshia, are here to make sure we succeed and the young survive, thrive, and prosper." I meet the eyes of every Dark One before me. A few lift their chins. The four traitors stare at the floor.

'Riley, the other guards are about to arrive. Make sure they have a magical ward placed on the traitors to prevent them from using any of their Dark One abilities. I've already told Samini to keep the others separate.'

Riley nods and moves to the door we entered through. I hear the mind-talk as he escorts the guards inside, each carrying magical charms for the traitors. The sight of silver-warded handcuffs is a relief — they'll stop the traitors from using their hands and arms as well. There will be no magic or Dark One ability used against us.

CHAPTER FORTY-FIVE

ONLY TWO DARK ONES REMAIN FROM THE ORIGINAL GROUP OF Old Ones and Council members — Augusta, and Frederick, a two-hundred-year-old councillor with eyes that have seen far too much. The traitors and Dark Ones against me have been escorted out in chains. For the few who are innocent, they are being escorted to be questioned separately.

Soon, the five of us are seated around a long rectangular table. Mum fusses for a moment, making sure everyone has refreshments and something to eat before we begin. It's such a Mum thing to do — offer snacks before interrogations.

But I need answers.

And I need them now.

My gaze shifts from Augusta to Frederick, then back to Augusta again. Before I can speak, I feel Mum brushing against my mind shields — a gentle tap, asking for my attention.

'Alexia, this woman... you said her name is Augusta. I cannot get over how much she resembles my grandmother — Annetta.'

'Ah, Mum. Augusta can breach our minds very easily. So be careful with your thoughts. And yes... Augusta is related to us as well.'

I turn my head toward Augusta, meeting her eyes directly. "Isn't that right, Augusta? Now you can explain to my mother just how related you are to us."

FINALLY, I FEEL STEADY AGAIN. THE ANSWERS I NEEDED HAVE been given, and for the first time today, I know my family is safe.

I reach out through the bond. *'Hey, babe. How are the twins?'*

Drake's relief washes over me like warm sunlight.

'Alexia... it's so good to hear your voice, baby. Is it safe to talk? What's happening?'

Guilt tugs at me — not because I kept him in the dark, but because I dragged him into danger simply by existing. But I refuse to risk our children. Not again. Not ever.

At least now I know they're protected. The security team interrogated the traitors and uncovered ten more Dark Ones — ten more threats to Darshia and the royal line.

'Drake, we had issues. Major ones. The Old Ones and Council... there were traitors. A lot of them. And they were willing to kill you and our children.'

His shock slams through the bond, sharp and horrified.

'Oh my goddess, Alexia. You detected them? Is that why you wanted me to take the twins and leave? What happened?'

'Yes. When I searched their minds, it was terrifying. These people were willing to do anything — anything — to drag Darshia back into the Dark Ages. They wanted to use me to get there. They're sick, Drake. Dangerous. And some of them manipulated Alexettia in horrific ways.'

A growl vibrates through the bond — pure fury. *'You have to be kidding me. Did you have Riley and the guards take them into custody?'*

'Yes. Twenty traitors in custody, all wearing warded charms. And I told Riley to keep them separated.'

'Good. When can we come home to you?'

'If you stay safe — now. But I still don't trust everyone here. Not all the Old Ones or Council members attended today. There could be more traitors hiding. Tell Devlain and Lucy. Stay together. And have Lucy prepare more charms — I have a feeling we'll need them.'

Drake's love hits me so hard I almost stand up and walk out of this room to find him.

'Will do, Alexia. I love you. See you soon.'

'Love you too. Keep safe.'

I close the link and refocus on the small group in front of me.

Augusta catches my eye — and winks.

Winks.

The audacity.

"You'll be together soon enough, Alexia," she says, far too amused. "Now, we have a birthday celebration and a Royal Coronation to organise. Big or small? Even if you choose small, you must still plan something for your royal subjects."

I consider her words — and an idea forms instantly.

"Regarding my birthday," I say, turning toward her, "I want something small and intimate. Just close family."

Warmth presses against my hand. Mum. She squeezes gently, and I give her a soft smile. She understands. After everything that's happened, I don't want a spectacle. I want peace. I want my family.

"Now that I'm a mother," I add, "I don't want to make a big song and dance about turning eighteen."

I glance at Frederick. His jaw twitches — a tiny tic on the right side. Interesting. He's hiding something.

I slip into his mind.

Alexettia used him. Blackmailed him. Manipulated him. He's unsure if he can trust me — and honestly, I don't blame him. But if he wants to remain on the Council, trust is non-negotiable.

"Now, regarding the Coronation," I continue. "I want the ceremony itself to be small. But afterward? A large town celebration for all of Darshia. It's time the people had a chance to breathe. To celebrate. To feel hope again."

Both Augusta and Frederick fall silent, thinking.

Augusta is already designing my coronation gown in her head — I can practically see the fabric swatches floating behind her eyes.

Frederick looks stunned, clearly expecting me to demand a grand spectacle like Alexettia.

Ha.

They'll learn soon enough.

I'm not Alexettia.

I'm Alexia — temporary Princess, soon-to-be Queen of Darshia.

And things are about to change.

CHAPTER FORTY-SIX

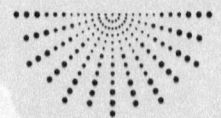

Feeling the heavy weight of the massive jewelled gown and its matching long cape dragging along the ground is definitely not my ideal way of spending my birthday. Each slow step toward the bright, sunlit balcony reminds me just how far from normal my life has become.

My mind drifts back to this morning — a small family celebration that already feels like another lifetime. Yay me, officially eighteen... even though I swear I feel about forty after everything that's happened. The moment was warm and intimate and over far too quickly. At least we'd managed a proper celebration two days ago for Drake's eighteenth — a real gathering, full of laughter, food, and the people we love. That memory wraps around me like a soft blanket now, a reminder that before the crown, before the chaos, I was just Alexia with her family.

Within minutes of the birthday breakfast ending, I was rushed off to be pampered, prepared, and fitted into this beautiful off-the-shoulder coronation gown of royal blue satin. A low-cut jewelled bodice, short sleeves, and a train long enough to trip a small army. Gorgeous. Heavy. Annoying.

The atmosphere beyond the balcony doors builds and intensifies. I can already sense thousands of people gathered below, waiting for their first glimpse of me. Their excitement vibrates through the stone walls, buzzing against my skin. All these people are here to see me — to witness their new Queen step into the light.

Drake moves up beside me with our daughter, Alley, tucked safely in his arms. I turn and smile at him — he looks so damn proud — then my gaze softens at the sight of our baby girl. Her tiny head rests on his shoulder, rosebud lips parted in sleep.

Over my shoulder, Mum beams at me, her eyes glittering with pride. Damien is wide awake in her arms, taking in everything with those alert little eyes. On my other side, Dad creeps closer, snapping photos with every step, nerves radiating off him like heat.

The closer I get to the balcony doors, the louder the crowd becomes — a living wave of sound.

"Babe," Drake whispers near my ear, "enjoy these moments while they last. I have a feeling tomorrow is going to be hectic."

"Drake," I sigh, "our lives are going to change constantly. This might be the only quiet moment we get before the public claims me."

He leans in, kisses me softly. "I love you."

A disturbance behind us pulls my attention. Lucy and Devlain slip into the foyer, both looking far too pleased with themselves.

"What are you two doing up here? I thought you'd already gone down to join the crowd."

Lucy wraps her arms around me. "A-Babs, where else would I be? Right by your side, you silly woman."

Her warmth settles my nerves instantly.

"Hey, I'm Queen of Darshia now," I tease. "Me — Queen. You — best friend."

Lucy snorts. "Okay, Ms I-Am-Queen. Get your Queenie arse out on that balcony and greet your royal subjects."

Thank the goddess for Lucy. She always knows how to pull me back from the edge.

"Yes, ma'am," I laugh.

I turn toward the open doorway and step into the sunlight.

The noise hits me like a wave — cheers, claps, shouts of excitement. The hairs on my arms rise. The atmosphere is electric, alive, pulsing with energy.

Wow.

That's all my brain can manage as I stare out at the sea of people. Thousands of faces. Thousands of voices. All here for me.

Dad keeps snapping photos like a man possessed. The royal photographer appears, capturing me smiling and waving before I ask for a shot with the crowd behind me. I might be Queen, but I'm still young enough to love a good selfie moment.

I step up to the podium. Adjust the microphone. The crowd quiets, a hush rolling outward like a ripple.

My heart thunders. My palms sweat. I pray I don't faint. Or vomit. Or both.

Alrighty. Let's get this party started.

I smile and project my voice. "Welcome, and good afternoon, everyone."

Thousands of eyes lock onto me.

Breathe, Alexia. Breathe.

"Thank you for attending today's celebrations. Today marks a moment of great importance — not just for my family and me, but for all of Darshia. A day that will be remembered in our history."

Faces brighten. People nod. Some cheer. Confidence trickles back into my veins.

"For those who do not know me... I am Queen Alexia Smithlyn of Blue Darkness. Of the Royal Blue House." I pause, letting the words settle. "The new Queen of Darshia."

The crowd erupts — louder, brighter, prouder.

"Together, we will embrace the modern world and its technology. We may be an old Dark One country and realm, but we will no longer remain in the shadows while others move forward."

I scan the crowd, gauging reactions.

"Darshia residents will have every opportunity to learn. To grow. To prosper. Our young will be encouraged to marry outside our walls — to find their soulmates."

I glance at Drake.

He gives me that panty-dropping smile.

My knees wobble.

Lucy clears her throat behind me, reminding me I'm mid-speech.

Right. Focus, Alexia.

"Over the next four weeks, I invite all residents to bring forward ideas to improve Darshia." I glance at a group of teen girls. "What do we need? What can we build? How can we grow?"

The group of teenagers perk up — good. They'll have opinions.

"Women and men will work side by side in all careers. Women will have the right to learn to fight, to protect themselves and others."

Several women nod fiercely. My heart lifts.

"We have much to learn and much to improve. Our children will continue to learn our history — including the old language — but they will also learn about the world beyond Darshia. They will be encouraged to study, work, and grow in other realms, and human countries, with other Entities, and cultures."

I take a breath, feeling the weight of the moment settle around me.

"I am here to improve Darshia's way of life, strengthen our economy, and protect our people. Long live the residents of Darshia."

I raise my voice. "Long live Darshia!"
The crowd explodes — thunderous applause, cheers, chants.
The sound shakes the balcony.
They chant my name.
Over and over.
Long live Queen Alexia.
Long live Queen Alexia.
Long live Queen Alexia.
And for the first time today…
I believe them.

CHAPTER FORTY-SEVEN

THE SHARP, CHEMICAL BURN OF ANTISEPTIC SLAMS INTO MY SENSES at the same moment a white-hot pain tears through my body. I jolt awake with a scream ripping out of my throat. My eyes snap open.

Drake is beside me.

Relief hits first — thank the goddess I'm not alone — but then I catch the look on his face. Tight. Worried. Bracing.

Reality crashes into me.

Oh, crap on a stick.

I'm in the hospital.

My gaze drops to my belly — still round, still full, still very much pregnant.

I look back up at Drake, and he answers the question I haven't managed to form.

"Baby... you're in labour. Our baby is coming."

I'm what?

In labour?

Me?

A brutal wave of pain wraps around my body, squeezing, crushing, stealing my breath.

Ahhhhhhhhhhhhhh—OWWWWWWW.

Eight ragged breaths later, my brain finally reconnects to my mouth.

'How in the hell am I in labour? Since when?'

Drake hears the thought before I can speak it. "Alexia, the doctor thinks you've been working too hard. You fell into bed exhausted this afternoon, and your mind basically shut your body down to protect itself."

I shake my head. *No. Maybe. Probably.* But I'm not admitting that.

Drake continues, "Your waters broke about thirty minutes ago while we were in bed. And let me tell you, getting a warm gush of water against your body is not something I want to experience again anytime soon. The doctor thinks you've been in labour for a while. Did you have back pain today? On and off?"

I nod slowly.

'Yeah. This morning. Twinges. A dull ache.' I thought I slept funny.

"Well, Alexia… that was most likely early labour."

Ha. Fantastic.

"How did I sleep through all this?" I manage to ask out loud — right before another savage contraction rips through me. I scream again, loud enough to shake the walls. My whole body locks up, and all I can think is how long is this torture going to last?

Two nurses burst into the room, followed by Doctor Brean. They rush to the end of the bed, lifting the sheet covering my lower half.

Oh great.

Bare skin.

No PJs.

And I'm in one of those stupid open-backed hospital gowns.

Who undressed me? And why does childbirth require this level of humiliation?

Doctor Brean crouches between my legs for a quick examination. I stare at the ceiling, pretending this isn't happening.

Not embarrassing at all.

Nope. Totally fine.

He stands, snaps off his gloves, and smiles like this is a casual morning chat.

"Good morning, my Queen. Not long now until your baby is born."

Morning?

I glance at the wall clock. Five past midnight.

Morning…my arse. It's still nighttime.

And as for his other words — *not long now* — is supposed to be reassuring…I don't think so — at all.

If I weren't currently being ripped in half by my own uterus, I would freeze him where he stands for that comment.

"PUSH. YOU NEED TO PUSH."

Grrrrr.

Oh, my actual goddess.

I am pushing, damn it.

It feels like my entire body is being ripped in half. If one more person tells me I'm "nearly there," I swear I'm going to shoot someone. Speaking of shooting—*where is my gun?*

Sweat beads along my forehead, dripping down my cheeks as another brutal contraction slams into me. Pain tears through my body, violent and unforgiving. I crush Drake's hand in mine, squeezing so hard I feel his bones grind together. He flinches.

Good.

This is his fault.

I'm in agony.

He's lucky I don't rip his balls off.

"Come on, baby," Drake says, voice breathless with excitement. "I can see the head. Our little girl is nearly here."

'I've changed my mind. I want to go home. Someone else can do this. I'm the Queen — don't I have people for this?'

I glare up at Drake. He meets my eyes and immediately shakes his head, because of course, he heard that thought.

'Alexia, I love you, my beautiful wife. And it's too late to change your mind. Our daughter will be here before we know it.'

'Drake, I don't think I can do this.'

'Alexia, you can. Take a deep breath and push. You're stronger than you think.'

He nods at me, steady and sure, and somehow that helps. I drag in a shaky breath, brace myself, and push as the next agonising contraction rips through me.

One contraction.

Two.

Both of them hell.

And then—

A cry.

Sharp. Loud. Furious.

My beautiful baby girl bursts into the world, her lungs announcing her arrival to the entire maternity ward. Seven pounds, four ounces. Forty-six centimetres long. A tiny angel with wisps of dark hair and eyes that match mine perfectly.

She's here.

She's real.

She's ours.

And every second of pain suddenly feels worth it.

A COUPLE OF HOURS LATER, I'M SHOWERED, WRAPPED IN CLEAN bedclothes, and finally resting in a private suite at the Darshia hospital. The room is quiet, warm, and dim, and for the first time since the chaos began, I'm alone with my sleeping baby.

I sink back into the pillows, cradling a sweet cup of tea in my hands and nibbling on slices of fruit-loaf toast. After four hours of intense labour, this moment feels like heaven.

Thirty-eight weeks of pregnancy.

Hours of pain.

And now… peace.

I can finally breathe. I can finally move on to the next stage of my life — being a mother to three beautiful children.

My gaze drifts to the cot beside me. Alex is bundled tightly in her baby blanket, a tiny pink beanie covering her head. She sleeps so soundly, her little chest rising and falling in soft, steady breaths. The sight pulls a huge smile across my face, warm and full.

My thoughts drift to the twins. I missed their first breaths, their first cries — the emergency caesarean stole that from me. But they're safe, healthy, growing… and that's all that matters.

The room is so quiet it almost hums. Drake left to check on the twins and grab some rest, and for a moment I debate whether I should sleep too. But the tea is warm, the toast is good, and the silence feels like a rare gift.

I finish the last sip with a sigh.

Just as I set the cup down, I sense Lucy outside the door — her energy brushing against my mind. She lifts her hand to knock.

'Lucy, come in — but keep quiet. Baby Alex is finally sleeping.'

'Oh, shit, Alexia. Warn me next time.'

I clap a hand over my mouth to smother a laugh.

The door opens slowly, and Lucy slips inside, eyes scanning the room like she's checking for threats. Her baby boy, Dorian, sleeps against her shoulder, wrapped snugly in his blanket.

I whisper, "Hello, Lucy. How are you doing?"

I haven't seen her in a week, and I've missed her — her smile, her sarcasm, her ability to make everything feel normal. She gave birth to Dorian just over three weeks ago, and between being Queen and being pregnant, I've barely had time to breathe, let alone spend time with my best friend.

Lucy settles into one of the leather recliners, smiling wide. "Congratulations to you and Drake on the birth of your new daughter," she whispers.

"Thank you, Luce." I smile back. "I'm a little tired, but it's good to finally stop and rest."

I lift my cup, forgetting it's empty, and set it aside. With a quick mental nudge, I ask a nurse for another tea.

"After the week I've had negotiating with half the kingdom, this cup of tea is the best thing in my life right now. How are you finding motherhood? How's baby Dorian?"

Lucy glances down at her son, then over at Alex, then back to me. "It has its moments, but I'm adjusting. I don't know how you did it with twins. Alexia, you're amazing. I'm just glad Devlain has been there for us."

"Of course he has. He loves you both — don't ever forget

that." I glance toward the door, expecting him to appear. "Speaking of Devlain… where is he?"

Lucy opens her mouth to answer, but a nurse slips in quietly with a fresh cup of tea, swaps it for the empty one, and disappears again.

After a slow sip of hot tea, I notice Lucy shifting Dorian into a better position. The little bedbug has woken up and is staring up at his mumma like she's the entire universe.

She still hasn't answered my question.

And she's avoiding my eyes.

"How's the breastfeeding going? Any trouble?" I ask gently.

I don't need her to say it.

It's written all over her face.

She's thinking about quitting.

"Oh, Alexia girl, where do I start? Trouble — just a little. My nipples are sore. I don't know how you managed to feed two babies at the same time."

I take another sip of tea, hiding a smile. Me managed? If only she knew what those early days were like. I'd been unconscious while Drake and the nurses expressed milk for the twins. They'd even tried placing the babies at my breasts to encourage them to latch.

"Lucy, it took practice. A lot of it. When you can, air out your nipples and let them dry properly. Do you want help? I can show you, or I can call a nurse."

She shakes her head and opens her top, unclipping her maternity bra. Her nipple is already leaking, and she tries to guide it into Dorian's mouth.

I set my cup down and move closer.

"Hey, Lucy… can I suggest something?"

She looks up, eyes already cringing, then back down at her fussing son.

"Hey. Look at me."

She lifts her gaze, tears gathering. I sit on the arm of her chair and rest a hand on her shoulder.

"I'll help you through this. It gets better. I promise."

She nods, swallowing hard.

"Okay," I say softly. "Pass me Dorian while you get comfortable."

She hands him over, and he gives me a look that clearly says feed me now. I raise an eyebrow.

In my Queen voice, I tell him, "Dorian, you, my little nephew, need to learn patience. Your mumma is learning, and so are you. Behave."

Lucy snorts a tiny laugh.

I grab a spare pillow from my bed and hand it to her. "Here. This will help."

She settles it across her lap, adjusts herself, and I pass Dorian back.

"Lay him where you want him," I explain. "Not the other way around. And when he latches, get more of the breast in his mouth. You want good suction."

Lucy nods, focuses, and tries again. This time, Dorian latches properly, sealing around her nipple and sucking like a starving little gremlin.

Within seconds, I see the shift — the hindmilk hits, and he struggles for a moment before settling into a steady rhythm.

"Lucy, breathe slowly when the hindmilk releases. It can feel intense. Deep breaths. It gets easier."

She looks up at me, relief softening her features. "Thanks, Alexia. I've been struggling. Sometimes I feel like giving up."

"Luce, I'm sorry you've felt that way. And listen — it's your choice. If breastfeeding doesn't work for you, don't let anyone guilt you. Your body, your decision. Try using the pillow. Try the better attachment. If it still hurts, use a bottle and formula. Or express with a pump and feed him your breast milk via a bottle."

She pulls a face, thinking. "Really? A pump? I'd still be feeding him my milk… just from a bottle. I think I'll try that. Thanks, Alexia."

"You're welcome. And if you do express, Devlain can take over night feeds."

We both giggle at that.

Alex stirs in her cot. I stand and scoop her up, feeling the wet nappy instantly.

"Hello, my baby girl," I whisper. "You're wet. Let's fix that, then you can have a feed."

She blinks up at me, tiny eyes bright, and I melt.

I take her to the changing table, swap her nappy and clothes for dry clean ones, then settle into the other recliner to feed her. When I look up, Lucy is watching me — and the diamond rings on her finger sparkle under the soft hospital lights.

My mind drifts back to her small wedding two months ago — the same chapel Drake and I married in. Then their Joining Ceremony, private now, no Queen required as witness. Thank the goddess.

I glance between us — two new mums, sitting in the same room, breastfeeding our babies. It still feels surreal.

Alex finishes quickly — probably annoyed about being wet earlier. I lift her upright, resting her against my shoulder. Even half-asleep, she lets out a loud, impressive burp.

Lucy bursts out laughing. "Oh boy, Alexia… Alex might be a girl, but she sure burps like a male."

Right on cue, Dorian burps too, then snuggles into Lucy's shoulder. We both laugh again.

"Lucy, can you believe how far we've come? In one year, we graduated high school, got married, had babies… and discovered a world full of Dark Ones and other paranormal entities."

Lucy frowns. "Are you calling witches entities?"

Oh crap on a stick.

Backpedal, Alexia. Backpedal fast.

"Well... not exactly. Witches are just one type of paranormal I've encountered. Let me finish. The Old Ones call all paranormal people, creatures, animals — Entities."

"What do you mean, people, creatures, animals? What exactly is out there?"

Oh crap on a stick. I did not want to do this right now.

"Lucy... look. As Queen, I deal with all kinds of entities. Thousands exist outside our borders. Ghosts — different types. Shifters — all kinds of animals. And I've even met an elf. Six foot, muscled, tall, dark, incredibly handsome, pointed ears."

"No shit. An elf? And shifters? Oh my. And we're married and missing out on all these creatures of muscles," Lucy laughs.

"Lucy, Lucy, Luce... our husbands might have something to say about the muscles part."

As I say it, I sense Drake and Devlain approaching.

I grin. "Luce, change of subject. The said muscles are about to walk in."

"Really? Bugger," she mutters, quickly covering her breast before turning toward the door.

CHAPTER FORTY-EIGHT

I SEND DRAKE A QUICK MIND-MESSAGE.

'Baby's asleep, be quiet coming in' — just as the door eases open.

Drake steps inside, moving carefully, one of the twins perched on his hip. Devlain follows right behind him with my other twin in his arms.

The moment I see them, my whole chest warms.

Alley's little head pops up, eyes wide, scanning the room for me. Damien does the same, his dark lashes blinking fast.

The second they spot me, both twins erupt in excited toddler babble.

"Mu-mum! Mu-mum!"

"Hiyaaaa, Mumum!"

Drake crosses the room and leans down, kissing me softly. The warmth of him, the tenderness — goddess, I needed that.

"Hello, baby," he whispers against my lips. "I brought you some little visitors."

I smile at Alley, then Damien. "Hello, my little ones. Did you miss Mummy? Daddy and I have someone here for you to meet."

The twins look at Lucy, then at Dorian in her arms. Alley lifts her chubby hand and points proudly.

"Aun Luc… an' bube Dain!"

"That's right, sweetheart. Aunty Lucy and your little cousin Dorian."

Damien's gaze shifts to Alex in my arms. His whole face lights up. He points with a tiny finger.

"Buby! Mumum… buby Aless?"

"Yes, Damien," I whisper. "This is your new baby sister, Alex. She's sleeping right now, so you both have to be very quiet. Can you be a big boy and not wake her?"

Damien nods his little head so seriously it almost makes me laugh. "Yeh, Mumum. Shhh."

Drake settles onto the arm of my chair, giving Alley a closer look at Alex. Devlain moves to my other side with Damien.

"Remember," I say softly, "gentle hands with the new baby. Just like you were gentle with cousin Dorian."

Both twins nod again — adorable, solemn little bobbleheads — glancing at sleeping Dorian as if reminding themselves of the rules.

Alley leans toward me, so I kiss the top of her head. She sighs happily and melts back into Drake's chest, letting out a tiny yawn.

Damien sees the kiss and immediately starts wiggling in Devlain's arms, wanting his turn. I lift my free arm, and Devlain places him carefully onto my lap. I wrap my arm around him before he can wiggle himself right off and wake Alex.

"Thank you, Devlain," I say.

"You're welcome, Alexia. I never miss a chance to hang out with my little nephew. Us boys need to stick together."

He grins at Damien before returning to Lucy's side, settling on the armrest and wrapping an arm around his wife and son.

Damien leans forward, trying to get closer to Alex.

"Buby Aless, Mumum," he whispers excitedly. "Aless... seepy."

In a soft whisper, I say, "Yes, Damien. Your baby sister is sleeping." I lean down and kiss the top of his head. His baby-soft hair brushes my lips, warm and familiar. "Damien, you're a big brother now. Big brothers look after their baby sisters. Do you think you can do that?"

He nods, tiny and serious. "Yes, Mumum."

"Good boy. You have two sisters to protect now. You're going to be a very busy little man."

Damien reaches out with his chubby hand and rests it gently on Alex's back. He beams up at me. "Me... big brotha now."

I smile. "That's right, baby. You're a big brother. Two sisters to look after."

He glances at Alley sleeping in Drake's arms, then back at Alex, nodding proudly. "Big brotha."

I look up at Drake and smile, sending through the bond, *'I love you.'*

His panty-dropping smile hits me full force, and my body reacts instantly. Seriously, I just had a baby and he's already making my knees weak.

'I love you, my beautiful, amazing wife,' he replies through our mate bond, leaning down to kiss me. His lips brush mine, soft at first, then deeper — sending warm, delicious tingles through my whole body.

A tiny voice interrupts us. "Dadada... kiss Mumum."

Drake smiles against my lips and pulls back. "Yes, little man. Dad gives Mummy a big kiss. Do you want a big kiss too?"

Damien nods eagerly. Drake and I lean in and kiss either side of his head with an exaggerated mwah. Damien giggles, then yawns, snuggling into me. His eyes flutter shut, and he falls asleep with his hand still resting protectively on Alex.

I look around the room, heart full. That's when I notice Devlain sitting quietly with his phone out, snapping photos of us.

I send him a message. *'Thank you, Devlain. I wanted photos of the twins meeting the baby. Can you send copies to both Drake and me?'*

'Of course, Alexia. Drake asked me earlier to take some. When I saw you both busy with the twins, I knew you'd forget.'

'Thank you again. They only meet their baby sibling for the first time once. My brain is slow today — it's been a long day.'

I sense my parents approaching the room.
Gods, this almost feels like old times.
I reach out to Mum, via my mind.

'Hello, Mum. The babies are asleep, so you'll have to be quiet.'

'Oh, Alexia... I was hoping the twins hadn't arrived yet.'

'Sorry, Mum. They're here. And their baby sister is fast asleep. Dorian too. Lucy and Devlain are with me.'

'You sound like you have a full room of visitors. Should we come back later?'

'No, Mum. Come in. Ask a nurse for a couple of chairs and bring them with you. And have them call the kitchens for refreshments.'

It isn't long before my parents settle into the room. Mum immediately starts snapping photos of all the sleeping babies — of course she does — while a nurse slips in quietly, gathers the wet baby clothes and dirty nappy, and disappears again without a sound.

At some point, exhaustion wins.

I must drift off, because the next thing I feel is strong arms wrapped around me. Warm. Familiar. Safe.

Drake.

I blink through heavy eyelids, searching the room for my babies. Baby Alex is curled in Mum's arms. Alley is tucked against Dad's chest. Damien is fast asleep in Devlain's hold. All three of my children, peaceful and perfect.

Drake has moved us to my bed, settling behind me, his arms wrapped securely around my waist as he props me gently against the headboard.

'Hmmm... I love you, Drake,' I murmur through the sleepy fog in my mind.

'I know,' he answers softly, *'and I love you. Go back to sleep. I'll watch over you and our babies. And we've got plenty of eager helpers here too.'*

A giggle bubbles up, lazy and warm, and a smile spreads across my lips. I look around the room through half-open eyes — my parents, Lucy and Devlain, the babies, Drake. My family. My circle. My heart.

Surrounded by love, wrapped in Drake's arms, my eyelids finally give up the fight.

I let them fall closed and sink into a deep, peaceful sleep.

EPILOGUE

SEVENTEEN YEARS LATER

"Alexia, are you sure about this?"

Drake's voice cuts through the quiet of my office. I glance up at him, then back down at the mountain of written requests cluttering my oak-carved desk. Dozens of private schools begging — practically grovelling — for our daughter Alex to attend.

"Drake, I've spoken with Alex. I'm not hiding something this important from her. She has the right to know what's going on."

Annoyance flickers in his eyes, tangled with concern. "Alright. And what exactly has our daughter suggested about all this?" He gestures at the avalanche of applications like they personally offended him.

My voice lowers. "Drake, you know the agreement. When Alley turns twenty-five, she becomes the next Queen of Darshia." The words leave my mouth... but something inside me stutters. A quiet, unsettling whisper.

For some reason, I don't believe Alley will be the next Queen of Darshia. Not with this betrothal business looming over her. Not with the way fate seems to twist around our daughters. But this is not the moment to unpack that.

I scan the room, suddenly sensing the girls nearby — yet I feel them one second, and the next they are gone. Were they walking by my office? Were they attempting to eavesdrop in the shadows… shaking the feeling off, my gaze settles back on Drake.

"And if Alley doesn't, for whatever reason, then Alex will take the throne instead. They both know one of them will rule. Until then, I continue to lead. We've made sure both girls have the same training — combat, negotiations, diplomacy, everything they need to become Queen. We've never favoured one over the other."

"Yes, yes, Alexia, we've treated all our children the same." Drake rubs a hand over his jaw. "But why does Alex want to go to our old school? I didn't think they would rebuild it. Why does she want to live among humans?"

I sigh, shoulders dropping. "Drake… you sound like you've spent too long away from the human world. Alex wants a chance to live outside Dark Ones and Paranormal Entities for a while. Honestly? I think it'll be good for her."

"I don't know, Alexia. What about her safety?"

"Drake, she'll have bodyguards. Two. And this time, one will be female."

He grumbles under his breath. "Looks like you've thought of everything."

"No. Not everything." I lean back in my chair. "I thought I'd leave the security arrangements — and where Alex lives — up to you."

Drake frowns. "What? Alex should live in our house. Next door to your parents."

"Yes, she should. But she'll still need guards. Personal bodyguards. And that, Mr Smithlyn, is where you come in. You've worked with Riley for years. You know the training, the recruits, the ones we can trust. And my parents can act as her guardians for school. We still look far too young to have teenagers her age."

"Teenagers," Drake mutters. "We have four of them. Four, Alexia. And yes, we look too damn young to have any."

"Yeah, yeah." I wave a hand. "I'm just relieved the pregnancy after Alex wasn't twins again. That would've broken me. At least Damien has Dane to do boy things with instead of drowning in sisters, and their dolls and cars. And Lucy and Devlain having their own set of twins after the birth of Dorian. Still wild."

Drake circles the desk, pulls me up from my chair, and wraps me in his arms. His breath brushes my ear, warm and distracting, sending a shiver straight down my spine.

"Alright, Alexia," he murmurs. "After talking it through, I think I've calmed down. But tell me honestly… do you really think Alex will be okay?"

Drake's muscled body presses against mine, his hard length nudging my hip, and for a moment my brain short-circuits. Instead of rubbing my thighs together, I press against Drake as my leg wraps around his waist.

Goddess, focus, Alexia.

Alex. We're talking about Alex.

"Yes, Drake. Alex will be fine. Living in the human world will be good for her. She needs it. Her magic is progressing fast, and her lessons will continue. She's prepared herself more than most adults ever do."

"Alexia, I just worry. That's all. I'll miss our baby girl."

I wrap my arms around him, feeling the tension in his shoulders, the quiet ache beneath his words.

"Oh, Drake… we'll all miss her. And she won't be far. She's not going overseas. She'll be five minutes away through the portal — at our house or staying with my parents. But honestly? With the way she's maturing, I think our rebellious daughter will choose our house."

And thank the goddess for that.

The Darshia boys have been circling her like hungry wolves. If one of them were her soulmate, we'd know by now.

Yes — getting Alex out of Darshia is the right move.

I do not want her losing her virginity to some hormone-drunk Dark One boy after a party. She deserves love, not a careless fumble with someone who won't matter in the morning.

Mental note: Re-evaluate the sex-education curriculum.

Teenagers today... ha.

"We need to think about how we're going to enrol Alex," Drake says. "Her Darshia school isn't on the human education department's list. Her grades won't mean anything."

"Ah, I wondered when you'd ask." I smirk. "As it happens, an old acquaintance still works at the school."

Drake frowns, digging through old memories. I wait a beat, then put him out of his misery.

"Drake, do you remember our old school secretary? Ms Lexington?"

His eyes widen. "Oh yeah. How is Ms Lexington? Why is she still there? I thought she'd have moved on ages ago."

"Oh no. Ms Lexington married an interstate witch. They have two children now. And she runs the school. She's the acting Principal."

"Wow. Good for her. But did we ever find out what she is? What entity?"

I shake my head. "No. Still a mystery. But it's time we found out. Whatever she is, it'll be interesting. And honestly? It's time we let our little girl grow. Who knows — Alex might find her soulmate."

And I feel it — that quiet tug in my chest.

Alex will meet him soon.

The question is... will he be human or an entity?

MY THOUGHTS DRIFT TO ALLEY.

The betrothal.

The one decision in my entire reign I never truly get to choose.

Alley is barely out of nappies when Drake and I are cornered into the agreement — a political union between Darshia and Silver, sealed in ink older than our bloodlines. Our daughter promised to Prince Philip. Not for love. Not for tradition. For law.

An ancient decree carved into the bones of our world:

If two ruling Dark One bloodlines refuse a political union when demanded, war follows.

War.

In this century.

In a world finally learning to breathe without fear between humans and paranormals.

I would burn that law to ash if I could. But I can't. Not without lighting the fuse myself.

So the betrothal stands — a quiet chain around my daughter's future.

It only activates if neither Alley nor Philip finds their soulmate before her twenty-fifth birthday. A loophole. A sliver of mercy. A chance for her to choose her own life.

A chance for her not to become Queen of Silver.

Though one way or another, she will wear a crown — Silver or Darshia. The only question is which realm claims her.

And yet… fate keeps its distance.

Every attempt to bring Alley and Philip together collapses in on itself — missed portals, political crises, sudden illnesses, storms that appear out of nowhere. Every path between them snaps like a frayed thread.

Two magnets flipped the wrong way.

Sometimes I swear the universe is whispering not this one.

Sometimes I feel Alley's destiny tugging in a completely different direction.

Sometimes I wonder if Philip's is too.

But the law doesn't care.

The threat doesn't care.

And the clock keeps ticking.

If neither finds their soulmate by the time Alley turns twenty-five, the betrothal locks into place like a trap.

The union becomes binding.

The marriage becomes mandatory.

And Darshia avoids a war — at the cost of my daughter's freedom.

A cost I never wanted her to pay.

The law that governs us leaves no room for negotiation. No mercy. No escape. It was forged long before my grandmother's grandmother ever drew breath — a decree built from blood and fear to stop Dark One kingdoms from tearing each other apart.

Refuse a demanded union, and war erupts.

Immediate.

Unavoidable.

Catastrophic.

I didn't choose this for Alley.

I didn't choose this for any of my children.

But the moment the demand was made, Drake and I had two options: agree... or watch our people die.

So we agreed.

We signed the ancient parchment. We sealed it with our blood.

And we prayed — desperately — that fate would intervene before the deadline arrived. And strangely... it has.

Every attempt to unite Alley and Philip fails. Not delays. Not postponements. Failures. Complete and absolute. As if destiny itself is shoving them apart. As if it's screaming not this one.

As if Alley's future lies somewhere else entirely.

But the law doesn't care about destiny. It doesn't care about soulmates. It doesn't care about my daughter's happiness. It cares about obedience. About alliances. About preventing war.

And unless fate delivers a soulmate to one of them soon… Alley will be forced into a marriage she never chose.

And I — her mother, her Queen — will have to stand there and watch it happen.

Because the alternative… is war.

And I am absolutely not looking forward to that conversation.

THE DAY HAS BEEN SET; WE'LL TELL ALLEY THE DAY AFTER HER nineteenth birthday. It would be poetic if she and Philip turned out to be soulmates — they're close in age, and stranger things have happened. But deep down, something in me whispers that Alley's path leads elsewhere… and Alex's path leads straight to the throne. The Darshia Throne.

I don't say any of that to Drake. Not yet. My instincts are screaming at me to hold it back a little longer.

The brush of Drake's warm lips against my neck pulls me out of my thoughts. My head tilts back automatically, giving him more access as he trails slow, deliberate kisses along my skin. His mouth finds my jaw, then my lips, and the kiss deepens — warm, hungry, familiar in all the ways that undo me.

If I were wearing socks, they'd be blown off halfway across the room.

Over fourteen years as best friends and then seventeen years together as a couple, and his touch still lights me up like I'm a hormone-crazed teen again. His smile, his hands, the way he knows exactly how to pull me out of my head and straight into him… goddess, it still works every time.

Heat curls low in my belly, spreading through me in a slow, delicious wave. Whatever we were discussing dissolves into static.

My body focuses on one thing — Drake. His closeness. His warmth. His mouth moving against mine with that slow, devastating confidence that always makes my knees weak.

He lifts me effortlessly, my back meeting the wall with a soft thud. His body presses into mine, solid and sure, and the world narrows to the sound of our breathing and the way he whispers my name like it's a prayer.

My fingers slide into his hair, tugging him closer. His hands roam my waist, my hips, drawing me in until there's no space left between us. The tension builds — hot, electric, impossible to ignore — and I melt into him, letting the moment take over.

The rest... blurs into heat and breath and the kind of intimacy that only comes from years of loving someone with your whole soul.

When the world finally settles again, I'm wrapped in Drake's arms, both of us breathing hard, foreheads pressed together. His eyes are warm, hazy, full of that look he saves only for me.

"You never stop surprising me," he murmurs, brushing his thumb along my cheek. "I love you, Alexia. I never want to let you go."

I laugh softly, still catching my breath, still feeling the echo of him everywhere. "No wonder you don't want to put me down," I tease, glancing between us.

He smirks — that devastating, panty-dropping smile that should be illegal. "Can you blame me?"

I reach out with my senses, checking the hallway, the office, the surrounding rooms. Someone was close earlier — I felt it — but now the space is clear. No footsteps. No curious teenagers. No staff.

Just us.

I look back at Drake, raising a brow. "Well, my ever-sexy husband... maybe we should take this to the lounge and finish what you started."

He arches a brow right back. "What I started? Really, Alexia?" His voice drops, low and warm, sending a shiver through me.

I smile, leaning in until our lips almost touch. "Yes, Drake. I'm sure. And you know what?"

He hums, waiting.

"I love you, too."

Thank you so much for reading **Dark Surprises**.

I am honoured you have selected this book.

I hope you enjoyed being submerged in the world of **Dark Surprises** - The second instalment of Sex, Lies And Family Secrets, as much as I enjoyed creating the world of Alexia and Drake, along with Lucy and Devlain.

Without you, my writing would have no meaning. Thank you, make sure you grab the third book and continue to enjoy the characters in the world of Darshia.

If you enjoyed reading this book, please consider leaving a review where you purchased it. This will help other readers make a choice to select this book.

The best way to say *thank you* to your favourite author, is by leaving a review. Even if it is only three little words 'I like it' - 'I enjoyed it'

Please visit me at: http://www.mltompsett.com

And sign up to receive my newsletters, for giveaways and the latest news on my books.

I would love to connect with you on Facebook: https://www.facebook.com/M.L.TompsettAuthor

ACKNOWLEDGMENTS

Once again, this journey has been a long one, but one I am glad to have travelled and once again completed. It is time for a well-earned rest.

Friends, family and loved ones, you all know who you are, without the generous words of wisdom, encouragement and sounding boards; I would still be typing away and debating should I travel down the road of publishing, once again. Thank you, for your ears and your reading abilities.

To my boys, thank you for allowing me to type and create, design, and hovering over my trusty laptop, including driving you all mad with the world of Alexia and Drake, all things in the world of romance – love you guys, don't ever forget it. Big hugs and kisses.

To my beta readers, I am sorry for your headaches, annoyance, and interruptions in your lives due to my constant onslaught of material to read. Standouts: Anthony, Michele, Alli, Kylie, Emma, Rashelle, Sally, and Gwen. Thank you, for your input is always welcome.

To my special people, thank you for your appreciation of our friendship and my ability to drive you mad with my writing talk — Anthony, Sharon, and Robin.

With your assistance, Reece, I can continue to create fantastic book covers. Thank you. Big hugs and kisses to Jay, too, for your valuable input and assistance.

To you, all my beautiful readers, thank you for taking the time to pick my book up and read the pages of Alexia and Drake. I hope you enjoyed the story and the drama of Alexia. If you enjoyed it, won't you please take a moment to leave me a review at your favourite retailer? I look forward to your comments.

This journey has been a long road travelled.
Just think, from the beginning - thanks to a fantastic song by Shakespears Sister, a haunting ballad - named - STAY. My imagination soon created the characters Alexia and Drake and their battle to remain together, and a faraway kingdom named Darshia. All this drama materialised in my head, and here we are — THE GUY NEXT DOOR, which continued with this book — DARK SURPRISES and three more books - YOU NEVER KNOW - IT'S YOU - WHAT YOU KNOW.

Once again, your little typist with a wicked imagination of fiction, fantasy romance — *M. L Tompsett*

Just remember — your mind is only open as much as you allow it.